# WHEN DAWN RISES

## THE CRIMSON SUN SERIES

JALEN NOEL

*For everyone who watched The Vampire Diaries
and wanted Elena to have both brothers
—and maybe Elijah, too—
happy reading.*

October 26th, 1694

He has locked himself somewhere in this castle. His heartbeat beat, beat, beats within the walls, as though they themselves are alive.

I should have known my beloved would be the first to betray my heart. To run away with the fantasy that he could ever actually escape. Geoffry and he have always been fickle things. What I did not foresee was Vincent choosing to hide from me like the coward I see him for now, dooming himself to torturous desiccation and rot, rather than succumbing to my desires like the others have done so willingly.

The day that I met the young human, Vincent James Buchanan, he stood out as an asset. His broad shoulders, strong jaw, calloused hands of a hard worker, and prominent muscles made him the perfect candidate for my army. Not to mention he had the perfectly damaged mind I needed to sink my claws into. It was not difficult to seduce him; he is an easily charmed man. Nor was it hard to convince him to kill the duke he knew as his father. The older man had not been a good father, neglectful and abusive, so my young Vincent had ripped his head from his body without remorse.

A fortnight has passed. That is a fortnight of his heartbeat driving me to insanity, and I find myself with no choice. I have to leave and take all of my darlings with me. The eight of them remaining are loyal, but even they can't stand being here, surrounded by his ever-slowing heartbeat.

We will leave and go to my manor in France. I don't want to leave without him, but I have no other option. Either we all go mad, or we leave him here for eternity.

What I know with absolute certainty is this: if Vincent James Buchanan someday gets out of this castle, I will hear of it. I vow, here in this journal, that I will hunt him to the ends of this earth to get him back. And if he will not love me as he once did, I will remove the limbs from his body and rejoice in the sounds of his agony.

# CHAPTER 1



The headlights of the car coming toward me are blinding as I squint through the sweat and dirt coating my face. The rolled piece of paper—the one that just might change everything—is tucked safely in the cylindrical case in the passenger seat.

"I'm not kidding, Joel," I start. "I think this might actually be something!"

My best friend, Joel Anderson, sighs over the speakers of my car.

"That's what you said last time."

He's right, of course. He almost always is.

"But this time, I'm ninety-nine percent sure it's true," I rush out, desperate to reassure him.

It's three in the morning. I need assurance that he'll get out of bed to unlock his door.

There's something about driving along the desolate roads of farmland that unsettles me. Or maybe that's due to the fact that the most undeniable piece of evidence that vampires exist is sitting in the passenger seat of my Honda Civic.

Thirteen years. That's how long I've been looking for irrefutable proof.

Thirteen years. And now I have it.

Well, sort of irrefutable. It's a very important piece of the puzzle that will *lead me* to irrefutable proof. Close enough.

I shrug, though he can't see it, and do my best to convince him to turn his brain on and wake up by the time I get there. When I hear the shuffle of his feet and the faucet of his bathroom sink turn on over the speaker, I hang up.

This is it. This is the moment.

Vampires are out there, and now I'm that much closer to finding one. I'm not talking about Dracula, hiding in a cave with deathly pale skin vampires. Nor am I talking about ones that sparkle in the sun and prey on moody teenagers. I'm talking about the real, live thing.

From what we've gathered so far, they are pretty much exactly like us—humans. They need to eat to survive, a.k.a. they need to drink blood. I guess that's the only similarity aside from physical attributes.

I haven't found a definite answer as to whether they can be in the sun or not, but if this goes the way I plan, I'll find out soon enough.

I park haphazardly in the gravel driveway and rush up to the door, banging a million times before he opens it, cursing at me in the threshold. I practically run up the front porch steps of his large two-story home. For a rich guy, he's got a very humble abode.

"Do you have to disturb the peace of my mental state this early in the morning?" he asks, rubbing a hand down his face.

His short black hair is a disheveled mess atop his head, and he's still wearing his pajamas—low hanging sweatpants and a t-shirt.

"You need to read this." I ignore him and step inside, brushing past him to squeeze through the door. Carefully, as though it will crumble at my fingertips, I pull the journal page out of its case and set it on the coffee table. Joel puts on a pair of glasses and picks it up.

Forty minutes pass, and he's read it eight times over. He hasn't said a word, and it annoys me beyond measure.

"Well?" I prod.

"This is," he starts, pausing to consider his words before continuing, "incredible."

An embarrassingly high-pitched squeal escapes me as I wrap my arms around him, locking him in an aggressive squeeze. I stand from the sofa and do a little happy dance, which makes him chuckle and shake his head.

"I leave for Germany tomorrow afternoon," I blurt out.

"Wait… what?"

"I bought a ticket already. I'm finding this thing. I'm finding a vampire."

He's looking at me like I've grown a second head.

"Izzy, I get that you're excited, but you leave *tomorrow*?"

He gently sets the paper on the wood-framed glass coffee table. For the first time since I told him that I believe in vampires, he looks dumbfounded at my words.

"Yep, so I'm going to need you to look after Augie for a few days. Pretty please?" I bat my eyelashes.

"Okay," he says, slowly coming to terms with this situation. "Fine. Bring August over in the morning. Just one question."

I nod at him to go on.

"How are you going to find this mystery castle?"

That is a fair point. In all my excitement, I hadn't realized I would need that information. If only I'd found the rest of the journal and not just one tattered old page.

"I don't know," I admit.

He raises his eyebrows, his bright blue eyes staring judgingly into my soul. Joel has always been my voice of reason. Whenever I want to jump, he is always the one to remind me there could be jagged rocks poised to kill me at the bottom of the cliff.

During my second year teaching at the university, I stumbled upon an article written by a woman in Romania claiming she was attacked by Dracula and he had to talk me out of booking a flight to interview the poor woman. He convinced me that a simple email would do just fine, and I was promptly emailed back by her PA telling me she had suffered a psychotic episode after not taking her meds. Which, quite frankly, was too much information to give some random stranger, but it kept me from pursuing that story any further.

"Right. Let's take our time with this. If this really is about a vampire, we need to do our research and find out where this journal is from. I'll take it to work and run it through some databases tomorrow. Maybe there is something that'll match."

The perks of having a millionaire tech CEO for a best friend. He has the entire world at the tips of his fingers.

"Thank you!" I wrap him in a spine-crushing hug. I head for the front door, throwing a final comment over my shoulder before shutting it behind me. "Oh, and Joel. If you hurt that paper, I will bury you alive and help look for the body."

"Get out of here, you vamp junkie. I'll call you if I find anything."

August does figure eights between my legs as I water the plants on the kitchen windowsill. Not many of them are thriving, thanks to summer's fickleness as autumn threatens to creep in. Erika insists I throw them out and buy seasonal plants, but I've been nursing these plants back from the dead for three years, and I'm not giving up on them now.

"Oh my god, you're a hero," my roommate exclaims as she walks into the kitchen. She goes straight for the French press, pouring herself a hefty mug of coffee and adding a little bit of the too-sweet creamer that she swears by.

"Good morning," I chuckle.

"It's not good yet. I still need to drink this," she says, lifting her mug to her lips. Her mid-length hair is styled in sandy blonde curls, some pieces pulled out in the front to frame her face. She's got on a three-piece beige cashmere suit, with a skirt rather than pants, and black heels that would be listed as my cause of death if I were the one wearing them.

"Anything exciting happening at work today?" I ask. The outfit is even nicer than what she usually wears to work—a pencil skirt and neatly tucked in blouse.

"We have some ranch owner from California coming in today to discuss partnering with us. I honestly don't know why Monique wants us all dressed to the nines when he's probably going to show up in a bolo tie and boots, yet here I am." She rolls her eyes.

"What does a ranch owner want with a magazine like yours?"

"Who knows? I just do whatever Monique tells me, plus I'm not interested enough to ask questions."

She finishes her coffee and leaves the dirty mug in the sink. Augie nuzzles against her leg and she sneers at him, stepping away and dusting off her ankle like he's a disease ridden rodent. I've never understood why she dislikes my cat. It's been like this since she moved in. She's had six and a half years to get used to him, and yet she still treats him like his mere presence will curse her with bad luck. Hence why Joel will be looking after him when I leave town.

I pick up a clump of his black fur off the floor and throw it in the garbage before taking my now room-temperature coffee into my bedroom. I really need to start making the coffee *after* I water the plants.

Sliding my headphones on, rubbing my fingers over the necklace permanently secured around my neck, and setting up my microphone, I prepare to press record on my computer. Every morning, after I make breakfast and water the plants, I record my podcast. By this time, Erika is gone, either at work or grabbing brunch at some trendy spot in the city. Augie has found a routine of napping on my bed, so he isn't a bother. And Joel is so swept up doing CEO things that he never calls. It's the perfect time to record without interruptions.

I'm thirteen minutes and twenty-four seconds in when Joel's face lights up my screen. I pick up on the first ring.

"Hey, I'm in the middle of recording The Daily Fangclub. Is everything okay?"

"I found it!" His voice blares through the speaker.

"You what?" I ask.

"I found the castle you're looking for. Izzy, this is it! Hold on, I'm sending you the location now."

He sends me a pin on a map that doesn't even have a name listed. I zoom in using the satellite image setting to see the crumbling remains of a long abandoned castle nestled deep in the woods. I can't believe it. We found it.

"It was a dutchie back in the fifteen and sixteen hundreds. Guess what name it was registered under in these files?" He pauses. "Buchanan."

"That's the same name on the paper! Oh my god!" I squeal, because this is it. This is the breakthrough we needed. "Ohmygod, I think I can still make my fight. Joel, you are the most amazing friend in the entire world! I love you! I've gotta go pack."

I jump up from my chair and run to the bed, where Augie has nestled into my pillows, scoop him up, and spin with him for a minute. "Augie, we did it! When I come back, you're gonna have a new vampire daddy! Hell, maybe *I'll* have a new vampire daddy."

# CHAPTER 2



Germany is a beautiful country. If I wasn't on the most important mission of my entire life, I would definitely stop every fifteen minutes to sightsee and do touristy stuff. However, I have a full tank of gas and a lifelong dream to fulfill. No pressure or anything.

The long flight wasn't nearly as bad as I expected. I sat between a kind old woman who fell asleep while knitting a scarf and a slim scholarly looking man who kept his nose in his book the whole time. Getting through TSA at the Boston Logan International Airport was probably the most stressful part of the whole trip.

Joel manufactured some false papers for me that would allow me to travel with a padded bag carrying bags of blood. I had to print the papers at the apartment and swing by his office to pick up the blood. He assured me the blood wouldn't go bad, since it's whole blood and not red blood cells, as long as I fed them to the vampire within seventy-two hours after pick up.

Once I landed, the elderly lady gave me a piece of taffy, and I rented a car from the airport. The employees there were kind enough to help me set up navigation on the car's touch screen, and then I was on my way.

Trees go on for miles in all directions as I follow the winding path. After an hour and a half of listening to music sung in German, because I couldn't figure out the Bluetooth in this car, I turn down a dirt road that ends at the bottom of a large hill. Upon the small mountain sits the castle. Was a Fiat 500 the best choice for this? Probably not. But it's affordable and has decent gas mileage.

The further I get into the woods, the thicker the trees get. It's strangely surreal being this far out in nature. I enjoy an occasional hike back home, but I've never been so many miles from civilization before. I'm all alone out here—well, except for the vampire that's hopefully starving beneath the ruins I'm about to park under. It's thrilling.

The hill that I have to climb to reach the castle looks like it'll be a terrible time. The landscape is covered in jagged rocks that stick out every which way, steep inclines, and fresh mud from the recent rain. Nonetheless, I strap on my backpack, double-check that my shoes are tied, and tally-ho up the damn thing. I am hyperaware that I'm potentially about to walk into the arms of a severely hungry vampire whose primary diet consists of, well, *me,* so I'm extra careful not to cut myself on any rocks. I'm breathless by the time I reach the top.

"I should've done more cardio to prepare for this," I say, winded.

Once I'm sure I can breathe again, I come out of the crouched position I'm in and look out at the crumbling stone structure before me. It's, for the most part, still standing. That, in itself, is impressive. On the east wall, there is a sprawling stained-glass window with only a few broken panes. I find where the door must have been on the south side. The entryway must have been grand when this place was in its prime. There are weathered paintings along the walls, too ruined to tell what they depict, and sconces every couple of feet, and climbing vines consuming everything.

I pull my flashlight out as I venture deeper into the Buchanan Dutchee, staring awestruck at every little detail. Ahead of me, there is a set of grand stairs that lead to the second floor. They're crumbling, from the looks of it, but I venture up them anyway. The sound of falling stones stops me from taking a step further once I reach the top. Had I gone another foot forward, I would have fallen straight back to the first floor. A large chunk of the floor up here is missing, stopping me from going further into the second floor.

Back on the first floor, I look around to find any sign that might point me to where this tomb might be. There's a set of stairs, in what looks to have been servant quarters, leading beneath ground level. Something about that strikes me. If I were hoping to escape a woman who had preternatural hearing, below her home is likely where I'd go. The journal described the sound of his heartbeat being heard in the walls. With an old castle like this, I'm sure if one locked themselves beneath, the sound of their heartbeat would travel through the stone.

Besides, if the writer of the journal was the woman of the estate, the likelihood of her venturing down into the servants' quarters was slim to none.

It's pitch black down here, and for the first time since arriving, chills run down my spine. Joel called me this morning when I landed to re-mind me how reckless what I'm doing is, and that notion is setting in now that I'm descending too-dark stairs into the unknown lair of some three-hundred-something-year-old vampire.

"This isn't scary at all, Izzy. It was a *great* idea to come here alone with nothing but a flashlight and a water bottle to protect yourself."

The sound of my voice echoes along with the distinct drip of water. The dripping is ominous and makes my stomach churn with the contents of my breakfast.

I yelp when I hear something scurry across the floor, whipping around and pointing my light in that direction. I don't see anything, but then another scurrying thing flits across the floor, and I exhale.

Obviously, there'd be rats down here.

Breathe.

It's fine. Totally fine.

*Smack.*

I slam face-first into the wall in front of me, having stupidly pointed my flashlight at the ground to look for rats. Rubbing my head, where there's sure to be a lump later, I look up and light up the wall.

Only, it's not a wall. It's a sealed door. The outline of it is clear after many years of weathering and crumbling. I run my finger along the crack between the wall itself and the door. When it was first sealed, it mustn't have been noticeable to the naked eye, but the years have taken their toll.

Luckily, I came prepared and packed a crowbar in my pack. Considering this Vincent guy went to all the trouble to hide within the castle walls to get away from this chick, I figured he might go to some extreme lengths.

The door breaks off in bits and pieces as I pry at it, chunks of stone scattering around my feet. After about two hours of chipping away at it, I've made an opening big enough for me to fit through. I take off my pack and set it against the wall, taking out only essential supplies. Hugging the blood bags to my body like my life depends on it, I enter the tomb.

It's even darker in here, somehow, and the air feels thicker. The beam of my flashlight reflects back at me as it shines on something. Upon closer inspection, I find a large glass coffin in the center of the tomb. The glass is weathered and aged, not allowing me to see what's inside, but I have a pretty damn good guess.

How the hell did this guy get a glass coffin down here without anyone noticing?

I set the blood bags on the ground next to the coffin and use all the upper body strength I have to slide the lid open.

Inside is the severely desiccated corpse of a very real vampire. Humans don't decay like that.

His lips are shriveled, his skin taught against his bones, and his hair is dull against his pale complexion. I cut the first blood bag open and hold it to his lips, waiting for enough of it to register in his starved brain and render him awake. Sure enough, his lips part, and I carefully feed him the rest of the bag.

Slowly, signs of life begin to appear in his features. His eyes become slightly less sunken, and his lips plump up.

Vincent James Buchanan is a beautiful man. You might not know it through the tattered clothes, dry, dull skin, and massive eye bags he is sporting right now, but I can see him.

That's what matters.

He's real. And I can see him.

Despite the obvious look of being woken up after essentially sleeping for three-hundred and fifty-something years, he has that look about him that women want and men want to be. Square jaw, crystal blue eyes, and wavy black hair. His pale skin is covered in slightly overgrown stubble, but when he reached the point of hunger where all of his organs shut down and his body stopped performing all of its necessary functions, it stopped growing. Interesting.

The blood bag I'd given him is empty, but he's trying to suck every last drop out of it, like a toddler with a juice box. Picking up the fifth, and last bag of A positive, I move to take the empty one away. He snarls at me and captures my wrist in a vise grip.

"I—" I start, eyes wide as I take in the beautiful predator who's about three seconds from shattering my wrist. "I have another one."

His head tilts two degrees, so similar to how a curious animal would, and I lift the very full blood bag in the air. He lets me go and takes the bag. It's only when I feel the sensation of viscous liquid covering my exposed skin that I realize he may have been a little overexcited. And that he definitely overestimated the integrity of that bag.

Bile rises in my throat as I gag, thanks to the blood now dripping off my eyelashes. I've never had an issue with blood, but at the moment, I no doubt look like Carrie, and the feeling of someone else's blood seeping into my hair is enough to make me want to vomit. I try to choke it back, hoping I don't make the situation any worse by puking in the small puddle that's formed between us. I take a deep breath and—

Nope. Blood. I inhaled blood. It's in my nostrils.

I hurl.

"Oh my god," I grumble as the scent of vomit mixes with iron, filling the room with the most unpleasant odor known to man.

"Can you walk?" I ask. When I'm met with dead silence, I huff and get off the floor. "Come on, I need you to get up. Please."

I grab his arm and try to haul him up with no success. I feel another wave of nausea, and I definitely do not want to make things any worse than they are, so I turn on my heel and march out of the dark tomb.

My back slams against the stone wall, knocking the breath out of me.

I blink back the sudden pain in my skull to find Vincent inches away from my face, with his fangs bared and eyes unnaturally bloodshot. He rears back, probably preparing himself to take a good chunk out of my carotid, and I panic.

"Please! Stop! Stop! I saved you! Vincent, I woke you up!"

He blinks. It's not much, but it's something.

"That is your name, right? Vincent James Buchanan. You were trapped here in 1694. I found you. My name is Isobelle Axford, and I would really appreciate it if you didn't turn me into a human Capri Sun right now," I say, rushing my words more than usual.

"Iz," he tries to speak, but it comes out gravelly and strangled.

"Here." I hand him a water bottle. "Drink, it might help."

He chugs the whole thing in under a minute. There's still a crazed look in his eyes that tells me he's way too hungry for my own good, but the fangs are retracted and the whites of his eyes have cleared.

"Isobelle," he rasps.

A giddy smile breaks out on my face. This feels like a victory.

"Yes! Yes, that's my name. Oh, god, this is so exciting. I found a living, breathing—Well, I guess you weren't doing either of those things *when* I found you, but I found a vampire. A real life freaking vampire!"

His throat bobs up and down as he gulps, his eyes glued to my throat.

"Shit. I found a vampire, and I'm covered in your version of butter pecan ice cream."

I miss when the blood coating my entire body was simply disgusting. Now it's both disgusting and a threat to my life.

"Okay, let's get out of this structural hazard you call a castle and to a hotel. We need showers."

I grab my backpack I had dropped by the entryway and start navigating us out of this place. My car is peacefully waiting at the bottom of the hill, where I left it, and I groan at the steep hike to the bottom. I basically had to rock climb to get up here, and the idea of twisting my ankle on the jagged rocks sticking out of the ground nearly makes me want to stay here forever.

"What is that?" Vincent startles me. The yelp I let out is only slightly embarrassing.

"That's my car. It's like a horseless carriage." At least I think that's what they were called during the industrial revolution. "Try not to think too much about it. You'll have whatever the immortal equivalent of an aneurysm is."

Despite the fact that I'm out of breath just looking at the hill, I start making my way down. I dodge the first couple of rocks poised to take me out, make it to the first tree, then my foot snags on a root, and on my ass I go.

Once I'm done grunting and fussing about my ass being on the ground instead of my feet, I look up to see Vincent already at the bottom. Staring at me.

"You wouldn't be able to help me out here, would you?" I ask, squinting against the sun now peeking out from behind the clouds.

He smirks. Actually smirks. I find myself smiling back, too amused at his human side finally joining the party to care that he's probably mocking me. In the blink of an eye, he's standing right in front of me, a large hand outstretched to help me up. Once I'm on my feet, he sweeps me into his arms and runs at supernatural speeds to the car.

"That was awesome," I say, still in shock from the fact that I just moved at vamp speed. I've been dreaming of that moment since my mom took me to see Twilight in theaters when I was nine.

He sets me down and grabs his throat.

"Oh, yeah. You're probably still hungry." He nods. "Can you consume animal blood?" That's never been clear in my research. In some versions of vampires, they can survive on just animal blood, and in others, it's not even considered a food source.

He nods.

"There are no humans, except me, obviously, around here for miles. If you need to, um, hunt before we leave, I'll give you some time."

He nods.

"Wait! Before you go darting around the woods, will you promise you'll come back?" I ask, desperately hoping he won't abandon me out here to murder a nearby village or something.

He simply looks me in the eye, holding my stare for an uncomfortable amount of time, and disappears. I guess I'll just wait here and pray he comes back to me.

The sun is gone when I hear the unnatural whooshing sound of my vampire companion returning to me. He's been gone for three hours while I've been freezing my ass off in the car.

"Oh, thank god. I totally thought you weren't coming back," I say in a rush, my shoulders relaxing at the sight of him.

"I nearly didn't," he says, his voice smooth and deep, with an amazing English accent now that he's nourished.

*Everything* about him is nourished.

I could tell he had broad shoulders and a strong jawline in his desiccated state, but I definitely did not notice how tightly he fills out his tattered clothes. His muscles seem to have gotten a little rejuvenation whilst he was running around, crushing the dreams of Bambis everywhere.

I open the passenger door for him and gesture for him to sit, scrunching my nose as he passes.

His time in that tomb did his hygiene zero favors.

Between his odor and the blood still coating the inside of my nose, despite some very intense scrubbing with a towel, this is going to be a very smelly ride.

"Why did you?" I ask, settling into the driver's seat.

"I do not know." His gorgeous face—a stark contrast to the sunken, Tim Burten-esque look from before—is serious as he stares out the windshield.

"It's a good thing you did. You clearly need someone to show you how a shower works so you can wash off the smell of death wafting from you."

Awkwardly, he pinches his shirt and brings it to his nose. His lip curls in disgust, and he drops the fabric. Smothering a laugh, I start the car and get going. There is an inn about twenty minutes away that seemed decent.

"How do you know of my kind?" he asks.

I tap the steering wheel and chew my lower lip for a few seconds, then say, "Movies."

He is quiet, and I remember that he has never even heard the word movie before.

"A movie is like a moving picture. And a picture is like a painting. So, imagine a painting that is moving... I'm not doing this right... Did you ever eat strange mushrooms when you weren't taking residence in creepy tombs?"

"Would the time I ate a poisonous mushroom intending to kill me count as eating a strange mushroom?" he asks. His face tells me he is serious, too.

"Who were you?" I ask, cocking my head.

"The son of a duke."

I choose to keep my mouth shut and let *that* process.

The rest of the ride to the inn is mostly silent. To my surprise, Vincent doesn't ask any questions about the car or the paved road. Though, I suppose when you have so many years to cope with the fact that you'll live several lifetimes, not much change would phase you. Maybe he expected things to be drastically different when he locked himself down there.

"This is our stop for the night," I say as we pull into the gravel parking lot of the inn. "Just wait here, okay?"

"Why?"

"Have you seen yourself? The sight of you is enough to send a grown man to the grave."

He has blood on his chin and neck, tears and dirt all over his shirt and pants, and his shoes are falling apart at the seams.

"I haven't seen myself since I was thirty-four," he mumbles, mostly to himself, but loud enough that I hear him.

"What do you mean?"

"My kind does not appear in mirrors."

In all of my research, I've only seen one article depicting a time when vampires couldn't see their own reflections, yet everything else said otherwise. There was something about pure metal or something like that.

I shoot a message to Joel, which he responds to immediately, asking him if he remembers the article. As luck would have it, he does.

"Silver-backed mirrors," I murmur. "I have to check us in, but after, I *need* to show you something."

The fair-haired man behind the concierge desk greets me with a cheery smile, one that falters when he sees the blood soaking my clothes and coating my face. Compared to the picturesque, cozy German setting of the inn, I look like a creature from a horror movie.

"Can you believe some random kids threw this stuff on me?"

He looks me over once more and returns the smile to his face, though it's less cheery now. When he starts speaking to me in German, I realize he didn't quite understand my lame excuse.

He gets me checked in easily, despite the language barrier. I can't blame him. There mustn't be very many Americans coming to these parts of Germany.

"One more thing," I say, spinning on my heel to face him again. "Do you have any spare clothes lying around?"

He cocks his head, so I type the question into my translator app.

"*Oh ja. Wir haben ein Fundbüro. Hier*," he says, waving a hand for me to follow him. I don't have a single clue what he just said, but I follow him anyway. He leads me to a small closet around the corner with a sign that says '*Fundbüro*' on it. Inside are a few boxes with clothes and forgotten items spilling out of them. I reach for a box and look at him to make sure he's okay with me going through them. He nods encouragingly.

"Thank you."

After much rummaging, I go back outside holding a 3XL Oktoberfest t-shirt, XL gray sweatpants, and a pair of men's slides. I would have grabbed underwear and socks, but I didn't trust the cleanliness of the clothes in those boxes. The items I did grab were the ones that looked like they'd fit and that smelled the best.

"Follow me to the room and try not to draw attention to yourself." Not that that's possible. He gets out of the car, once again towering over my five foot seven inches. Shutting the door, I grab his hand and tug him behind me.

As expected, the concierge gapes as Vincent trails me through the lobby and up the stairs to our room. If I didn't know where he just came from, I'd gape, too.

"Costume party," I say over my shoulder in hopes that he'll understand that and pray he'll believe me and not call any authorities.

Locking the heavy wood door behind us, we find ourselves in an antique-filled room. There are little wooden sculptures and vintage tea sets set up along various shelves along the walls. There is a velvet green recliner chair in one corner, a lamp in the other, and one large, four-poster bed centered against the wall.

Temporarily ignoring the one-bed-for-two-people situation, I locate the bathroom. It definitely does not strike me as a bathroom you'd normally find in a hotel or inn. It looks more like a grandma's bathroom that hasn't been redecorated since the seventies, but it'll do. The large mirror over the sink is perfect for what I want to do.

"You said you've never seen your reflection, right?"

He stares at me, his expression blank, then responds, "Not since I was human."

"In your time, mirrors were made using silver as a backing. Silver is a pure metal. Nowadays, mirrors are backed with aluminum."

My smile goes from ear to ear, but he clearly doesn't get the message. I go to him and gently nudge him toward the bathroom.

"Look in the mirror."

He cocks a brow at me, but then he turns, and his face lights up with shock. For the first time in over three-hundred years, he sees himself.

"I truly look terrible," he muses. His hands roam his jaw and his hair as if he doesn't believe what he's seeing is real.

"Nothing a shower won't fix," I chirp.

"A shower?"

I open the curtain to the shower-tub combo and show him how it works. Turning on the water, I make sure it's warm, but not hot, for him.

"I'll go to the bedroom and you can undress. You just stand under the water and use a washcloth to wipe yourself down. Here." I hand him a washcloth from the linen cupboard. "Use this with soap on it."

He nods slowly, giving me hope that he'll efficiently wash himself so he doesn't smell like *that* all day tomorrow. I leave him with a warm smile and shut the door.

# Chapter 3



I stare at the pile of clothes on the bed, as though it's not my fault that they are out here and Vincent is naked in the shower.

He's naked. In the shower. And I have his change of clothes in the bedroom.

Taking a breath, I remind myself that I'm a grown woman, and it is not a crime to enter the bathroom to put the clothes on the counter. I knock twice and announce that I'm coming in before opening the door.

"I'm going to leave some clothes by the sink for you," I say, stepping into the bathroom slowly, like if I make a wrong move the ground might swallow me whole.

The water turns off.

Before I get the chance to scurry out and back into the safety of the bedroom, he opens the curtain, and all six foot something inches of him is in full frontal view. He's absolutely, breathtakingly gorgeous, with muscles straight out of a superhero movie. I work overtime to keep my eyes from roaming below the waist as I scramble for a towel to throw at him.

"Thank you," he says, and his accent, mixed with his nakedness, nearly brings me to my knees.

At least if I were on my knees I could look right at his—

"Yep! No problem!" I rush as I basically fall out the door and slam it shut behind me.

He comes out a minute later covered by the shirt and sweats, no nakedness in sight, and I allow myself to breathe. The shirt is much too large for him and covers where I'm sure the sweatpants outline the bulge of his penis.

Shaking off that thought, I take my own pajamas to the bathroom to quickly shower and change. Once my teeth are brushed and my hair is combed, I return to the room. I snag a blanket off the bed and head straight to the recliner.

"Do you not wish to sleep in the bed?" Vincent asks, observing my choice.

"I—Well, you've been sleeping in a tomb for three centuries; I figured I'd let you have the bed tonight. I can't imagine what that long in a coffin does to your back," I joke.

"It's a large bed, Isobelle." My name coming out of that mouth is just cruel. I'm trying *not* to have dirty thoughts about the first vampire I've met, thank you very much. "There's plenty of room for both of us."

Popping the leg rest up, I sink further into the velvety chair. "That's okay. You enjoy the king-sized comfort. I'll be fine in the chair."

With a curt nod, and what I think is a roll of his eyes, he lies down and lets his eyelids fall.

A few hours later, Vincent is softly snoring from the bed while I doom scroll on my phone. A text comes in from Joel, who I texted two hours ago, forgetting about the time difference.

Joel: You're sleeping in a chair after he literally offered to share the bed? Are you CRAZY?

I've already seen him naked. No need to make my life harder.

Joel: Haven't you been dreaming of hot vampire sex since you were like… 15?

That's beside the point.

Joel: Just fuck him and get it out of your system.

JOEL!

Joel: * shrugging emoji *

I turn the phone off and pull the blanket over my head. Leave it to him to make a situation like this worse than it already is.

I focus on the sound of Vincent's breathing and the soft purr of his snores as I try to fall asleep. The excitement from today has caught up with me, and I'm tired, but completely unable to sleep.

My only wish is that my mom could be here, so I could tell her that I found him. She would be ecstatic to know that vampires are real. I guess, if I'm right about her death, maybe she already did. All those years of watching cheesy vampire movies and shows, sitting on our cozy blue suede couch, have finally paid off.

I know I can't take Vincent to the Boston Police Department and present him as evidence that my mom really was killed by a vampire, but knowing that he's real is enough to prove it to myself. Everyone thought I was in denial, that I was lashing out because of the trauma of her loss, but I knew deep down that it wasn't some freak accident that did that to her.

Vincent is my salvation.

I no longer have to beat myself up trying to uncover the truth. Because of him, I know it.

With that thought stirring in my head, I doze off to sleep.

"What the bloody hell is that?" Vincent stares at the plane like it's about to devour him.

He stared at every passing house, bus, and towering building that same way. He only asked for an explanation once and was satisfied with it, oddly at peace with the amount of time that's passed between his last life and this one.

I've decided to treat the years he was entombed as though he were dead. I tried asking him what desiccation was like this morning, and he pretended as though I weren't even in the room. Clearly, he doesn't want to talk about it, so I won't push it.

"This," I say as I climb the stairs to Joel's private plane, "is an airplane. It's like my car, except it moves through the air."

"Like a bird?" he asks, still staring incredulously, and I'm praying none of the workers nearby notice.

"Yes, like a big metal bird."

Hesitantly, he follows me in and takes a seat in one of the large recliners. Joel's money will never cease to impress me, no matter how long I've had to get used to it. His biotech company took off so quickly that he was practically instant-rich. When you're a genius and come up with revolutionary means of research and development, that happens. He'd never admit how smart he is, but he knows it.

"Good morning, Miss Axford and guest," the pilot, Sam, greets us as he exits the cabin. "We will be taking off in about fifteen minutes. It is a bit over eight hours to Boston, so please, make yourselves comfortable."

"Sounds good. Thank you, Sam."

"Will either of you be needing anything for the flight?" he asks.

"No, just some privacy." I realize how that sounds too late. Sam works hard to keep his brows from shooting up any higher than they already have. "Thank you," I mutter, my cheeks heating.

He nods and reenters the pilot's cabin.

I wait until the plane starts moving, preparing for takeoff, before I delve into the many questions burning the tip of my tongue.

"I wanted you to be able to rest last night," I start, "but, to be honest, I have a million questions I need answered."

"What kinds of questions?" Vincent's brows furrow.

"Vampire questions."

I occupy the seat directly across from and facing him, so I get a front-row seat to each of his expressions. He's frustratingly hard to read.

"Fine, I will do my best to answer any question you may have."

My smile beams straight at him.

"If you answer mine first."

Of course there's a caveat. I guess I can't blame him for wanting answers from me, too.

"Okay, ask away," I say, though I'm instinctively on the defensive.

"How did you know where I was?" he asks. Simple enough.

"I found a journal entry from 1694, in the archives of an abandoned mansion in southern New Hampshire, that mentioned you locking yourself in a castle," I say. "My friend, Joel, managed to narrow the possibilities down to the one I found you in by searching your name, Vincent James Buchanan, and cross-referencing it with any known estates in the 1600s."

"Who did the journal belong to?" The severity of his rich English accent gives away more than his face. This is important to him.

"It doesn't say. Whomever it was felt betrayed by you, I could tell that much. I have it at my apartment if you want to look at it when we get there."

"I'd like that, thank you."

I nod, smiling sympathetically. I don't know what happened to him in his last life, but whatever it was had left a scar far worse than skin level.

"Is that all you wanted to ask?" I prompt.

"For now."

"May I ask mine?"

"Yes."

I swallow, nervous to actually get the answers I've been guessing at since I was thirteen. Not knowing but making inferences based on research is one thing; knowing the sure, solid fact is another.

"Okay, then. I guess I'll start with an easy one." I take a breath. "Obviously, the sun doesn't kill you," I'd figured out that much as we left the inn, "but does it have any effect on you?"

"No. Only if we're vulnerable or exposed for too long," he says, very matter-of-factly.

I consider this. Not really a straight answer, but better than any I've had. "How does someone become like you?"

"Like me?" he asks, one corner of his mouth turning up.

"You know what I mean," I say, brushing chestnut hair behind my ear.

"Yes, I suppose I do," he says, voice soft. "For one to become a vampire, the blood of another must be in their system when they die."

I dart my eyes around the mostly empty plane to make sure no one hears us.

"So, all you have to do is drink vampire blood, then die?"

"Drinking it works sometimes, yes. However, that method makes the blood less potent and there's a less likely chance for the person to wake up. The preferred method is to get the blood in direct contact with an open wound. It will immediately be soaked into the human's bloodstream in its most potent form. If the human dies within three days of exposure, there is a chance they will transition."

I process his words carefully. "But no guarantee?"

"Once the first day passes, the chances of survival decrease considerably."

Interesting. Three days is much longer than I expected, but I guess if the vampire blood is directly exposed to your bloodstream, it would take longer for it to get filtered out.

"So, when they wake up, they are just," I pause, skewing my face as I try to piece this together, "a vampire? Nothing else is required?"

"What do you mean?"

"They don't have to, like, drink human blood or anything like that?"

He stares blankly at me.

"It's just," I start, the need to not come off as some clueless idiot strong, "some of my findings suggest that something along those lines might be required for the transition to be complete."

He looses a breath. "No. The transition is complete as soon as the person awakens. Why are you so keen for answers, Isobelle? You do not wish to condemn yourself to an eternity of bloodshed as I have, do you?"

The thought has definitely crossed my mind. "It's not on my calendar at the moment, no."

"Good. I would not wish my existence on anybody. It is bad enough that I have had to survive it."

I don't press him on the matter. Instead, the plane settles into silence, and I rest my head against the seat. Though he didn't give me much of a look into who he is, he opened up just a crack. That's more than I could ever have asked. It was never a part of my plan to befriend the vampire once I found it, but he's rather charming and has been intriguing, to say the least.

I wake to a panicked feeling deep in my gut. It takes a few seconds for my surroundings to filter in, reminding me that I'm forty-thousand feet in the air.

Vincent is gripping the arm of his seat, holding a hand tightly over his nose and mouth.

"What's wrong?" I ask, my voice garbled from sleep.

His eyes flick to mine, bloodshot and multiple shades darker than the ocean blue they shone earlier.

He's hungry.

"Animal blood didn't do it for you, huh?" I say, trying to mask my fear with humor. On the inside, I'm melting in terror. Scrambling for my backpack, I curse myself for not thinking ahead. I stand, shifting closer to him so I can reach the overhead storage, and he growls. Animalistic and barely restrained.

He's barely holding on to control.

"Shit, I'm out of blood bags," I mutter. I'm not sure whether logical thought filters into the next words that leave my mouth, but I say them, anyway. "Feed on me."

"No!" His voice is carnal, more animal than human.

"Unless you plan on murdering the pilot and sending us to the ground at deadly speeds, you have to feed on me."

He shakes his head and pushes himself further into the seat as though he can bolt himself to it with sheer force.

"Vincent, you're not really in a position to argue this right now." I roll up the sleeve of my hoodie. "Do it."

He doesn't budge. *Of course* he is going to be a good vampire. Just my goddamn luck.

I kneel in front of him so that we're at eye level and gently place a hand on his wrist. "I trust you," I say as I push his hand away from his face. He lets me.

"I don't."

Our eyes meet, and I try to show him through just a look that he has my complete and utter permission. In all honesty, I'm shitting myself on the inside, but for the pilot's survival, and imminently, mine, I have to do this.

He concedes.

His hands are deliberately careful as he grips my sides and pulls me up onto his lap. Ignoring the buzzing radiating throughout my entire body, I watch as he slowly raises my wrist to his lips. Our eyes lock. He takes a deep breath, his restraint wearing ever so thin.

His teeth pierce my delicate skin.

At first, it hurts. The sharp sensation of his fangs biting into my flesh, followed by a targeted burn, causes tears to well in my eyes. As the burning spreads, crawling up my arm until it's searing in my shoulder, those tears fall. I accept the pain, and I force myself not to make a sound. He needs this.

Then something changes.

The pain turns into something else completely, something very opposite of pain. It trickles into my core, my entire body ablaze with it. I find myself craving it, the sweet sensation. At the edge of my senses, the pain is still there, but it's drowned out by the toe-curling, tingling sensation flooding my body now.

Biting down on my lip, I try to mute the insatiable moan that creeps up my throat. His other hand comes up to hold my head, his fingers gentle in their caress against my hair. He gently brings my face to his shoulder, allowing me to anchor myself to him. He keeps sucking, my senses locked into the action, never wanting it to stop, and I moan into his shoulder. His hand sweeps down the back of my head in a comforting motion.

Then his mouth leaves my wrist, the ecstasy in my body ebbing and fading with the loss of contact. Without my permission, I whimper. He continues caressing my head, his palm eventually resting at the nape of my neck as a heavy feeling settles over me.

I want to beg him to do it again, to take more, but my lips won't move the way I need them to. My eyelids grow excruciatingly heavy, and my entire body relaxes into the warmth of his beneath mine.

"Shh. Sleep, love," his voice filters through my grogginess. Everything goes black, and I fall into unconsciousness.

# CHAPTER 4



I wake in the dark. There's a sliver of light coming from somewhere, but I'm not entirely sure where I am and can't place it. My head is pounding, and I groan as my fingers rub my eyes. The more my eyes adjust, the more of the room around me filters in, and I realize I've been here before.

I'm in the spare bedroom I've claimed as my own at Joel's house. The sliver of light is coming from a small crack in the curtains. And there's someone in here with me.

My eyes take a minute to focus, but when they do, I find Vincent perched in a rocking chair in the corner of the room. He's asleep, his head resting against the back of the chair, the column of his throat exposed. He is still wearing the shirt and sweats from the inn.

Then, everything comes flooding back to me.

Oh. My. God. He fed on me, and instead of it hurting—aside from in the beginning—like I expected, it felt like he was eating me out, rather than eating *me*. Warmth creeps into my cheeks as I spot the bloodstains on his shirt.

I must be absolutely mental. My blood is staining his shirt, and instead of being repulsed, I'm blushing. But hey, I'm just a girl. Who knows what makes my head tick.

Wait, how did we get here?

I sit up, and another groan rasps up my throat. My whole body feels like it just ran a marathon.

When I look across the room again, Vincent's eyes are open. They're soft, yet annoyingly unreadable. The last words I remember him saying on the plane come to the forefront of my memory.

*Sleep, love.*

"You're awake." He doesn't move to get up, nor does he let much of any emotion into his tone, yet somehow, I feel like a weight has just been lifted from his shoulders.

"How long was I out?" I ask, trying to scoot to the edge of the bed. My muscles ache and burn with every movement. "And why do I feel like I was run over by a herd of buffalo?"

"Two days."

I blink harshly, looking at him as though that will make what he said any different.

"What?" I say, my voice coming out high-pitched and louder than I intend.

"I am sorry, Isobelle. I was overzealous. It won't happen again."

"How is this your fault?" I retort.

"You slept so long because your body needed to recuperate from the blood loss. *That* was my fault."

If I remember correctly, *I* threw my veins at *him*. I point out as such, and he stares at me in silence. This man is infuriating. The least he can do is give me *something*. Some kind of emotion. I'm drowning in the desert over here.

"How did we get here?"

I decide it's not worth the headache.

"I asked the pilot where to take you to rest. He contacted the man of the house, Joel, and he came to get you."

"How did *you* get here?" I can't imagine him walking off the plane with an unconscious me in his hands went over very well. Sam would have blown a fuse, and Joel would have come for his throat.

"I followed the horseless carriage the man brought you here in. He didn't want me in here, so I forced my way in. It wasn't difficult. He's weak. Even for a human."

I snort out a laugh. He said that with the straightest face; I know he means it.

"I'm sure Joel would love to hear that," I say.

"He comes in here much too often for my liking. I told him you were only in need of rest, but he insisted you needed medical observation."

What? Medical observation by who?

Speak of the devil and he shall appear. Before I can ask anything else, Joel opens the door and steps into the room.

"Christ, it's dark in here," he mutters. "Izzy! You're awake!"

I'm wrapped in a tight embrace, wincing a little at the bone deep ache that causes, and he sits beside me. I see what Vincent meant by medical observation as my eyes catch on the blood pressure cuff and stethoscope in my best friend's hands.

"How often do you come to do that?" I ask, pointing to the medical tools.

He ducks his head a little. "Every three hours."

"Much. Too. Often," Vincent drawls.

"I'm not a big fan of how much time *you've* spent here, either, creep," Joel bites.

"Where else would he go?" I ask rhetorically.

"Anywhere." He looks over at Vincent. "Back to the tomb whence he came."

"Wait, how often do you sit in that chair just… watching me?" I ask.

Vincent doesn't answer.

"Every goddamned minute for the last forty-seven hours," Joel responds for him.

Forty-seven hours. He's sat there for literally two days straight. I can't tell if that's creepy or really sweet.

"Oh my gosh," I rush out, "Joel, this is Vincent. *The* Vincent. The *vampire* Vincent."

"Yeah, I gathered that, Iz," he deadpans.

"Don't do that," I whine, rubbing my temples.

"Do what?"

"Don't ruin it! Pretend you didn't know or something. I want you to be as excited to meet him as I have been to introduce you."

His lips press into a down-turned line as he tries to hide a smile.

"That might have been the case had he not nearly killed you."

Rolling my eyes, I huff out a breath. God, I feel like I have the worst hangover ever.

"Fine, fine." He cracks that boyish smile I know too well. "I can't fucking believe you finally did it, Isobelle Axford. I can't believe you finally found your vampire."

He looks at me, the smile on his face spreading from ear to ear.

"I'm so goddamn proud of you."

My own smile widens and tears well in my eyes because I know he is. He has been in my corner since the day I told him my theory about what killed my mother. Never once was there judgment or cruelty.

I was the girl who cried vampire, and he was the only villager who had my back.

"Thank you." I nod curtly.

"Vincent," I turn to face the brooding man in the corner, "this is Joel. He's not the dick I'm sure you think he is. He's my best friend, and if you plan on sticking around—which I really hope you do—it would be great if you both could get along."

Vincent gets up and comes this way, clearing his throat.

"It's a pleasure," he says, bowing his head.

"Wish I could—"

He cuts off at seeing the glare I shoot at him.

"Nice to meet you." Joel rolls his eyes. "I have to get to the office. I've spent the last two days here. Can't wait to see what fires were started in my absence."

He gets up and heads for the door, leaving Vincent and me alone in the dark room. But before he leaves, he spins around and says, "And no more *blood sharing*. Please. I can't handle you taking another two-day recovery nap."

He says 'blood sharing' like he knows exactly what happened, and at the memory, heat rises to my cheeks. There's no way he could know what I experienced on that plane. Once we hear the front door shut, I swallow my nerves and ask what I've wanted to since I fell asleep.

"Why did it," I pause, unable to think of how to say this, "feel like that?"

"The blood sharing?" Vincent clarifies. I nod. "That is, unfortunately, how it always is if you don't struggle. Our fangs release a venom that triggers the human nervous system and turns it into something pleasurable. It's all a part of the facade our species needs to convince prey that we're not a threat."

Well, that's unsettling. Is that how he sees me? Prey? I hope not, but it would make sense. I'd never thought of it this way, but we *are* two different species.

A predator wouldn't sit in that old chair for forty-seven hours until its prey woke up.

"Do you think of yourself that way often?" I ask, looking to where he's standing at the foot of the bed.

"How do you mean?" He cocks his head.

"Like you're not a person. Like you're something... *other*."

His jaw feathers, and he looks at me with perfect seriousness when he says, "I am something 'other', Isobelle. Don't make the mistake of thinking otherwise."

"Okay, then riddle me this," I start. "Are you capable of sadness?"

"Yes," he answers hesitantly.

"What about joy?"

"Yes."

"Anger? Love? Grief?"

"Yes."

"Passion?"

"Your point?" he asks, crossing his arms over his chest. The action makes his already intimidating stature look twice as massive.

"Then you're not as 'other' as you think you are. All of those things are very human, Vincent."

His lips press into a thin line.

"Don't discredit yourself because of whatever happened in your past. You are as human as I am. You just have a unique diet," I add the latter in an attempt to lighten the mood. This conversation has become uncomfortably serious.

He doesn't laugh.

I decide to get up so I can brush my teeth, shower, and get into some fresh clothes. After sleeping for two days, my armpits are sticky, and the sensation nearly triggers my gag reflex. I swing my legs over the side and get to my feet, only, it doesn't feel like it should. The ground feels unsteady, and the world around me wobbles a little.

My knees turn to Jell-O. Just as I'm about to topple to the ground, a strong hand grips my elbow and another wraps around my waist.

"Christ," he curses under his breath. "You must do everything with caution for a while. Your body is exhausted from reproducing the blood you lost."

"Well, I need to shower. I feel disgusting, and I can't even imagine how I must smell to someone with super senses."

"Could you perhaps take a bath? It would likely make you feel better, as well as offer more security. The idea of you on your feet for any duration unsettles me at the moment."

I consider this. A bath would probably be good for my muscles, especially if I throw some Epsom salt in there. I nod. "A bath sounds good."

He guides me back to sit on the edge of the bed and heads for the connected bathroom.

"I'll draw one up."

The energy needed to ask him how he plans on figuring out how to do that is not within me, but imagining him soaking himself trying to do it makes me smile. It's strange to be so tired, knowing how long I slept for. I guess I'll have to be selective as to when he can feed on me in the future.

Just then, my phone chimes.

> Joel: There are blood bags in the standing fridge in the basement, and I left my credit card on the counter. Please, for the love of God, go buy that man some new clothes.

I smile at the message, grateful that Joel is always thinking ten steps ahead. I'm sure Vincent will be thrilled to update his wardrobe. Hopefully, after a bath, some coffee, and a proper meal, I'll feel well enough to make the drive into the city to take him shopping.

"The bath is ready, I believe," Vincent announces, reentering the room.

He helps me up and keeps a hand beneath my elbow the entire way to the bathroom. I have half a mind to ask why he's helping me so much and why he watched me sleep for forty-seven hours, but I decide not to look a gift horse in the mouth.

"I think I'll be able to undress myself, Vince. If I need something, I'll call for you."

He assesses me, then nods and turns for the door.

"Thank you," I add, before he shuts the door behind him.

The Epsom salt I keep under the sink is thankfully still there. I pour a generous amount of lavender-scented salt into the tub and carefully slip out of my clothes. I make a mental note to wash the bed sheets later today, since they've had me and my dirty clothes in them for so long.

The bath is the perfect temperature—hot enough that it stings a little getting in, but cool enough that it doesn't burn. A candle, a book, and a glass of wine would be perfect right now, but this will do. I'm still a little high on the fact that I found a vampire, something I've been working toward for thirteen years.

As I scrub myself down, I make sure to pay extra attention to my lady bits, a little disgusted by the fact that the effects of our blood sharing were still there. God, that's abhorrent.

I soak in the beautifully warm water for who knows how long, but get out when my stomach starts incessantly grumbling. Wrapping a towel around me and cursing myself for not learning my lesson, I leave the bathroom to find clothes. Vince is standing at the far side of the room, a book in his hand that he must have plucked from the bookshelf there.

The room isn't anything exciting. There's a half-full bookshelf in the far corner, a desk covered in random clutter that I've accumulated over the years, a rocking chair, a bay window that I'm obsessed with, and an overly fancy four-poster California king-sized bed. I fought hard to get Joel to let me put my own bed sheets on the bed, a cream-colored set that makes the room feel a little warmer with its stark white walls.

I've done what I can to make the room feel more homey by filling it with succulents, books, clutter, a few blankets from home, and such. The house itself could use some homeliness. Joel spends the majority of his time in the office working on whatever needs to get done, so he doesn't care much about having a cozy home. The walls vary from charcoal gray to white depending on the room. Bathrooms, bedrooms, and closets are all white, hallways and the living room are light gray, and the kitchen and dining room are charcoal gray. There's minimal wall decor, a mirror, a clock, or an abstract art piece here and there. I've slowly been sneaking pops of color in, like the yellow blanket I draped over his black couch last week.

"Um, do you mind stepping out while I change?" I ask shyly. Vince looks up for the first time, his gaze raking down my body in a way that sets my core ablaze, and nods. He closes the book, sets it on the desk, and goes out into the hallway.

I rummage through the dresser drawers and pull out a pair of jeans, a simple white V-neck, and undergarments. I'm unsure why I choose to wear a white, lacy matching set, but I try not to think about the decision too much. I bring my hand up to my neck to make sure my necklace is still there before throwing my hair into a low pony.

I emerge from the room to find Vincent waiting for me, ever the gentleman, so I lead him downstairs to the kitchen. I light up when a familiar feline rubs against my ankles.

"Augie!" I exclaim, bending down to pick up my beloved black cat. "Oh, how have you been? I'm glad to see Uncle Joel kept you alive all this time."

August nuzzles his face into my cheek and purrs softly.

"I missed you, too."

I set him down, and he moves straight for Vincent, trailing figure eights around his ankles.

"That's August, my cat. I promise he's friendly," I say. Vincent looks rigid as he watches August like the feline is about to pounce. "You hungry? For human food, I mean. You can eat human food, right?"

It takes him a minute to answer, attention still locked on Augie. "Yes, I can. And I would be grateful for some food."

"Perfect. I'll whip up some eggs and bacon. You like toast?"

His attention is back on my cat, so I decide to make him some, anyway. The scrambled eggs turn out perfectly, thanks to the tutorials I've been studying for the past month on YouTube. I serve up two plates and set them on the counter.

"Milk or OJ?" I ask.

"What is OJ?"

"My bad, it's orange juice. I think today I'll have to start showing you how to act a little more modern."

"I'll try it. Thank you," he says, taking a seat at the counter.

I pour two glasses of orange juice, and we eat our meals in comfortable silence.

# CHAPTER 5



Vincent is looking through the men's fashion magazines I gave him like they've offended him. I found them in a very sterile looking basket in Joel's bathroom, and I thought letting Vincent look through them would help me get a grasp on what we're looking for. So far, there's been no luck. I was hoping he'd at least show a preference as to what style he likes, but he's bared a grimace at each of them.

"You have to remember that you're not in the seventeenth century anymore. These are very twenty-first century outfits," I point out, hoping he'll just pick *something*.

"Must all of modern fashion be so relaxed?" The judgment in his tone is palpable.

I look through the magazines he hasn't browsed yet and pick a business one out.

"What do you think of this?" I slide the magazine full of men in three-piece suits to him.

For the first time since bringing the pile out here, he doesn't grimace.

"These are not atrocious," he says. I smile because that feels like the biggest win of my day.

"Business casual it is," I say. I know he's looking at the very un-business casual section of the catalog, but in no world can he walk around dressed like he's attending an important meeting every day.

I grab the magazine and pick my keys up off the table by the front door.

"Come on. We're going shopping."

Vincent follows me out to the car and slides into the passenger side. He buckles in, like I showed him, and settles into the seat. I connect my phone to Bluetooth and hit shuffle on my 'Upbeat Jams' playlist.

"Modernism lesson one: music," I say cheerily. There's nothing that boosts my spirits like music, and I'm happy to share some of my favorite songs with him for the first time.

It takes him a while, but eventually, he stops raising his brows at every boom of the bass and every shift in the beat. For most of the ride, he just sits and listens.

"For both our sakes, when we get there, just let me do most of the talking. Actually, unless it's absolutely necessary, let me do all the talking," I say. "There are going to be a lot of things that are new to you, and will probably be a shock, so just trust me on this, okay?"

"Okay."

"And if you get, um, hungry," I glance at him before continuing, "I packed a small cooler of blood bags in the trunk. Just remember not to squeeze them so hard this time."

I clutch my necklace at the memory, using it as an anchor to keep away any lingering nausea.

"What is that necklace? You never take it off."

I purse my lips, clutching the charm again before opening up to him.

"It was a gift from my mom. She gave it to me when I was a baby." I lose a shaky breath. "It's an Italian horn. It's supposed to ward off evil spirits and bad juju."

"I was sure I recognized it. Why do you touch it so much?"

"I feel like it's a connection to her. I've never taken it off—-I've always felt it protected me."

He nods, looking from me to the road ahead. He doesn't ask anything else, just listens to the music and watches as trees turn to buildings. We take a small detour as cops direct us away from a scene. They form a blockade so that onlookers can't see anything, but I can't help but wonder what it could be. There's a lot that happens in this city. It's hard to avoid, yet having such a large gathering of officers in one spot piques my interest.

There's one spot left on the street in front of the tailor shop. I know the area well, as I've come here with Joel often. On days when I'm feeling particularly lonely, we often run errands together or spend the entire day at his house. Every so often, he'll come to my apartment, but he and Erika don't get along, so I try to avoid it.

"We'll ask them to take your measurements, then we can pick some stuff out. I'm so excited!" I squeal.

He follows me into the sleek store, dirty looks immediately shooting in our direction at Vince's attire. Ignoring a rude comment from an elderly shopper to our left, I walk up to the nearest sales associate and ask about getting measurements. He directs us to a small stage surrounded by mirrors in the back corner and pulls out measuring tape. He works swiftly, recording measurements of Vincent's chest, torso, shoulders, arms, and everything in between. By the time he's finished, I have a list of measurements and corresponding sizes for Vince.

Now, we get to hunt.

I love shopping. Not that I've ever had the money to just buy whatever I want, but even just browsing racks is fun for me. It's always been a good way to take my mind off my work when things get frustrating. I love shopping even more when it's for other people.

"If you see anything you like, just hand it to me. I'll also pick out things I see that I think will look good on you. You would *kill* in a sweater and some slacks."

"I don't plan on killing anyone in anything, Isobelle," Vincent's voice pitches low.

"That's not—" I pause, laughing. "It's a figure of speech. It just means you'd look really good."

"Oh."

I try to smother the grin on my face but I can't help it.

After an hour of browsing and me trying to convince Vince to pick something out—spoiler alert, he doesn't—I have a pile of collared shirts, cable knit sweaters, slacks, and a few designer t-shirts. We are directed to the dressing rooms, where I wait in the seating area for him to emerge in each new outfit. "Isobelle?" he calls after three minutes.

"Yeah?" I call back.

"Could you," he starts, "help me?" he asks almost begrudgingly.

"With what?" I stand and move toward his door.

He opens it and stands in the doorway with unzipped pants and an unbuttoned shirt, looking like Zeus fallen from Olympus. I hurriedly shove him back into the decent-sized fitting room and shut the door.

"Um, you can't button it?" I ask.

"These buttons are so small," he grumbles.

"It might take some practice." I smile softly. "Here, let me."

I move to button the top button, and he goes still, looking down at me with such intensity that my skin heats. My knuckles graze his muscles as I move on to the next button and the next. Okay, so the grazing might be a little intentional; I'm just a girl.

"Um, the pants have a zipper and a button. Just pull the zipper up until it stops, and the button's a bit bigger than the ones on the shirt," I say, biting my lower lip as I take a step back.

He watches me, then turns to the mirror and gets the pants buttoned and zipped. Thank God for small mercies.

"I think you should try tucking in the shirt," I say, tilting my head as I look over the outfit.

He tucks it in, and I tell him to wait while I go grab something, returning moments later with a brown belt. He looks at it like it's a snake.

"You put it through the belt loops on the pants."

He takes it from me and attempts the challenge. And fails miserably. I step forward and take it from him.

"Like this." I push the end of the belt through the first loop and keep going. By the time I reach the back loops, I'm pressed firmly against him. The warmth of his body radiates over my skin. "There," I squeak and step back.

He looks over himself in the mirror, his expression unreadable.

"Well?" I prompt. "What do you think?"

He doesn't say anything. Instead, he assesses himself and nods.

I take the win.

He spends the next hour trying on outfits. I spend the next hour helping with buttons, covering my eyes while he changes, and trying to gauge whether he actually likes the clothes I picked out.

We end up buying everything, including the outfit I insist he leave on. We also tack some underwear and socks on to the bill. He looks a million times better in the khaki slacks and navy button-up than he did in his oversized shirt and sweats. We walk to the shoe store around the corner and get a few pairs of dress shoes, casual lace-up sneakers that he can wear with almost anything, and a pair of athletic shoes. Next, we hit the sportswear store a block over to grab some casual clothes for him to sleep and bum around in.

Once I feel satisfied with all our purchases, we walk back to the car. The sun is just starting to set and my stomach is grumbling. Our excursion took longer than I expected, and I didn't realize I'd skipped lunch.

"Are you hungry?" I ask. He gives me a look, so I add, "*Really* hungry?"

He seems to consider something before saying he could use a bite. I grab one of the bags out of the cooler and hand it to him once he buckles up. I've never been more thankful to have tinted windows.

"You drink that, and when you're done, we can pick up dinner," I say, trying to be casual about the man literally drinking blood in my passenger seat. I know he's sucked my wrist the same way he's sucking it back, but it feels weird watching him drink it like a skinny marg.

After making a call to Joel to see what he wants from the Chinese drive-thru we love, we take off down the streets of my favorite city. It's a whole other place at night, with all the lights turned on and people bustling through the streets. Vincent is entranced by the view outside his window the entire time.

I steer smoothly through the LED-lit streets. The multi-colored lights blur past us, and I decide I could get used to this. I hope Vincent decides to stick around because now that I've got him, I don't know what I'd do if he left.

# CHAPTER 6



Sunlight pours in through the open blinds, every little dust particle in its stream visible. I stretch my arms above my head and blink a few times as I welcome the day.

After dinner last night, I was completely tapped out, still slightly suffering from my blood sharing hangover. This morning, I feel like a brand new person.

Vincent slept in the guest room across the hall from mine—there are three other guest rooms on this floor and one downstairs. Joel's house will always have me in awe. It's completely unassuming from the outside—simple wood paneling and a wrap-around porch concealing the mansion that lies inside.

I drag myself downstairs after brushing my teeth and follow the smell of coffee to the kitchen. Joel's already up, sitting at the counter with a coffee in hand. He's looking over the contents of a folder when I bid him good morning.

"How's your wrist?" he asks without looking up.

"Straight to business, huh? No 'Good morning, best friend in the whole world. How'd you sleep?'?" I move past him and walk around the island to the coffee pot.

"Has it healed yet?"

Rolling my eyes with my back to him, I answer, "It's scabbed over. I'm sure it'll leave a scar."

He *hmphs,* but doesn't deem to say anything else.

"It's not a big deal, Joel. I basically forced him to feed on me."

"Oh, yeah, because that's the logical thing to do forty-thousand feet in the air with no medical aid." His tone is biting.

"It was me or the pilot. Besides, I'm fine. Will you just get over it, please?"

He glances up for the first time, his icy blues searching for something in my eyes.

"I have a work trip coming up soon. Will the two of you still be here while I'm gone?" he asks.

"No, I was planning on taking us to my apartment after breakfast today."

He's extra dick-ish this morning, and I'm not liking it one bit.

"I'm sure Erika will be *thrilled.*"

I bite my lip, holding back the words fighting to leave my mouth, then Vincent walks in. He's dressed in slacks and a button-up combo again, clearly having changed out of the plaid pajama pants he wore to bed.

I make a show of gasping. "You buttoned your own shirt!" I exclaim, and he rolls his eyes. "I'm so proud," I say, mimicking a mother whose child just tied their shoes for the first time.

"Good morning," he says, taking a seat on the opposite side of the counter from Joel.

"Look at that, Joel. The three-hundred-year-old knows how to say good morning."

Joel mutters something I can't hear and remains focused on his work.

"Coffee?" I offer Vince.

"Please, thank you."

"Do you like it bitter or with sugar and cream in it?"

"I've only ever had it bitter. It was an Italian delicacy last I had it."

I ponder the course of history and the period in which Italians gained access to coffee. I had to take many niche history classes during the course of my degree, such as Italian History. If I remember correctly, they started bringing coffee to Italy in the early 1600s. Just before he sealed himself beneath the castle.

"What was your status before you sealed yourself away?" I ask while pouring his mug.

"I was the son of a duke my entire life, so I grew up with privilege. However, when I joined Vivianne's ranks, we were treated very much like royalty. We were not, not even Vivianne had any royal blood, but we were revered the same way a king was."

"Is Vivianne the woman you hid from?" I ask, immediately regretting prying into his past. He's been so respectful of mine.

"Yes, she's the one who turned me."

I nod rather than say anything else and serve him his coffee. Joel has remained unnervingly silent, typing on his laptop like a madman.

"After we get some breakfast in us, I was thinking about going back to my apartment. You don't have to come, of course, but if you want to, I'm sure I can make some room," I say into my coffee mug.

"You don't live here?" he asks.

"No," I chuckle. "Joel was just nice enough to let us stay for a few days. I live in the city."

"Okay."

Okay? Okay, what? Okay, yes, I'll follow you to your apartment because I'd follow you to the ends of the Earth, or okay, have fun moving?

"Great." I rock back on my heels and sip my coffee.

I guess I'll know his answer when I'm packing the car.

"I suppose it's a good thing that I did not take anything out of these bags," Vincent says as he descends the front steps.

He's coming with me.

Beaming with joy, I bounce on the balls of my feet and say as casually as possible, "I guess so."

We finish loading his things into the back seat and then grab the cooler of blood bags that Joel packed for Vince. It's about a three to four weeks supply according to Vincent, and I know we can't leave them in the cooler for that long. I have enough funds in my bank account to stop by an appliance store and buy a mini fridge on the way, because in no world am I putting blood bags in the refrigerator I share with Erika. I'm having a difficult enough time trying to think of what to say about Vincent living with us.

We listened to another one of my playlists the entire way to the store and to my apartment, August curled up by Vincent's feet while I drove. He carries the mini-fridge and cooler upstairs with minimal effort, and I follow him with my backpack and his shopping bags. As I twist the key in the lock, I send up a silent prayer that the place isn't a wreck after leaving Erika alone for so long. She's not a problematic roommate in any way, but she has a habit of not cleaning up after herself whenever I'm gone for a few days.

To my relief, the place is clean.

"Welcome to my humble abode," I say, ushering Vince through the door. "My room's this way."

He follows me and sets the fridge and cooler down in the center of the room. The living room and kitchen are open, light spaces in the apartment. The wood floors are a lighter stain, and all the accent colors are bright. My room is the opposite of that Pinterest-worthy aesthetic. The walls with the window and bedroom door are painted off white to complement the two other walls that are exposed brick. My bedding is pale yellow with a few matching accent pillows, and the rug covering most of the hardwood flooring is white. My 'L' shaped desk in the corner is a recycled vintage cherry wood piece, housing my recording station, computer, a few piles of books, and files full of research that I've printed out.

I always wanted a bay window, and unfortunately, this apartment didn't come with one, so I bought a pastel purple loveseat to put under the rather large window. In the corner nearest that, is my massive book-case. Of course, I have an entire shelf dedicated to the Twilight books and merch I've bought over the years. My Carlisle Cullen Funko Pop is one of my prized possessions.

Vincent scans the room, not saying anything but clearly cataloging every little detail. It's a large room as far as apartments go; Erika definitely noticed the size difference compared to hers when she saw it for the first time. I have a storage unit filled with my parents' things that my mom had bought before she died. When I turned eighteen, her lawyer contacted me and told me about it. The last, and only, time I went there, I remember seeing a couch with a built in pullout bed. I think that couch was upstairs in my dad's office in the house I grew up in. I'm sure if I move some stuff around, we can fit it in here.

"You can sit anywhere. I'm going to set up the mini fridge before we run some errands," I say, getting to work unpacking the fridge.

Turning on the TV just to make some background noise, I decide to put on the news. For a man who's not exactly caught up with the times, I figure that'll be a good way to start. I'm putting in the second shelf when I hear an interesting story come on.

"Rachel Gregory, a student attending Boston University, was attacked yesterday evening, walking to her apartment. Authorities have yet to identify a suspect, but they have released a statement regarding these murders."

The middle-aged reporter's face is replaced by the Boston Police Department chief.

"We are putting all available resources into catching the killer. We have yet to find any evidence leading us to the suspect. The manner of these murders is unlike anything we've seen in this city before. The victims have all been found almost completely drained of blood, with teeth-shaped wounds on their bodies. This leads us to believe that these are demonic ritual killings, and the Boston Police Department has considered the possibility of cult activity."

The woman reappears on the screen.

"Rachel makes the fourth victim this week."

She moves on to another story, but I'm still mulling over what the chief of police just said.

Vincent has been with me every minute since landing from Germany.

"You didn't..." I look at him, guilty already for even asking. "Right?"

"I've been with you, Isobelle."

"I know. It's just... four people dead this week, and it's only Tuesday."

Pulling up the other cases on my phone, I find the first murder was committed on Sunday afternoon. Three girls and one guy have died. The flashing red and blue lights from the police on the street yesterday come to the forefront of my mind. What if we drove past a homicide scene and didn't even realize it?

Bodies drained of blood.

Bite wounds.

It *has* to be a vampire.

The cops can't be blamed for immediately assuming that these are demonic and ritualistic killings. That's exactly how vampire killings have been labeled for centuries. In medieval times, vampire attacks were blamed on radical heretic groups. In the Renaissance era, witches were to blame and then burned at the stake. Innocent people have been punished for vampire's sins for no other reason than vampires being sloppy.

"What are you thinking?" Vincent's voice cuts through the thought spiral I was about to go down.

"Nothing. I'm just kinda in shock, I guess."

"Why?"

"I've lived in this city my entire life. It's been thirteen years since there has been any sign of vampires here. Yet, I bring you here, and bam! A homicidal vampire starts roaming the streets."

"Thirteen years?"

"Yeah, that's when... That was the last time anyone was murdered like this."

I finish setting up the mini-fridge and plug it in near my desk. It's big enough to fit the fourteen blood bags Joel sent us with, thanks to some maneuvering.

"I'm going to go pick up a couch for you to sleep on. I doubt you'd find the loveseat very comfortable. You can read a book, or I can turn on a movie for you to watch while I'm gone, if that's alright with you?"

"Isobelle. You just said that there is a homicidal vampire prowling the streets. Do you really believe that I am letting you go out by yourself?"

Fair point.

"Okie dokie. I'll run to the bathroom real quick and we'll head out."

The stuff in the storage unit is coated in a thick layer of dust, a harsh reminder of how sorely I've neglected what's left of my parents. I'm sure their graves look as abandoned as their things here. I run my index finger over the top of my old box TV, the butterfly stickers I'd stuck to the sides still there. Out of curiosity, I press down on the VHS feeder on the front and out slides The Princess Diaries. My mom and I used to have Movie Night Mondays, and I remember being so excited to watch this with her. She had wanted to watch the Titanic double feature, but I convinced her to watch this with me. She fell asleep in my twin bed that night, her arms wrapped around my body.

"All of this is yours?" The sound of Vincent's voice makes me jump.

I wipe away the tears that had fallen and take a steadying breath before answering.

"Technically, yeah," I shrug.

"Why is it not in your apartment?"

"There's no room." That's partially the truth. There isn't any room for most of this stuff. The part I don't say is that, the idea of looking at any of this again is sure to make me break down crying. Standing here now, surrounded by old memories, I'm focusing very hard to hold it together.

"This would look much nicer than your ugly dining set," he says, examining the mahogany dining table cluttered with boxes.

"Gee, thanks," I nearly laugh.

The small dining table we have at home is a circular one made of glass and framed with white metal. Erika bought it, but I don't think it looks terrible. Especially when one of us stops at the store down the street to buy flowers to put in the center.

"Ah!" I exclaim, squeezing between more boxes and upturned furniture. "This is what I was looking for!"

Moving boxes out of the way, I realize this is going to take us a while. The couch is tucked in the very back corner of the unit, which means, to get it out, we'll need to move at least half these things into the hall. While Vincent is apparently measuring the thickness in millimeters of the dust coating everything, I start moving what boxes I can lift.

"Hey, guy with superhuman strength, I could use a little help with these," I say over my shoulder, setting the third box in the hall.

"Apologies. How can I help?" He's at the entrance of the storage unit instantly.

"Start moving boxes and stacking them with these. Just don't block the walkway. Oh my god! Careful! God, you almost gave me heart palpitations."

Moving much more deliberately, he begins stacking boxes.

"Some of this stuff is fragile, so please remember your own strength." I sigh, pinching the bridge of my nose.

Ten minutes in, I notice something silver sticking out of the top of a messily packed box. Pulling it out, I find a dusty picture with a silver frame and dust it off. It's an old picture of my mom, dad, and me sitting on a picnic bench. My mom's emerald eyes are transfixed on me as I laugh at something my dad is doing. Her dimples, the ones she gave me, are prominent on her cheeks as she smiles at me. My dad is laughing, too, his eyes squinting while his grin spreads from ear to ear.

Dammit, I miss them.

"Isobelle," Vince breaks my daze, his hand firmly finding my shoulder. "Are you well?"

"Yeah, yeah. I'm fine," I say, wiping away my tears. "I just need a minute."

I respectfully pull out of his grasp and walk down the hallway, turning the first corner to try to find the vending machine. A bottle of water would do me some good right about now.

After taking a few more corners, the glow of the vending machine lights up the hallway ahead of me. My arms are wrapped around me as I walk the final stretch under the flickering LEDs overhead. There's a crash down the hall, and I jump, squeezing my arm more tightly around myself as I punch the buttons 'B7'.

For a fleeting moment, the LED lights completely turn off. No buzzing, no flickering, no nothing. They turn on at the exact moment my water falls into the dispenser, and I find myself jumping for the third time since we got here.

With shaky hands, I unscrew the bottle cap and take the first quenching sip.

*Knock. Knock. Knock.*

What the hell was that? It sounded like something hard tapping on one of the metal doors to the storage units. My heart is beating out of my chest, and my breathing is coming in short bursts.

In the distance, I can hear the sound of boxes shuffling on the concrete; Vincent is still at my parent's unit. There's someone else in here.

The knocking sounds again, reverberating off the walls. I tell myself that it's nothing to worry about, that this is a public storage facility and that plenty of people could be here doing the same thing I am. But a large part of me tells me there's a masked killer around the corner on a mission to scare the shit out of me before shoving a machete through my chest.

Of course, the vending machine is right up against a dead end, so I have nowhere to go but back to where I came from—the direction of the masked killer noises. Thanks to the scary movies one of my foster parents used to watch all the time, I know better than to yell for Vincent. Or maybe I should. Would he be able to find me fast enough to stop the machete wielder before I'm brutally slain?

I recap my water and start down the hall.

Turning the corner, I swear I see the silhouette of a man, but the lights flicker and I blink and he's gone. *It's just your mind playing tricks on you, Isobelle. Breathe.*

Walking at a pace that makes my calves burn, I try to remember the directions I need to take to get back to the unit.

*Knock. Knock. Knock.*

It's behind me now. Against my better judgment, I turn around to see the silhouette again.

Shrouded in shadow is a tall, considerably built man with tousled hair.

I open my mouth to say something, but no sound comes out. This could be it. These could be my final moments, and I can't even think of any cool last words.

He drags his fingers along the ridges of the unit doors as he creeps forward.

"Don't worry, this won't hurt." His voice is deep, sultry, like a finely aged brandy. He is towering over me before I even have time to blink.

"You're him, aren't you?" I look up into the most vivid hazel eyes I've ever seen. "The cult killer on the news."

His thickly framed eyes darken, and a smirk tugs at his lips. Life-threatening proximity aside, he's beautiful. His bronze skin, dulled by the lighting in this cheaply maintained building, is covered in tattoos from his hands to where his sculpted arms disappear beneath his black t-shirt. He has a light five o'clock shadow spanning his jaw and upper lip, leading to his messy black hair. There's even a little brown mole on the side of his neck.

My very existence is threatened by his presence, yet I'm drawn to it like a moth to flame.

"Is that what they're calling me?" he croons.

A strong force pushes me back, away from the beautiful predator before me. I look down to find Vincent's arm across my body, tucking me safely behind him.

"Get away from her," he growls.

If Vincent is Zeus personified, this man is Hades in every sense.

He doesn't even bat an eye in Vince's presence.

"I'd get out of my way if I were you, old man. Before I make you." His tone is cold and menacing.

Vince tucks me further behind him to where I can't see the attractive stranger. There's a terrible snapping sound and Vince falls to the ground.

"Vince? Vincent!" I drop to my knees to examine him. There's a weird shaped lump on his neck where the man broke it. I mouth the words "oh my god" and stare in horror.

"What did you... How did you..."

"Who the hell are you?" he asks, stepping over Vincent's body. "And how do you know him?"

I slowly rise from the floor, my chest a hair's breadth away from his.

"I don't think you have any grounds to be asking *me* questions!"

He ducks his head so we are eye to eye.

"Who. Are. You?"

"My name is Isobelle Axford. It's only polite to tell me yours." Maybe I'll at least get to know the name of my murderer before I go. Maybe I'll be able to *The Lovely Bones* this shit.

"Creed."

"*What* are you?"

"You know the answer to that already, clearly." He glances at the pile of Vincent on the floor.

"Maybe I want to hear you say it," I say, forcing my voice not to shake.

He scoffs, that smirk returning.

"Why are you here? Why randomly show up in this city of all places and start killing people?" I ask.

A muscle in his jaw ticks and he purses his lips.

"Okay, well, if you're not going to kill me, do you think you can do me a favor?"

His brows raise in amusement.

"Could you tone it down a little? No, tone it down a lot. I have worked very hard to find my friend that you just KOed, and I'd like to keep his supernatural existence a secret. Having you prowling Boston leaving bodies thrown here and there isn't exactly going to help in the long run."

He stares into my eyes for a long moment, my breath catching as he does.

"You're brave."

"Thanks?"

"Your boyfriend will be fine. He's just getting some beauty sleep."

"He's not my boyfriend." I'm not sure why I say it. "Not that it's any of your business," I mumble.

"Sure."

He keeps me pressed between his body and the wall, unmoving, and I'm unwilling to push him off. There's still a good chance that he'll rip into my throat.

"Um," I say, my voice uncharacteristically breathy. "Could you possibly help me put him in the car?"

"Scared of getting caught in here with a dead man, Isobelle?"

I gulp at the sound of my name rolling off his tongue.

Finally, he steps back. The space between us allows me to take my first full breath since our initial exchange. Strangely, I miss the proximity.

If I went to therapy, I'm sure someone with a PhD would have a heyday divulging into that train of thought.

He easily hoists Vincent's limp body over his shoulder.

"Lead the way, *princesa*."

Once Vincent is laid across the backseat, I go back into the storage facility to put the boxes away. Creed follows me.

"You can go now, thanks," I say.

"You clearly came here for a reason. It'd be shitty to let you go home empty-handed."

"Like you care about being shitty."

"I don't know what you mean. I'm as un-shitty as they come." He feigns puppy eyes. Although, his puppy eyes have a lot more sex appeal than most.

"Fine. You can help me move these boxes so I can get to that couch."

"That's what you had your white knight doing while you were off getting water?"

"Um, yes."

He rolls his eyes but starts moving boxes into the hall. In no time at all, the path to the couch is clear enough to get it out of there. He lifts the couch completely solo and bares the weight of it on his shoulder.

"Were you planning on strapping this thing to your car?" he asks, his tone mocking.

"I guess so." In all honesty, I hadn't thought that far.

I'm sure I have bungee cords somewhere in my trunk. I fish them out while Creed balances the dusty couch on the car. He figures out how to secure it while I replace the boxes.

"Thank you," I say.

"Yeah, sure. Don't get your thong in a twist over it."

I slide into the driver's side and find Creed sitting comfortably in the passenger seat.

"What are you doing?" Instinctively, I glance back at Vincent.

"Relax, *princesa*. He's got a couple hours left of his *siesta*."

"I'll ask one more time. What are you doing?"

"Someone has to get sleeping beauty out of the car, and I doubt that'll be you."

He has a point. If he's telling the truth and Vince really won't wake up for a few hours, my only other choice is to leave him in the car.

"I'm gonna regret this," I say to no one, and I put the car in drive.

# CHAPTER 7



After vacuuming all the dust off the couch, Creed not-so-gently dropped Vince on the warm brown cushions. He then proceeded to stay at my apartment, snooping and occupying my sofa. It's been two hours, and already I'm counting down the minutes for Erika to get home. While I don't look forward to explaining the two men now occupying our apartment, I know that her being here will take Creed's attention off of me.

She's a flirt at heart, and Creed is her favorite flavor of the male species. Tall, dark, and fifty shades of good looking.

The top sirloin I picked up from the grocery store on the way here sizzles in the pan, the aroma of it filling the space.

"Smells delicious," Creed mutters into my ear, his body suddenly pressed against my back.

I elbow him in the ribs and turn sideways to push him away. He's been all up in my business since he set Vince down. He reaches for the lid of my rice pot but pulls away quickly when my wooden spoon slaps the back of his hand.

"If you ruin my dinner, I'll turn this thing into a stake and kill you… whatever your last name is. I'll kill you dead," I threaten.

"Careful when you threaten me, *princesa*. It gets me hot." He over enunciates the 't'.

"You're repulsive."

"Keep lying and maybe you'll convince yourself that's true."

Rolling my eyes, I turn back to the steak.

"Martinez," he says after several beats of silence.

"What?" I ask.

"My last name." He glances down at my hands. "It's Martinez."

"Oh," I mouth.

Erika loves my Baja Bowls, so I figured that would be a good buffer for the 'by the way, two men are going to be occupying our home for the foreseeable future' talk.

I'd love to kick Creed out, but it doesn't seem like he plans on budging any time soon.

"What'd you season the steak with?" Creed asks, eyeing the red powder covered meat.

"Chipotle lime seasoning."

He '*hmms*' and leans against the counter.

At last, the sweet sound of the door opening and clicking shut graces my ears.

"Mmm, smells good, Iz! Are you making—oh." She stops when she sees Creed. "Who is this?"

Creed looks at her over his shoulder, her shock turning into pure girlish excitement.

"This is Creed. He's a friend from work."

"Here I was thinking you worked with a bunch of old guys," she says, eyes still on Creed.

Augie chooses now to hop up on the counter and nuzzle into Creed's forearm. He purrs as he rubs his body against the tattooed extremity.

Creel pulls away, and August has to regain his balance to not fall off the countertop. Giggling, I swoop my cat into my arms and scratch the top of his head.

"I really don't understand your issue with him. I thought you were a big scary man," I mock. Since the second August made his first appearance, taking a liking to Creed, the man has avoided him like the plague.

"Not a fan of cats," he bites.

I set Augie down to flip the steak.

"Will you be staying for dinner?" Erika asks, still in her Creed-induced trance.

"I'll stay as long as you like," he answers, leaning his forearms on the counter to face her.

She gives him a sultry smile and retreats to her room to set her things down. This is going to be *great*.

"If you so much as think about hurting her—"

"You'll whittle some other household appliance into a stake and drive it through my still-beating heart." He smiles.

"I'm serious. She's off limits."

He gets a mischievous gleam in his eyes as he smirks back at me.

"Are you offering?"

"If you plan on sticking around like it seems you are, I have an unending supply of blood bags for you and Vince. So let's make the whole of Massachusetts off limits," I counter in a hushed tone. "That's no fun."

"Too. Bad."

This man will be the death of me. Speaking of men, Vincent emerges from the hallway, trailing after Erika.

He makes eye contact with Creed, and every ounce of oxygen leaves my lungs.

"Who's this, Izzy?" Erika asks, but I'm too busy sprinting across the living room to answer.

I grab Vincent's arm and get on my tiptoes.

"It's okay. Please, just be calm until after dinner," I whisper in his ear. I know I'm asking for more than I deserve, considering Creed snapped his neck and is a mass murderer, but I can't risk involving Erika in this mess. "Creed, can you turn off the burner on the steak, please?"

He smirks, that gleam back in his eyes, and turns to face the stove.

Erika clears her throat.

"Oh, right. Erika, this is... my cousin from England."

"I didn't know you had cousins in England. I actually didn't know you had cousins at all. Or any family, really," she mumbles that last part.

"Yeah, neither did I!" I blurt. "I did one of those DNA things, and low and behold, here he is!"

"Does your cousin have a name?" she asks, batting her eyes at Vince. *Classy.*

"Vincent," he says, reaching a hand out. He gently grasps Erika's fingertips and brings her hand to his mouth, placing a brief kiss on her knuckles. She, of course, blushes like a fool.

Can she not just pick one? Or maybe neither?

I'm not usually the jealous type, and I have no grounds to warrant jealousy, but I feel the pang of it in my gut all the same.

"E-Erika," she stammers.

"It is a pleasure."

She's practically drooling.

"Does anyone want wine?" I ask, my hands finding my hips. "I'll get wine."

"This is tasty," Creed says after swallowing a bite of his food.

"Thank you," I say.

"She makes this all the time. It's my favorite thing she makes, not that much else she cooks is great." The latter was unnecessary, and I find myself clenching my teeth a little too aggressively. "Do you cook, Creed?"

I don't pay attention to his answer, instead my focus is on Vincent and his flared nostrils. Clearly, he's not going to let this go, and I am not looking forward to what will come when Erika goes to bed.

I down my second glass of wine and pour another one.

"Rough day, Iz?" Erika asks. I'm shocked she's torn her eyes off of Creed long enough to notice.

"Rough evening."

She makes a feeble attempt to smother a smile and turns back to Creed, who is enjoying the attention.

"What do you think of the meal, Vince?" Creed asks, turning his gaze to the seething man across from him.

"It's delicious."

"Really? I haven't seen you take a bite."

Without hesitation, Vincent shovels a mouthful into his mouth. I take my chance when Erika looks away to squeeze his hand on the table and give him a pleading look. He huffs out a breath. Sliding my hand back across the table, I busy myself with eating.

"Does Isobelle bring male friends over often?" Creed asks Erika, and I snort, nearly choking on my food.

"No. No one but the only friend she has aside from me." I take a big gulp of my wine.

"*A friend*, huh? How long have they, you know?" He wiggles his eyebrows.

"Oh, god, no. They're not together," Erika chuckles. "He's gay, unfortunately."

I'm sure Joel would love to hear about her disappointment in his choice of bedroom buddy.

"And what about you?" Creed asks.

"A lady never kisses and tells," she replies, a coy smile on her face.

This has to stop, or I might whittle that stake for my own heart.

"Promises, promises," Creed says.

I stomp on his foot, and he whips around toward me. His eyes roll at the warning glare I shoot him, but he stops playing who-has-the-better-innuendo with my roommate.

Erika continues to ask both of them questions throughout dinner. By the time she excuses herself to shower and get ready for bed, I've finished four and a half glasses of wine, which, surprisingly, didn't make their conversation any more tolerable. However, I seem to have traded one tiresome conversation for another, much more hostile one.

"What the bloody hell is he doing here?" Vincent asks, his snarl directed at me.

"Can we take this to my room?" I ask, tired and a little dazed from the wine.

I get up and head down the hall, the boys on my tail, shutting my bedroom door behind them.

"Vincent, Creed. Creed, Vincent." I plop down on my bed, head spinning a little. "Vincent, Creed is very sorry for breaking your neck. Creed, tell Vincent you're sorry."

"Unlike you, *princesa*, I don't find myself in the habit of lying."

"You're a killer. You shouldn't be anywhere near her," Vince bites.

"Who are you to be making her decisions?" Creed steps up to Vince. "And can you honestly tell me you don't have a ledger of your own, old man?"

"Boys, boys, please," I mumble, slurring my words. "Can't you both be civil?"

"I'll be civil when he is no longer in this apartment," Vincent says through gritted teeth.

Ugh, I can't handle this level of testosterone.

I lie back until my head hits the pillow. One of them says something, but the call of sleep is too loud to hear it. They'll probably sort it out themselves, right? They are grown men.

I wake up with a gnarly headache and a jumbled recollection of what happened after dinner. I know Vincent wasn't happy, and I know Creed didn't like Vincent's tone. I can't remember much else.

Speaking of the two vampires I invited into my home, where are they?

I sit up, the sun's rays hitting my face, causing my eyes to burn. I block the light with my hand and find Creed asleep on the loveseat. His head is tilted backward, and his mouth is wide open. He looks a lot less intimidating this way. Vincent ended up sleeping on the couch. He also looks so perfectly vulnerable in this state. His dark hair is messy and sticking in every direction, his shirt is thrown on the floor, and the contours of his back muscles are outlined in the sunlight. A belly sleeper.

They must have found some sort of resolution to their issues. Good. I don't want to wake them up, so instead of getting out of bed, I reach over to my shelf and grab the book I started before leaving for Germany.

I'm lost in the pages when I feel the weight of the bed shift. I'm not sure how much time has passed, but I'm not willing to give up this perfect fantasy world to see who's awake.

"What are you reading, *princesa*?"

His morning voice is nearly enough to pull me out of the story. I tilt the cover up so he can read it, but he snatches the book from my hands instead.

"Hey," I whisper-shout, not wanting to wake Vincent.

"With gentle hands, he caresses my inner thigh. His fingers making their way to my slickened center—"

I cover the pages with my hands, cheeks burning with heat.

"Let's not," I say and tug the book from his hands.

"Want a play-by-play?" he asks, gleaming hazel eyes meeting mine.

His hand rests on my knee, his eyes never leaving mine as he starts trailing his fingers up my thigh. My breath hitches in my throat.

Vincent groans from the couch and I scramble out of that bed faster than I've ever scrambled in my life.

"Morning, sunshine! I am going to go make breakfast. And coffee. I need coffee."

I practically run from the room and put the kettle on the stove. While I wait for that to boil, I get started on my eggs. Despite what Erika thinks, I'm a great cook. Self-taught, but great.

The kettle whistles, and I add it to the coffee grounds in the French press.

After the eggs are done, I toast some bread in the pan and serve three plates. Erika's already at work, probably pissed that she had to stop to get coffee on her way in. Creed and Vince come dragging themselves down the hallway a moment later.

"What's wrong with you two? Stay up too late resolving your spat?"

"Maybe I stayed up too late watching you sleep," Creed suggests.

"I made breakfast," I say, dropping the amused look on my face.

"Thank you, Isobelle," Vince says as he grabs his plate from the counter.

I pour three coffees, two black and one with honey and milk. Creed grimaces at his when I hand it to him.

"Make it like you make yours." He hands it back to me.

I raise my brows and crane my ear toward him.

"Please," he adds, a condescending smile on his face.

"Gladly."

They sit on the barstools, and I eat standing on the other side of the counter. August is curled at Creed's feet.

"So," Creed starts around the food in his mouth. "Why'd you let me stay last night? You've got no reason to trust me. For all you know, your roommate is dead in her bedroom right now."

"I didn't think I had a choice."

"Not true. I see at least four more wooden utensils you could have threatened me with."

I shove a forkful of eggs into my mouth.

"I could ask you a better question," Vince chimes in. "Why did you stay?"

I turn a curious look toward Creed, eager to hear his answer. Instead, he bites off a mouthful of toast and sips his coffee.

# CHAPTER 8

*Izzy*

"Vincent, will you please just relax and watch the movie while I take him?" I'm exhausted from this conversation.

When Creed asked me for a ride earlier, I didn't consider that Vincent might take offense when I asked him to stay in the apartment for a bit. The opening credits for Twilight are playing on the living room TV that he's supposed to be watching.

"Consider this a study hour for you. Learn how people act in the real world," I say, hanging my purse over my shoulder.

He groans and glares at me, but finally, Creed and I make it out of the apartment.

"Twilight is hardly how people *act in the real world*," Creed says, air quoting that last bit. "Unless you want him moping around like a moody teenager."

"It's pop culture. It'll at least help him acclimatize."

"Sure, but if we come back and he's brooding in your bedroom corner, I'll drive your wooden ladle through my own heart."

I laugh. "Just wait until he finds my highlighter."

A crooked grin spreads across his face, one corner of his mouth slightly higher than the other. Large smile lines appear on his cheeks, charming enough to make a part of me melt just looking at them.

*Get it together, Isobelle. He legitimately almost killed you yesterday.*

As we descend the stairs, because whoever built our apartment building was a psychopath and didn't install an elevator, I decide to ask Creed where it is I'm taking him.

"The storage place."

I halt with my feet on two different steps.

"I'm sorry. The same storage place we were at yesterday?"

"Unless we were at another one yesterday, yes."

"And why do you need to go back to the storage facility?" I ask, briskly moving down the steps to catch up to him.

He doesn't skip a single beat when he says, "I need to get my car."

"Your car?"

"You having a stroke back there, *princesa*?"

"You're telling me you had a car yesterday and still made me drive you here?"

"How else was I going to get some quality time with you?"

"You don't even know me."

"Doesn't mean I can't seduce you." He winks.

"There will be no seducing. Nope. Nuh-uh. No way."

He spins on the ball of his foot to face me, causing me to damn near slam into him. His arm comes up beside me on the rail as he leans forward, the two of us at eye level, even though I'm a step above him.

"You sure about that, *princesa*?" he says, deep and full of promise.

I gulp back the sudden ball in my throat.

"I saw how you were looking at your roommate last night. If I didn't know any better, I'd say you were jealous."

"Or concerned for her safety, you know, given that you're a wanted killer and all."

I put on the best show of my life to seem confident and unafraid. The truth is, I'm both buzzing with nerves—fear—and getting a little slick between the legs.

"If that helps you sleep at night, sure." He leans closer, his lips brushing my ear as he says his next words. "But the scent of your arousal says otherwise."

His teeth softly clamp and pull at my earlobe as he retreats, turning around and continuing down the stairs. As he hits the second-floor awning, I'm still frozen on the steps where he left me. When my thoughts finally catch up to me, I storm down the steps, practically running.

"Hey!" I catch up to him, grabbing his arm and turning him toward me. "What the hell was that?"

"Don't act—"

"Don't you *ever* corner me like that again!" I shout, jabbing a finger in his face. "Who do you think you are that you assume I'm okay with what you just did back there?"

"I'm not a fan of liars, Isobelle. So, if you want to spew them, run back upstairs to your perfect little white knight watching chick flicks in your living room."

"What right do you have to tell me I'm lying, Creed?" I speak through gritted teeth.

"Look where you're standing."

I snap out of the red-rimmed focus I have on his face to realize that I've stepped so close to him that our chests touch. My mouth is barely an inch from his, where his head is tilted to look at me. "If you were telling the truth, you wouldn't have gotten this close."

"You're infuriating."

"And you're still standing there."

Shoving his chest, I step back and walk out the door.

Creed looks positively miserable in the passenger seat of my car while I sip my frappe that I stopped for and sing along to music by three women that men like him typically can't stand: Taylor Swift, Sabrina Carpenter, and Billie Eilish.

His misery brings a smile to my face.

My insides still seem to be confused by what he did in the stairwell, but my brain has at least found some sound logic. Were his actions okay? No. That's why I'm tormenting him with my music. Did I hate the way his actions made me feel? Also no. That is why I'm still giving him a ride.

Between him and Vincent, my hormones and emotions are out of control, and I am going to need to find a way to fix that ASAP, because it doesn't look like they'll be going anywhere any time soon. I haven't had the bravery to tell Joel about Creed yet. To bring home a vampire who is capable of killing me at any minute is one thing. To admit to allowing a vampire into my home who has been terrorizing the city is entirely another. He supports me in a lot of things, but that is one thing I have a feeling he'd protest.

"You missed the turn."

"Did I? Oops," I say, smiling at him.

"We can do this all day, *princesa*. I'm not apologizing."

"I didn't ask you to." And I don't want him to, either.

"Good. Now, can we cut the bullshit and get me to my car? I have somewhere I need to be."

"What? You got a hot date waiting on you?" I ask.

"Would you care if I said yes?"

"No." I answer too fast. Would I care? I've known him for less than twenty-four hours, yet he's like a magnet for my attention. Honestly, I *was* jealous when he entertained Erika's ridiculous flirting last night. I'm not even sure I like him, but something in the back of my head is telling me that I would care. I'd care very much. And that frightens me.

"What'd I say about liars, Isobelle?" His eyes darken, and I purse my lips, focusing on the road instead of him.

"Izzy. Just, please, call me Izzy. Most people do."

"Vincent doesn't."

"Vincent's... different." As in, he's lived an entire lifetime in a time that I couldn't even imagine actually living in.

"Izzy. I like it. Makes me feel special," he drawls.

We turn into the parking lot outside the storage facility. It's a weekday, so it's mostly empty.

"Which one's yours?"

"I parked around the back. You'll know it when you see it."

I pull around the back side of the building and immediately know which car is his. I stop next to a cherry red Chevy Impala, casually parked along the cinder-block wall. From here, it's in perfect condition. The paint job is pristine, and the interior leather matches the exterior coloring. It's gorgeous.

I'm not much of a car person, but even I'm swooning over his vehicle of choice.

"*That's* yours?"

"You like what you see?"

"I mean, how can I not?"

"Stop lying to me," he pauses to lean over the center console, "and maybe I'll give you a ride."

With a wink, he gets out of my car and into his.

I spot a pack of cigarettes on the dash and raise a brow at him.

"You smoke?" I ask, nodding to the discarded box through the open window.

He glances at it, then shrugs. "I quit."

My brows raise as I give voice to my shock. "Really?"

He seems like a guy who would smoke, not a guy who would smoke, then quit.

"Long time ago," he drawls.

I shrug and begin to roll up the window.

"Race you home!"

I take off before he even has his engine running. Not that I meant it seriously, because he has somewhere to be and I have no desire to get arrested today, but speeding off and leaving him in the dust brings me a specific sense of giddiness.

Fifteen minutes later, I'm jiggling the key in the lock to my apartment. I think the locks may need to be replaced, but I don't care enough to take it up with our landlord. Upon entering, I find Vincent sprawled out on the couch, fully immersed in the movie, Erika angrily mumbling to herself in the kitchen, and Joel working around her to get plates and silverware from the cupboard.

"What are you doing here?" I ask, not sure whether it's intended for Erika or Joel.

"I thought I'd bring you guys some lunch," Joel answers first.

"That client we were supposed to meet with from California stood us up. Again. He came in for his initial meeting and we couldn't come to an agreement, so he was supposed to come in yesterday but didn't. I emailed him yesterday afternoon to invite him in today, and he still didn't show up. Now my boss is pissed and taking it out on me because everything is my fault, as per usual, and I can't find the hay slinger anywhere!" Erika huffs and leans on the counter.

"Oh. And, thank you."

"So, he doesn't get the deal. I don't see how that affects you," Joel chimes in as he plates some food.

"Did you not hear a thing I just said? My boss is mad. When the boss is mad, Erika suffers. Got it?"

He rolls his eyes and brings the food to the table. It looks like subs from my favorite sandwich place in town. It's a really cute mom-and-pop place run by the DiMarco family.

"I got one for you, too, creep," Joel tells Vincent. Looks like that's going to stick for a while.

You watch a girl sleep for two days just one time, and suddenly, you're branded a creep.

"Oh, have you met Vincent before?" Erika asks.

Internally, I panic because I hadn't realized I needed to come up with a five-tier story about who Vince is and why he's here when I told her he was my cousin. Externally, I smile in Joel's direction and pray he saves this like he usually does.

"I picked him up from the airport with Izzy. I wanted to make sure he wasn't going to murder her or something like that."

Not the best save, but a save, nonetheless. Erika shrugs and grabs her sub just as her phone rings in her back pocket.

"Hello?" Her greeting is followed by a lengthy string of unintelligible ranting. When she hangs up, the color has bleached from her face, and she quickly wraps her lunch back up. "I've got to get back to the office. Thanks for the sandwich, I guess," she sneers.

"Is everything okay?" I ask.

"I'm not sure, but if I don't get back in like five minutes, I am so fired."

Her work is at least fifteen minutes away.

The door slams behind her, and I follow her trail to lock it.

Roughly an hour after Vince, Joel, and I finished lunch, Creed had knocked on the door. Explaining to Joel that I had welcomed yet another vampire into my home was difficult enough. Imagine the judgment I faced when he had found out that Creed is the cult killer. He might have actually tried to kill me had my bodyguards not been there to rip his head off for doing so.

We've watched a total of three movies, each one a vampire movie that I love, which has allowed for a lot of time to get comfortable around each other. Joel seemed content that Creed wasn't going to kill me and left half an hour ago. Erika is still MIA. Creed and Vince are settled in the living room with me, Vince on the other end of the couch, and Creed in the large armchair next to us. I poured Vince a glass of the whiskey I keep set aside for rainy days to try to calm his nerves. Getting asked what I'm doing or where I'm going every time I stand up is a lot, especially when I'm so used to living with a roommate who doesn't care what I do or when I do it.

Before Erika, I lived alone. The minute I turned eighteen and got out of the foster system, I got a car with the money I'd saved up over the years and awaited high school graduation so I could move into dorms at college. By the time that happened, I had access to all of my parents' money. I made a down payment on this apartment right away.

Looking around now, I've come a long way since those bare-walled days.

"Someone's here." Creed's head snaps toward the door.

"Who?" I ask.

"I don't know."

"It's a vampire," Vince adds.

Another one? What am I, some vamp magnet? I find one, and suddenly, they're all coming out of the shadows to occupy my life.

I push off the couch and march for the door, Creed's hand clamping down on my arm before I can take more than two steps.

"I'll be fine. Besides, if they try to hurt me, I'm sure the two of you will be at my defense in half a second." *Because you're both crazy and have been hovering all day.* The latter goes unsaid.

His eyes burn holes through my skull, but he eventually lets me go. I cautiously open the door to find a tall blonde leaning on the doorframe, blisters covering patches of his skin. He looks up, his golden brown eyes meeting mine.

"Help me." That's the only thing he says before losing his grip on the doorframe and collapsing on top of me. For once, I'm glad to have two super-abled men attached at my hip because I don't go tumbling to the floor under his weight.

As Vince lifts the stranger off of me and Creed pulls me into his side, I can't help but stare at the man.

"What are those blisters?" I ask.

"One hell of a sunburn," Creed answers.

Vince hauls him over his shoulder and holds him in a fireman's carry.

"Take him to my bed." He nods, and I trail behind him down the hallway. "He needs blood, doesn't he?"

"Yes," Vince says, lying the man's limp body on the bed.

"And a shit ton of it. I'm going to go out on a limb and say he's new, judging by the severity of the burn," Creed adds.

"New?" I look up at him.

"As in, just turned. Whoever did it clearly didn't tell him anything about the transition."

I look over at the blonde man again, taking in the soot and blood-covered state of his jeans, button down, and blazer. His face, while beautiful, is coated in dirt and dried blood. Something happened to him, and whatever it was, wasn't good.

"Rest assured, *princesa*," Creed sidles up beside me, "I didn't look that shitty when I turned."

"Thank you, Creed. I was so worried," I deadpan, rolling my eyes.

"Keep that attitude up and I'll give you a reason to be."

Lips pressed into a thin line, I watch as Vince slowly looks toward us. I don't mind Creed's dirty quips, but they seem to grate Vince's nerves.

"So, that's what the sun can do to you?" I ask.

Vince grits his teeth, then answers, "Yes. When we don't have enough blood in our systems, our bodies are weak. Sun exposure will turn our skin red, then, if exposed long enough, blister like this."

"Hence why baby vamp here got it so bad. I doubt he ate anything after waking up." Creed crosses his arms over his chest. "But why the fuck did he come here?"

"Why did you come to Boston?" I volley. He considers that for a moment, then shrugs.

"We need to get him blood, so when he wakes up, he doesn't try to feed on you, Isobelle."

Vince is right, of course. I don't feel like being treated like a five course meal today. At least not in *that* sense. I check the mini-fridge and find six blood bags remaining.

"Will this be enough?"

"It'll have to be." Vincent collects the bags and takes them to the bed. He opens one and starts pouring it slowly into the stranger's mouth. It takes a minute, but eventually, he drinks. After bag two, he's able to hold it to his own mouth as the blisters start to heal. After bag four, he sits up and desperately reaches for bag five.

Then he spots me.

Before Creed or Vincent have time to restrain him, he's pressed against me. Looking down at me with striking brown eyes, he seems to fight something inside himself. Like his instincts are battling beneath his skin.

"Creed, don't." Vincent's tone is biting, but I can't remove my gaze from this tall man. Partially because I'm frightened, but also because there's a gravity about him that begs me not to look away. "He won't hurt her."

"How the fuck do you know that? Don't hold your fucking hand up to me, *viejo*, unless you want it severed."

"He won't."

If I could find my voice, I'd ask how Vince is so sure that this man means me no harm. Then the blonde says a single word that sends my head spinning.

"Mate."

I sobelle paces in front of Creed and me, while Logan, the stranger who collapsed at the threshold, watches her like a helpless child. His wide eyes and gawking expression have remained permanently fixed on her silhouette since he decided to say the one word I've been avoiding since putting everything together.

That day, when she woke up after I fed on her and I had to hold myself back from ripping Joel's head off just for being close to her, was when it all snapped into place for me. Any sane man would not have watched a girl sleep for two days on end. I was not a sane man then, and I never will be again. I have a mate. Mated men are never sane.

"Is somebody going to explain what the hell he just said?" Isobelle asks, feet pounding against the wooden floor as she takes ten steps to the left. Ten to the right. Ten to the left again.

"I mean, he's, what, ten minutes old? He doesn't have a single clue. I doubt he even realizes what he said." She sticks her hand in Logan's direction.

Creed chuckles. "Well, *princesa*, I believe he called you his mate."

"I got that, Creed, thank you. What on God's green earth does that freaking mean?" Her pulse is pounding beneath her skin, her heart beating against her sternum.

"It means the mindless little fucker is attached to you until the day he dies. It's like marriage, but even more goddamn constraining."

"How would he even know that? He's been a vampire for all of a few hours."

"It is an instinct. It comes naturally to us, like a feeling rooted deep in our chest, whispering to us what it needs," I say.

"*Us?*" she questions, eyebrows raised. Her pacing finally ceases.

"Buckle up, buttercup. You are in for one hell of a culture shock." Creed crosses his arms over his chest and sinks further into the couch.

"What?" Isobelle's jaw slackens. Her eyes find mine. "What does he mean?"

"I didn't want to say anything, in case I was wrong. I've never heard of a vampire-human bond before."

"Wrong about me being your mate, too?" Her forehead wrinkles as her deep brown brows shoot up. She takes a step back.

"Not just his, baby."

"Great! So, I'm stuck with all of you until you die?" She huffs out a breath, then recoils. "I didn't mean it like that. It's just... this is a lot to take in."

"Beautiful," the kid murmurs, still transfixed with Isobelle.

"Want me to fix him?" Creed offers.

"Can you?" Isobelle asks.

Without any further conversation, Creed gets up, walks over to Logan, and punches him square in the jaw, knocking him to the floor. Isobelle jumps, drawing in a sharp intake of air. By the time Creed is back in the chair, the kid is shaking off the hit, rubbing his jaw.

"What the hell was that for?" Logan asks, looking at Creed for the first time. "Who the hell are you?" He looks around the room. "And where the fuck am I?"

"See," Creed gloats. "Fixed him."

"Y-you're name's Logan, right? That's what you told me before." Isobelle kneels in front of him.

"Yeah, who are you?"

"I'm Izzy. You, uh, said something before. Do you remember why you said it?"

The kid rubs the back of his neck, a slight blush reddening his face. "Well, I reckon, ma'am, I called you beautiful because I think you are."

"I—Thank you." Isobelle smiles sweetly at him, yet I don't want to tear the kid limb from limb. "I didn't mean that, though. I meant when you called me your mate."

"I, what?" he asks.

"You said 'mate' to me a little bit ago. Do you know why you said that?"

"I don't remember saying that, but I can't deny that that's what I want to call you. What's going on?" His eyebrows scrunch together. The poor lad hasn't a clue what has happened to him.

"What's the last thing you remember?" I ask.

It takes him a moment, concentration written all over his face.

"I remember driving through fields. Then I remember someone hitting me and my truck rolling off the road. I blacked out after that, and next thing I knew, I woke up here. Drinking out of blood bags like they were Bloody Marys."

"Oh, Logan," Isobelle breathes. I don't need Creed's abilities to know she grieves for him.

"He's not dead, for Christ's sake. The stench of your sadness makes me want to vomit," Creed says. Isobelle whips her head around to look at him.

"The *stench* of my sadness?"

"Oh, fuck. You didn't know I could smell that?"

"You can *smell* my sadness?" Skepticism oozes from her voice.

"Yup." He pops the 'p' sound and smirks at her.

I look at the kid as he watches Isobelle. He's going to be dependent on her for the first few weeks. A newborn attached to the mother's breast.

"I can only handle one bomb dropping at a time, so for now, I'm going to act like you didn't say that. Logan, you said you want to call me mate. Why?" Isobelle turns back to the kid.

"I don't know," he says slowly. "It's like, somewhere in the back of my mind, I know that's what you are to me."

"Is it that way for the two of you?" She looks between Creed and I.

"In a way," I say.

"What the hell does any of this mean? Vince, you always seem to have an answer."

"For us, having a mate is like the very fabric of our soul is eternally calling out to another. That longing is what drew Creed and Logan here, and what kept me from abandoning you. It amplifies tenfold when the mating bond is solidified, but the constant ache in our chests turns into something whole, complete, when that happens, rather than the longing we all feel now," I say, recalling from my past.

"Solidified?" Logan asks from his perch on the sofa.

"When mates fuck, it forms a complete bond. Until then, they're like two halves of a whole," Creed offers, a dark grin on his face.

"I'm going to move past that bit for a moment." She shakes her head. "Why don't I feel that *call* to any of you?"

This is where things stop making sense to me. She is human. We shouldn't have any of these feelings for her. It's unnatural.

"I don't know."

"What he's trying to say is that you're a fucking anomaly. A human with three vampires mated to her," Creed says, crooked grin still in place.

"This just keeps getting better, doesn't it?" She looks up to the ceiling and mouths something, then she clutches her necklace. "So, *if* I were to… make love to any of you, I'd bond myself to you?"

Creed scoffs, and Logan tries to hide a smile.

"It's not likely. You're still human. Until you *feel* the mating bond inside—you calling out for us—you aren't half. Right now, we are in a waiting pattern."

"So, I need to turn to complete the bond?"

"Yes."

"Say the word, *princesa*, I've got plenty of blood to spare."

She looks like she's considering his offer, and a spider crawls up my spine. I may have to live this insufferable eternity, but she shouldn't have to just for us.

"So, wait. I've been alive for twenty-five years. Why now? Why didn't Creed find me before?"

"I didn't feel anything until about two weeks ago."

Realization hits me like a fist to my gut.

"It's my fault."

Silence.

"When I bit you, it must have activated something. My venom mixing with your blood, it's like it lifted some metaphorical veil that was concealing you from us. That's why I didn't feel a pull to you, but simply a dull prickling sensation. Your blood hadn't been activated yet."

She *hmms* and stands from her crouched position. Ten steps left. Ten right. She repeats this cycle four times before stopping and sitting atop her bed.

"Where the hell is he going to sleep?" she asks, more to herself than any of us.

"I don't mind sharing the bed, *princesa*. Golden boy can take the loveseat." Creed winks and I grimace. I may be at ease with Logan's affection toward her, but Creed's crude manner makes my teeth clench. Isobelle doesn't seem to mind, so I keep it to myself.

"Nice try, but I'd prefer my bed to myself until further notice, thank you very much," she throws over her shoulder. His smirk only widens.

"Don't let me put you out, Izzy. I can go back to my hotel," Logan offers.

"Absolutely not. You just died and came back to life as a vampire. You're staying here."

"I-I died?"

Isobelle pinches the bridge of her nose, shoulders tensing.

"I'm so sorry. I shouldn't have said that. Well, I definitely *should* have said that; I just shouldn't have said it like *that*. Yes. You died. I assume in your accident, but somebody had to have gotten to you and got vampire blood in your system before you died. That's why you came back. That's why you felt a pull to come here."

"Oh," he says, eyes on his hands where they rest on his knees. "I guess that beats death. The permanent kind, I mean."

Isobelle laughs. The lilting sound of it soothes my nerves, her effortless smile attracting my gaze like a scent attracts a hound.

This woman will be my undoing, mortal or not.

# CHAPTER 10

## *Izzy*

I wake up to my back pressed against a warm body and a strong arm slung over me. The steady breathing of whoever it is moves my body as their chest rises and falls. I look down to find a tattoo-covered arm, lit by the sun peeking through the window, curled around my waist.

Behind me, Creed sleeps peacefully pressed against my body. When I fell asleep, he was lying on the pullout bed, his nose in a book he pulled off my shelf. Judging by how deeply he's breathing, he snuck into the bed a while ago. Logan is snoring from the makeshift bed he made for himself on the floor—a haphazardly thrown together pile of blankets and spare pillows. His limbs are splayed out over the collection. He's quite handsome now that the blisters, dirt, and blood are gone. His face is carved in a way that shows ruggedness, but also cut with a softness that's unnervingly disarming. His suntanned skin stands out against his golden blond hair, making him look like every girl's beachy wet dream.

If Apollo is walking the planes of this earth, he's asleep on my bedroom floor.

Vincent is asleep in what looks like a very uncomfortable position on the loveseat. His head is tilted back so that the column of his throat is exposed, his pulse beating against the pale skin of his neck.

Gingerly, I scoot out from Creed's grasp, careful not to make too much noise as I sit at the edge of the bed. I forgo slippers as I pad barefoot to the bathroom. As I catch a glimpse of myself in the mirror, long brown hair in an unruly mess atop my head and indentations from my pillow decorating my cheek, I wonder how the heck I got into this situation.

Two weeks ago, I was just a girl trying to find proof vampires exist. Now... Well, now, I'm a girl with three vampires who are mated to her, and therefore, stuck to me like glue for all eternity. A part of me wonders what it would feel like if I could feel the mating bond. Would it be intoxicating and wholeheartedly fulfilling, or would it be like a plague sewn into the fabric of my soul? They don't seem to hate me, so I'd like to believe it's most like the former.

I jump when I lift my head from spitting out toothpaste to find Creed standing behind me in the mirror. As I clutch my chest, he steps closer to me. His hard body presses against my back, covering me in his warmth, and he leans down to kiss the spot behind my ear. His fingers graze the nape of my neck as he sweeps my hair to the side.

"What are you doing?" I whisper.

He presses another kiss to my neck.

"You left the bed. I wanted to touch you. To smell you." His voice is deep and gravelly, heat budding in my core at the sound of it.

"What do you smell now?" I ask, the revelation of his heightened sense spinning at the forefront of my mind.

*The scent of your arousal says otherwise.*

He had said that to me in the stairwell, and I didn't bat an eye at the time. If he could smell my arousal and my sadness, what else can he smell?

"Bliss." His breath tickles my skin. "Frustration. Desire."

"What does that smell like?" I ask, my own voice breathy.

He *tsks*, like he couldn't possibly fathom supplying an answer to that.

"Well, when you're happy, you smell like fresh rain. Everything turns sour when you're angry. Bitter when you're sad. And when you're turned on," he whispers into my ear, his hand snaking under my shirt to squeeze my breast, "cinnamon."

"When I come…" I start, biting my lip as he pinches my nipple. "What do you think I'll smell like then?"

He chuckles, a deep and sultry sound, and grazes my earlobe with his teeth.

"Come for me and I'll tell you," he whispers, making eye contact with me in the mirror.

"We can't," I say, the moan I let out to finish that remark not helping my case.

As he continues to fondle my breasts, both hands beneath my shirt now, my resolve slips.

"Why not?"

A quiet moan escapes my throat before I can answer him.

"Because Logan and," I pause, holding my breath as he bites my shoulder, careful not to break skin, "and Vincent are asleep just outside the door."

"Then you better be quiet, *princesa*. Can you do that for me?"

I shouldn't, but I nod. A little voice in the back of my head is telling me I should stop this, but every fiber of my being is telling me to let him make me come.

He removes a hand from my breast to slide it down my stomach and beneath the waistband of my shorts. I'm not wearing any underwear.

A realization that makes him groan with approval. I gasp for air as his fingers slide over my folds.

"Mmm," he moans. "You're so wet for me, *princesa*."

I throw my head back into his shoulder as he strokes my clit, wet sounds intermixing with the heavy breaths entering and exiting my lungs. He strokes in circular motions, my clit swelling beneath his touch.

"You want more?"

I nod desperately. It would be embarrassing were I not at the mercy of his touch. Within seconds, I'm biting his neck to stifle my moan as he sinks his finger into my opening. He begins pumping in and out at the perfect rhythm.

"That's my good girl, staying quiet so we can have this all to ourselves. Right now, you're mine. And only *mine*."

His words alone bring me closer to the edge. When he adds a second finger and starts stroking my G-spot, my limbs turn to jelly, and I clamp my teeth over his neck even harder as I come undone.

The only thing keeping me from crumbling to the tile floor is his arm firmly wrapped around my waist.

I gush around his fingers, clamping and relaxing in a steady pulse until he removes them. I nearly come again as he brings his fingers to his mouth and sucks my mess off of them.

"Well?" I pant. "What's the verdict?"

"Words couldn't fucking describe the way you come for me, *princesa*."

He turns my head to face him and envelops my mouth with his. He takes everything I was nervous to give, and I relish every second of it.

When he stops kissing me and I regain control of my muscles, my mind immediately snaps back into reality.

"What about them?" I ask, jerking my head toward the door.

"What about them?"

"What are they going to think? How are they going to feel?" I've never had mates—just thinking that makes me want to gag a little—and I don't know how sanctioned being intimate with one, but not all, will make them feel.

"Fuck them and fuck their feelings. Until we open that door again, you're mine. I meant that when I said it. And I believe you need a shower, unless you want to walk back into the bedroom dripping from the orgasm I just gave you."

"We can't do anything in the shower, Creed. I mean it. Not until I understand this whole mate thing," I say, turning around to face him.

He holds up his hands. "Fine, I won't fuck you until you're screaming my name in the shower. Scout's honor."

"I highly doubt you were a Boy Scout," I deadpan.

He winks and starts the water.

I can't help but gawk at his body as he undresses; his hard muscles look like they belong in a superhero movie. He's got full-sleeve tattoos covering his arms, stopping and curling around the base of his neck and smoothly blending into his upper back. Painting the center of his back are one-and-a-half circles made of a series of vertical dashes. The outer circle is only half complete as it begins to encircle the smaller one on the inside. Along the top of his back, between the endpoints of his sleeves, is the Latin phrase "memento mori". *Remember you will die.*

I graze my fingers over the line tattoos, and he stills for a moment. It's so fleeting that I nearly miss it.

"What do these mean?" I ask.

He turns around and lifts me by the waist to sit on the counter.

"Who's touching who now?" He brings his eyes level with mine, and I get stuck in the depth of them. "No funny business, remember? Don't make this harder for yourself by rubbing your hands all over my body, *princesa*."

"You didn't answer my question."

He smirks, the amusement not reaching his eyes, and turns around to step into the shower. I huff out a breath and undress, following him in.

"You know, I was always too chicken to get a tattoo. Joel has one. It's a set of angel wings across his shoulders, and I was supposed to get one the same day. I kind of wish I had now that I think about it," I say, wanting to fill any silence there would have been, given that we are two adults naked in the shower together. It's not a big shower, either. It's a run-of-the-mill tub shower combo.

When I look up from my feet, to face the intimacy of the situation, I find Creed's blazing gaze directed straight at me. His nostrils are flared and his eyes are furious.

"Are you okay?" I ask, stepping back until my leg hits the faucet.

He's towering over me in a way that makes me feel utterly and completely small, his mass seeming to double in size with his ferocity.

"Who the fuck is Joel?" he seethes.

Um, what? He's standing here looking like he's about to rip my heart out of my chest because I mentioned Joel?

"He's my friend," I say, chuckling. "Are you jealous?"

"Your friend?" he says, still teeming with emotion.

"Yeah. He's my best friend." My face falls. "Why are you so mad?"

His fist slams into the shower wall beside my head, his body trapping me from moving away.

"Have you fucked him?"

"What? No! He's like a brother to me, Creed. And if it makes you feel any better, he doesn't exactly bat for my team."

"Maybe lead with that next time you mention some man you've fucking seen topless, Isobelle. For fuck's sake," he says through his teeth, eyes rolling.

"Why does it matter? You immediately went on the defensive. Are we going to talk about that?" Now I'm kind of getting pissed off.

"I know you don't get it in that human brain of yours, but you're my *mate*. Saying things like that without context is going to fucking set me off. Dammit, you need to understand that!"

"How am I supposed to understand any of this?" I ask, stepping up to him. I do my best to ignore the fact that my breasts are pressed against his abs. "I am just a human. I have researched vampires for almost half of my life, and there are still things I don't know. Like your freaky smell thing or mating bonds! So don't come at me expecting me to know things I couldn't possibly. I don't feel a special bond between us, Creed. You three do. I know this has all happened for you just as quickly and suddenly as it's happening for me, but don't you dare blame me for setting you off. Because, again. I'm. Just. Human."

His nostrils flare, and I think he's two seconds away from either killing me or kissing me.

Unfortunately—or fortunately—someone pounds on the door.

"Isobelle! Are you alright?!" It's Vincent, his fist hitting the door so hard I'm shocked it doesn't burst into a pile of splinters. "Bloody hell, Isobelle! Open this fucking door!"

"I'm fine! I promise, Vince. I'm alright," I shout, praying he doesn't break down the door and find Creed and I still pressed together in the shower. "Is *he* in there with you?"

The doorknob jiggles.

"What's it matter if I am?" Creed shouts back.

"You better not fucking touch her. I'll—"

"You'll what? Kill me? We both know I couldn't hurt her if I wanted to. Go back to the dungeon you crawled out of, old man."

I look up at him with wide eyes, lips pursed. It's like he lives to piss people off. He just flashes me a crooked smile and reaches around me for something. The shampoo cools the top of my head as he pours it over me and starts lathering it into my hair. I close my eyes, enjoying the scalp massage he's giving me, and turn around.

I've never showered like this with someone before. It's always been about sex, not simple intimacy. It's nice, the way he's scrubbing my head with his fingers instead of fucking me against the wall. Although, I'm not totally opposed to that idea. In fact, if Vincent and Logan weren't on the other side of this wall, that's probably what we would be doing right now.

"I can scrub myself, thank you," I say as I take the loofah from his hands. Part of my brain, the logical part, reminds me that, just minutes ago, his hands were very intimately acquainted with my vagina. However, the not-so-logical shy girl part is telling me that his cleaning any part of me with my loofah, covering me in soap suds, is far too much for one day.

Once the water is turned off and we are both thoroughly dried off, we find another dilemma.

"I told you before, I don't give a shit how they feel about what we just did."

Okay, then. *I* found a dilemma.

I have no clean clothes, and I need to leave this bathroom. Creed, on the other hand, has zero cares in the world and opens the door, strutting into my bedroom wrapped in nothing but a towel. As he grabs his backpack from beside the couch, I am left holding a towel over my naked body while Vincent and Logan look between us. Logan looks confused, and Vincent looks disappointed.

It could be worse. They could be looking at me with sheer and utter disgust. Like Erika is right now because, apparently, she decided to join the party, too.

"Good morning," I squeak.

She uncrosses her arms and storms into the bathroom, shutting the door behind her.

"Why the hell do you have three totally hot men in your freaking bedroom right now?"

"It's a long story," I say, pinching the bridge of my nose. "I've become a walking homeless shelter over the past few days."

"A long story? Do you realize that one of those very attractive men out there is Logan Jenkins? The rancher from California who almost made me lose my freaking job?"

Oh shit.

I did not know that Logan was that guy. I can't exactly explain his circumstances, either. Not that I understand them any better than she does. All I know is that he died and someone turned him and then he wound up on our doorstep.

"He didn't even recognize me when I walked in looking for you." She puts her hands on her hips as I look her up and down.

"No offense, but if I didn't live with you, I wouldn't recognize you, either," I say, taking in her satin pajama set, makeup-free face, and messy bun.

She rolls her gray-blue eyes and shakes her head. "Be honest, Isobelle. Did you have an orgy last night?"

I burst out laughing so hard that my stomach hurts. I can't even get the words out of my mouth before I hear Creed call from the bedroom.

"She wishes she did!"

"Shut… up!" I say between achingly violent laughter.

"You know what? Fine. Have fun hanging around with a bunch of strange men you don't even know." She turns and grabs the doorknob, looking over her shoulder before she opens the door to say, "And by the way, fucking your cousin is disgusting."

Then she storms out of the room, ignoring the suppressed smiles and snickers from Creed and Logan. Vincent is glaring daggers at Creed, and when he sees me, it amplifies.

"You told her Dracula was your cousin?" Creed snorts.

"I didn't know what else to say, okay?"

Still coming down from my laughing fit, I pad over to the closet and grab some clothes to change into. Thank God I teach remotely and don't have to dress all fancy to hold a class on campus. Today is presentation day, so I have to actually put on some makeup and brush my hair for work, as opposed to my usual routine of lounging in sweats with my hair in a ponytail while I grade assignments.

I change in the bathroom and reemerge wearing a blouse and jeans.

"I have to be in a meeting for my class at eleven o'clock today. Can I trust that you three can keep yourselves occupied and out of my room for a few hours?" I ask, paying special attention to look directly at Creed at the end.

"I can talk to Jenkins about his transition. Teach him a few things he'll need to know," Vince says.

"And I will be doing anything else," Creed quips. "I'm jonesing for a snack."

He flashes his hazel eyes at me and smirks.

"You do what you please, Creed. But I swear, if I see a single word of another person found drained of blood, I will kill you," I threaten.

"No dead bodies today. Scout's—"

"Don't." I point a finger at him.

"Promise," he says, crossing an X over his heart with his finger.

# Chapter 11



After three very long hours of listening to presentations about heresy and the unjust accusations thrown around in the mid-sixteenth century, I am starved. I walk into the living room to find Vincent talking to Logan about self control. I don't pay enough attention to catch more than a few words here and there, but it sounds like Logan isn't giving him a hard time for it. Creed is MIA, no surprise there. A part of me regrets not getting his phone number, but I assume he'll just show back up here whenever he's done doing whatever it is he's doing.

"You wanna grab a bite?" Logan asks as I search the fridge for something. I really need to go grocery shopping.

"Actually, yeah. I'm starving." To make my point, my stomach growls.

"I can tell." He smiles that sweet boyish smile of his. "I haven't been here long enough to know any good places. Wanna show me one?"

"I'd really like that. Vince, do you want to come?"

I wouldn't say it out loud, but I really think he should get out of the apartment. He desperately needs to be shoved headfirst into the modern world. That's how birds learn to fly—they just jump off the branch and flap their wings. Or die.

Mateo's is busy, as usual; every table taken by lunch goers. Gianni, Mateo's son, spots me from behind the counter and immediately comes our way.

"Little Izzy," he booms as he crosses the restaurant with his arms wide open. He wraps them around me in a bone-crushing hug. "When ya didn't come in last week, Pop and I got a little worried," he says in his thick Boston accent.

"I'm fine, but you might want to start worrying if you don't loosen this bear hug," I say, the sound of my voice only slightly strangled.

He releases me and claps me on the shoulder. Vincent comes up to my side, Logan not far behind him, and I realize that both of them might be about two seconds away from tearing Gianni's limbs off.

"Gi, this is Vincent and Logan," I introduce them. "Guys, this is Gianni. His dad owns this place."

"Aye, I own the place, too, honey," he says.

"Oh, so that's why you're still working the register and not in the office with your dad?" I jeer.

He chuckles and knocks my arm with his elbow.

"Good to meet ya," he says, and extends a hand to Vincent first. Thankfully, he shakes it without removing any major extremities. Logan does the same, throwing in a charming smile. "How do you two know our girl?"

My mom started bringing me here when I was just a baby. I honestly think my first time eating solid foods was in this hole-in-the-wall restaurant. Mateo went to Catholic school with my mom—the same school most of the Italian kids in the city attended. Naturally, when he opened this place, my mom came often just to see him. I've often wondered, if my mother had kept to her Catholic faith, if she would have asked Mateo to be my godfather, and if I would have been saved the ordeal of living in the foster system.

Gianni is only two years older than me and has been a good friend of mine since our sandbox days. Only, instead of a sandbox, it was the floor of his dad's office, and instead of buckets and shovels, we played with his parents' wedding cake toppers, which just so happened to be two Barbie dolls, custom-made to look like them. When I was nine, we even had a fake wedding in that office.

"They're old friends from school," I interject. I can't keep telling people Vincent is my cousin, and I'm not entirely certain that Logan is sound-minded enough not to blurt out the word 'mate' to anyone with ears yet. Earlier, Vincent mentioned that Logan is going to be a little dazed while he adjusts to the transition.

"We were in the mood for a bite, and Izzy said your joint is one of the best in town," Logan says, throwing an arm around my shoulders.

Gianni notices the blatant possessiveness, but thankfully doesn't speak on it. When I was in the only serious relationship I've ever been in, I brought the guy here to be vetted by the DiAngelos. Angelina, Mateo, Alena, and Gianni are like the only family I have left.

"And she's right," Gi beams. "Usuals all around?"

"Are you guys alright with that?" I ask.

"If you like it so much that they know the order by heart, I'm sure we'll like it," Logan answers.

Vincent shrugs and offers a polite sort of smile.

As Gianni walks away to work on our food, I send a silent thank you to whoever is listening for Creed not being here. I have a strong feeling that if he were, Gianni would not have walked away still in a good mood.

"Before you go all alpha jealousy mode on me, he's like a brother to me. I mean, he's basically a cousin. I swear there is no threat coming from him," I say, as I turn to face Vincent and Logan.

We all sit down at the table, and I am buzzing with anxiety over what they're going to say.

"Why would we act any kind of way, Isobelle?" Vince asks, a bored expression on his face.

"Well, it's just that, this morning, Creed sort of freaked out when I mentioned Joel." I turn toward Logan. "He's just my best friend, nothing else. And I realize that the way Gianni and I act with each other is a little... familiar. I didn't want you guys reacting the same way."

Logan squeezes my knee, stilling my leg from shaking. I hadn't even realized I was shaking it.

"You are your own person, Isobelle. We know you have your own life," Vince says, and I realize I was worrying over nothing.

"You really weren't thinking about tearing his head off when he hugged me?"

"I mean, I was a little bit, if I'm being completely honest," Logan chimes in.

"Comforting." I rest my head in my palms on the table.

"Three 'Izzy's' for the table," Gianni says as he sets food-filled baskets in front of us. The 'Izzy' consists of a salami and pepperoni sub with all the fixings that I love and a side of salt and vinegar chips. They make tons of other food—pizza, pasta, salads, and lots of the classic Italian mom-and-pop joint type stuff. But their subs are my favorite things on this entire planet.

Logan is the first to dig into his meal, red pepper relish falling out of the bottom of the sandwich. He moans in an uncomfortably sexual way with wide eyes as he tears off another bite.

"Hungry much?" I ask, brows raised.

"Vince said it would be this way," he says around a mouthful of bread.

I look at Vincent, who is looking at his sandwich like it's either crawling with worms or made of gold.

"Vince?"

"Hm? Oh, yes. He'll be quite hungry for the first several days. A steady balance of blood and regular food will satiate him," he says, still looking at the sandwich.

"Is your food alright?" I try to peer at the basket but see nothing wrong with the arrangement of food.

"Yes, just... What is this?" he asks slowly, like he's never seen a sandwich before. It occurs to me that he likely hasn't eaten a sandwich before.

"It's a sandwich. Or, this kind is called a sub. It's just bread with meat and sauce and veggies and stuff in between. You just pick it up and eat it, like this."

I take a bite out of mine and savor the combination of flavors I am so familiar with, yet every time I eat it, it's like I've never tasted it in my life.

"You eat it all together?" he asks, one black brow quirked.

"Yes."

"Where exactly are you from?" Logan asks, giving Vince a confused look.

"I was born in Scotland, but I traveled often throughout my life."

"No, I think he means *when* are you from, Vince."

"Ah." He takes a bite of his food—finally—before answering. "I turned in the year sixteen hundred and sixty-four."

"Pardon my language, but holy shit," Logan says, his jaw slackening. "Creed was right. You are an old man."

Vincent *tsks*, a small smile on his face as he rolls his eyes.

"How old were you when you turned?" I ask.

"I was four and thirty years."

Logan's brows scrunch together, and he stops chewing for a second.

"Thirty-four," I say. He nods and gets back to devouring his food. "What was your life like?"

I don't want to pry into his past—it's obviously jaded—but I feel like I know next to nothing about him. If he's going to be stuck to me forever, I feel like we should get to know each other better.

"It was nothing special. My father was a duke, therefore I was fortunate enough to have fortune and hearty meals every day. He wasn't around much, so I spent most of my childhood and early adulthood with the castle guard. I was an angry young man, and I think people noticed. That's why I was turned. One of the guards had a sister, who promised me everything I thought I wanted." He looks past me, like he's watching his memories on a screen behind my head. "I was naïve."

"What did she promise you?" I ask.

He answers with a single word.

"Strength."

I decide to leave it there for now. The haunted look in his eyes tells me this isn't something to hash out here. Though I want him to know that he can trust me, like I want to trust him.

"Buddy," Logan chuckles. "Have you seen yourself?"

I shoot him a look and he gets back to eating in silence.

After lunch, Creed called me—how the heck he got my number is beyond me—and met us at the apartment. He thought it would be a good idea to clean up whatever wreck Logan's truck was in before the authorities started sniffing around. We all loaded into his car—I got shotgun, of course—and tried to figure out where exactly Logan was when his car was wrecked, based on his memory. He doesn't remember much, but thankfully, it's enough to get us to where he rolled off the road.

The tire marks and torn up grass and dirt are there, but one very important thing is missing—the truck.

"I know this is where I was," Logan says from where he's standing on the asphalt. He refuses to come any closer. "I wouldn't forget that. How could I? I—This happened two days ago."

I get it, the trauma of coming back to the place where you died is probably a lot.

"Just plug your damn nose and come help us, farmer boy," Creed says from where he's looking at footprints.

"I can't," he says, looking queasy.

"For fuck's sake, there's barely any blood on the ground, you fuckin' daisy."

Vincent doesn't engage in whatever their argument is, and instead is crouched by some debris in the dirt. He follows the trail of it back up to the road, but not where the truck rolled off.

"I think Vince is on to something," I say, following him up the road. The debris trail continues the further we walk. "Maybe whoever turned you cleaned up the mess."

"Why?" Logan asks.

"Probably to cover their own tracks. It wouldn't help them much if the police went looking for you as a missing person," I say, squinting in the sun.

It's warm today, especially for spring. I drop back and wait for Logan to catch up to me.

"How are you feeling?" I ask him, lowering my voice to have some semblance of privacy.

"I'm good, just a little nauseous."

"Are you hungry? Is it the sun?"

The image of him covered in blisters comes to the forefront of my mind, and I want to banish it from my memory now, knowing how good of a guy he is. He's been nothing but a gentleman since he snapped out of that haze after waking up.

"No, I'm alright. I think it's just being here. It's a lot."

We haven't had time to talk about how he's dealing with all of this. It can't be easy to find out that you not only died, but came back as a blood sucking mythical creature, too. I don't know much about him, but I know from what Erika said that he has a ranch back in California.

"How are you holding up? You know, with... everything?" I ask as our steps fall into sync.

"Honestly? I'm not really sure how to process any of it. I mean, one minute, I'm taking a drive to clear my head and the next, I'm waking up on the side of the road and my skin feels like it's on fire. Don't even get me started on the whole vampire thing, because that in itself is way too much to understand."

We're quiet for a long stretch, the both of us walking side by side as we follow Creed and Vincent along the road. The sun is starting to set, and the sky is turning the most beautiful shade of orange.

"Just so you know," I start, resting my hand on his bicep, "I'm here for you if you ever need to talk. I can't totally understand what you're going through, but I'm a pretty good listener."

He smiles at me, his hand coming up to rub mine where it lays on his arm.

"Thank you, Izzy." The vulnerability in his eyes is gone within seconds and he drops his hand. "What about you?"

"What about me?" I cock my head.

"How are you handling all *this*? I mean, from what Vince told me, all of us just kind of came at you pretty suddenly."

I hadn't taken the time to really consider how I'm feeling about it all. Of course, it's overwhelming, but it's also, in a way, what I've been searching for for years.

"And the whole mate thing? What the hell is that about?" he asks, his smile leaking through to his voice.

"You tell me. You're the one who dropped the bomb on me," I say, jabbing him with my elbow.

He runs a hand through his blond locks. "Hey, I didn't know what the hell I was saying. Can't blame me for that."

"I'm just saying, it was quite the thing to say to a girl the first time you meet her."

"I guess it was sort of a bad first impression, wasn't it?"

I raise my brows and give him a "you think" look.

"Okay, then. Let me try again." He stops walking. "As myself, this time."

I stop walking, too. I can't help the smile that blossoms on my face as he adjusts his t-shirt and clears his throat. He offers me a hand.

"Hi, ma'am. I'm Logan," he says.

I shake his hand. "Nice to meet you, Logan. I'm Isobelle. But friends call me Izzy."

"Pleasure is all mine," he pauses and raises my hand to his lips, pressing a soft kiss to my knuckles, "Izzy."

The way he's looking over my hand to see my face brings heat to my cheeks. I chew on my bottom lip as he stands and sweeps a hair from my face.

"How was that?" he asks.

"I'd say that was pretty good for a first impression," I say, looking between his golden brown eyes and his rosy lips.

"Holy shit," Creed says from a few yards away. "The motherfuckers pushed the damn truck into the lake."

"What?" Logan and I ask at the same time. He vamp-speeds to see what the guys are looking at while I jog over.

He's right. There are tire tracks haphazardly covered with leaves and dirt going straight into the water.

"Well, that's one way to deal with the problem," I shrug.

"All of my stuff is in that truck. My phone, my clothes, my ID, credit cards, cash." Logan clutches the hair at the back of his head in his hands.

"Could we, I don't know, get it out? You guys have super strength, right? It shouldn't be *that* hard."

Creed grumbles something under his breath, and Vincent looks back at the water, seeming to assess the situation.

"I can't ask you guys to get in there and dig my truck out just to get my stuff back. It's okay, I can just get a new phone," Logan says, defeat lacing his words.

After everything he's been through, he deserves a win. I look between the others and decide to light a fire under their asses.

Rolling up my jeans, I march into the water.

"What the hell are you doing?" Creed shouts.

"If neither of you will help, then I guess Logan and I are doing this ourselves," I say, throwing my hair into a ponytail.

"Bloody hell," Vince groans and then I hear splashing in the water as someone joins me.

"Are you all fucking stupid? It's nearly sundown. In about fifteen minutes, there'll be nothing but darkness out here," Creed says.

"Then we better work fast," I throw over my shoulder.

"Fuck. Me."

# CHAPTER 12



It takes the four of us—honestly, the three of them—three hours to get the truck out of the lake. Logan is sifting through mud and water soaked things to find what he needs from the wreckage, and Creed is muttering an endless string of curses about his shoes being ruined. Vincent is covered from head to toe in algae, mud, and whatever else was in that water and hasn't had a single bad thing to say.

I think I'm starting to understand him a little better. He doesn't expose much of his personality or feelings, but I truly believe that he's a caring person at heart. He is dripping with lake slime and genuinely just seems content to have been able to help. He and Logan were the only ones who fully submerged themselves under water to push the truck onto the bank, while Creed stayed in chest deep waters to lift and pull from his end. I tried to help, but the three of them refused to let me do anything until the truck was on dry land.

"I can't fucking believe you got me to do this shit," Creed sneers from where he's trying to dust the mud off his pants.

"Will you calm down? It's just mud," I say as I hop into the backseat.

"These shoes are ruined," he bites.

I stop rummaging under the seats to look at him over my shoulder on all fours.

"Creed, you can buy new shoes. This truck and the things in it are all Logan has right now, so I would appreciate if you would stop talking if you have nothing positive to say," I snap.

He glares at me, but doesn't say anything else. I'm sure a guy like him isn't used to having women put him in his place. He has the looks of the devil and the attitude of a teenage girl on her period. A lot of women like that kind of thing in a man. The bad boy type who bows to no man and abides by no rules.

"Thank you," Logan whispers from where he's elbows-deep in the center console.

"Just ignore him. He's kind of an asshole," I say.

"No, thank you for helping me get my stuff back. You didn't have to ask them to help."

I brush a loose lock of hair behind my ear and offer him a genuine smile. He's too nice for any of this. Of all the men in Boston, he shouldn't have died.

He brings his thumb to my temple and rubs my skin, wiping mud off his thumb onto his shirt.

"You had a little something there."

"Thanks," I say, my voice a whisper.

I'm not sure how long we sit there staring at each other, but eventually, the sound of Vince's voice breaks us out of it.

"He left."

"Who?" I ask, hopping out of the truck.

"Creed. He got in his car and left."

"He stranded us here?" Logan asks as he follows me out of his truck.

"Are you kidding me?" My voice raises to shouting volumes. "It's pitch dark out here with no signal and no way of getting a ride, and he just left? All because of his stupid shoes!"

Logan's hand finds the small of my back and rubs circles in an effort to comfort me. I'd be lying if I said it didn't work a little bit, but I am still furious with Creed. What kind of selfish prick would just up and leave us in the middle of the night in the middle of nowhere?

"Do you have everything that you need?" Vince asks Logan.

"Yeah, I got what I could salvage."

"Good. We need to push the vehicle back into the lake and then we can run home."

A warm feeling spreads under my skin, butterflies erupting in my stomach.

*Home.*

He called my apartment home.

"Good thinking. Let's hope it's easier to get back in that it was to get it out," Logan says, then his hand leaves my back, and he and Vince get to work.

Creed and Erika are lounging on the couch when we get back home. I try to tame my wind-whipped hair before marching over there and laying into him, but there's not much I can do for that.

"What the hell is wrong with you?" I yell, blocking his view of the TV. "Seriously. Is there, like, something missing in your brain?"

"You guys made it back. I was starting to get worried," he says, feigning concern on his face.

"Don't you dare pull any bullshit just because Erika is here. You left us in the middle of butt fuck nowhere, asshole."

Logan comes up beside me and tries to coax me away, but my blood is boiling and I'm not walking away until there's some blood in the water.

"Isobelle, I have no idea what you mean? I couldn't find you guys, so I thought I'd drive the road, hoping to spot you."

Erika looks between us, confused and, quite frankly, entertained. She's trying her best to hide the amused smile creeping onto her face.

"You are so selfish. You don't care about anyone but yourself. What if one of us got hurt? What then? It would be *your* fault. I'm sure having that on your conscience wouldn't mean a damn thing to you, but deep down, you'd know it was your fault. If Vince or Logan had gotten hurt and we were fucking stranded out there for God knows how long, I would never forgive you."

"Well then, it's a good thing the three of you are intact, isn't it?"

"Come on, Iz. We made it back. It's okay," Logan says quietly enough so Erika can't hear.

"No. It's not okay." I look back at Creed, who's carelessly spread out on the couch, not a care in the world. "Can't you take anything seriously? Or is that not something you're capable of? You know, other people are affected by your actions, Creed. Maybe think about that the next time you decide to fuck them over."

His careless smirk falls, and he sits up straighter.

"I thought you liked it when I fucked you."

Erika's lips press together, and her eyes grow wide. Logan stills next to me, and Vincent appears at the corner of my vision.

"You asshole," I say through clenched teeth. My vision rims red. "Find somewhere else to stay tonight. Call me when your heart unfreezes, and we can discuss how this is going to work."

Without waiting another second, I turn on my heel and stomp off to my bedroom. I wait for Vincent and Logan to follow me in before shutting and locking the door. Moments later, I hear Erika laughing as the two of them continue on with whatever they were doing before we got here. "For the record, we didn't fuck. It didn't go that far," I say, seething as I pace the room.

I turn around to pace the other direction, and I bump into a solid wall of man. Logan's hands grab my forearms as he holds me still against him.

"Hey," he says, ducking his head so we're at eye level. "Don't let him get to you like this. You are an amazing, kind, caring woman. I've only known you for a day and I know that. You don't deserve to feel like shit because of that dick."

Tears well in my eyes, I'm not totally sure whether they are from anger or how nice Logan is.

He pulls me into his chest and strokes a hand over the back of my head.

"You know," he says, pressing his lips against the top of my head, "your accent comes out when you're angry."

"What accent?" I ask, the sound muffled by his chest.

"Your cute ass Boston accent. It's thicker when you're mad."

I can feel him smile against my head, and I hold on to the warmth that bleeds from his body to mine, burrowing myself into him and wrapping my arms around him.

"I have no idea what you mean," I lie.

I've had a slight accent since I was a kid; it's hard not to get one living in this city. For the most part, it's undetectable, but occasionally—like when I'm emotional or when I say certain words—the accent comes out. It's nothing even remotely close to Gianni's, probably because neither of my parents were from here, but it's there.

Logan rests his cheek on my head, cradling me in his arms and letting me stand there with him wrapped around me like a safety net. When I open my eyes again, Vincent is quietly sitting on the couch reading a book, as if the two of us aren't even in the room. I don't know whether to feel awkward or at ease with the fact that he's here to bear witness to the affection passing between me and Logan.

"Was I too harsh?" I ask as I unwrap myself from around Logan's torso. I move to step away, but he keeps an arm around my waist, tucking me into his side.

"No. I think you told him what he needed to hear," Logan says.

I look to Vincent. He has the book laying across his chest as he looks at me.

"Creed needed to know that you will not be walked on so easily. I think it was a good thing that you projected yourself so strongly," he says.

I'm glad they think I was in the right. What Creed did was wrong on so many levels, but I was a little worried that kicking him out of my room for the night might have been overboard. Speaking of, there is not enough space in this apartment for all of us.

"If you all plan on sticking around, I think we better find somewhere else to stay for a while," I suggest.

Trying to imagine a life where I am surrounded by them all the time is next to impossible for me at the moment. After all, I barely know them. But, if what they say about the whole mate thing is true, I don't think it's even possible for them to leave me be for longer than a few hours. I don't mind Vincent's company; he's wise and polite and doesn't cause me any trouble. I definitely can handle having Logan stick around, with his kind and gentlemanly ways. Creed is the problem.

There isn't a scenario where I see him fitting into this messed up puzzle harmoniously. He's hotheaded, selfish, and a complete jerk. He has his moments, sure. For instance, this morning was amazing, but I don't know if I could handle his episodes—like the one he had tonight—until the day I die.

I rub my hands over my face, digging the heels of my palms into my eye sockets.

"I need a shower." I step out of Logan's hold. "Actually, I need a long, hot bath. You boys make yourselves comfortable. I'm going to be awhile."

With that, I shut the bathroom door and draw the most soothing bath to ever have graced this apartment.

# CHAPTER 13



"Can we please just watch a movie in here?" Logan asks, procrastinating getting dressed.

It's been a week since we moved in with Joel. The boys all have their own bedrooms, which is such a relief from how cramped we all were in the apartment. Vincent has been like a ghost, roaming around the house reading, watching movies I suggest to him, and occasionally socializing. Although, when he does decide to talk, it's usually because Logan needs advice about being a vampire or because I have a question he has an answer to.

Creed has been in and out, sometimes gone for a few hours or a whole day. I managed to get him to agree to come with us tonight somehow.

"No, we can't. Joel has been more than kind this last week, letting us move in without so much as batting an eye, so we're taking him to this dinner and everyone is going," I say.

He considers this and nods, grabbing the bagged suit I picked up for him earlier from the closet and leaving for his room. I search my things to find a dress appropriate for the five-star Michelin restaurant that I picked out—one that I know Joel likes. It's a little out of my paygrade, but I love him and he's done so much for me. He doesn't know the boys like I do, yet he opened his doors to them because I asked him to.

It wasn't my proudest moment, asking him to allow me, plus three men, into his home. He didn't judge me for asking; he never would. He just asked when we'd move in and made sure the extra rooms were ready.

My head whips around as Creed knocks on the door, strolling in without waiting for permission. He has a bag in his hands that he sets on the bed.

"It'll look good on you," he says, leaning into the bathroom door frame. "It's your size. Wear it."

I have no words. I look between him and the bag on the bed, unsure of what to say. On the one hand, he picked out something for me to wear, had it dry cleaned, and brought it to me. On the other, he's been giving me the cold shoulder all week and is now demanding I wear whatever it is he brought me.

He watches me for a little longer before pushing off the door frame and walking out, shutting the bedroom door behind him.

Setting the purple maxi dress in my lap aside, I get to my feet and return to the bedroom. My hands shake as I gingerly unzip the bag. I don't know why I'm so nervous, or why my hands are shaky.

Maybe it's because this feels like a large stepping stone toward peace with Creed.

I gasp as I pull out the gorgeous emerald green dress. It's floor length, with a high slit going up one side and a folded scoop neckline. It is the most beautiful dress I've ever held. It's too much. And, thanks to Creed, it's mine.

I carefully select makeup that will complement the dress and curl my hair, pinning some of it back so it's elegantly out of my face. I have the perfect pair of black heels to go with the look and slip into the dress. As promised, it fits like a glove.

"May I help?" a certain accented voice booms from the door.

Vincent is dressed in a handsome fitting three-piece suit, looking like the royalty that he once was. His inky hair is slicked back, two strategically placed strands hanging over his forehead.

Nodding, I turn my back to him and sweep my hair over my shoulder. His knuckles chill my skin as he finds the zipper.

"This is much easier than the clothing women in my day had to endure," he says, knuckles grazing my skin the entire way up my spine as the zipper closes.

"I can't imagine seventeenth century corsets were very easy to get in and out of," I say.

He grabs my hair and lays it over my back again.

"They were not. However, you can trust that I was skilled then," he pauses, running a finger over the now zipped dress, "as I apparently am now."

Blush creeps onto my cheeks, and I thank God I have makeup on, obscuring the bright red I'm sure adorns my face at the moment.

"Were you... Did you, um, have anyone back then?" I ask.

"How do you mean?"

"Like a lover or girlfriend?"

Hearing myself ask that out loud sounds ridiculous. It wouldn't be very 'period romance' of the people of the seventeenth century to refer to someone as their girlfriend. If my knowledge based on period movies and shows, has taught me anything, it's that there was plenty of sneaking around, engagement, and marriage. There was no in-between.

He laughs, eyes averting to the floor for a moment before he looks back at me.

"There was one woman. I loved her with my entire heart," he says, sounding melancholy.

"What was her name?"

"Vivienne. Her name was Vivienne."

I rub my arm. "What happened?"

"I loved her, but she was just using me. She was no longer capable of love when she met me. I was naïve and couldn't see that."

He doesn't say any of this with bitterness. He says it like he says most things: with a soft tone. Looking at him, you wouldn't assume he has such a gentle nature. I'm sure there's much more going on beneath the surface, but until he opens up some more, I have no clue.

"She sounds awful," I say, reaching my hand out and grabbing his without giving the action much thought.

He looks down at the contact but doesn't pull away, then his eyes meet mine. A muscle in his jaw ticks, his gaze bouncing between my lips and my eyes.

"Hey, Iz, you ready? Woah," Logan says, entering the room. "You look beautiful."

Vincent gently pulls his hand out of mine and leaves without another word. He has a habit of doing that. Confusing me into wondering whether we've just had a moment or if he thought nothing of it.

"Thank you," I say, turning away from the empty doorway and toward Logan.

He looks quite handsome himself, dressed in the suit I picked up for him. Looking down, I notice a pair of black pointed-toe cowboy boots instead of the dress loafers I bought him. Seeing my eyebrows shoot up at the sight of the footwear, he holds his hands up.

"I know, you bought me those fancy old man shoes specifically for tonight, but they aren't comfortable. And these look just as nice as any other shoes the city slickers that go to this place will be wearing." He shoves his hands into his pockets and takes another step toward me. "I really want to touch you right now," he breathes, his eyes slowly devouring the way this dress accentuates my curves.

A few days ago, we had a discussion about boundaries. Vince explained to me that he's in his newborn vampire stage and that his lost puppy act would fade soon enough, but I couldn't handle him having a hand on me or being right over my shoulder all the time. He's been very good about respecting those boundaries. Keeping his hands to himself and giving me space for a few hours a day.

Right now, with the way he's looking at me, I wish we never had that conversation.

"Then touch me," I whisper.

I reach out and grab his hands, guiding them to my waist. He takes over and runs his hands up my sides, brushing his thumbs under the curve of my breasts. My skin prickles where he traces my body, my nipples hardening beneath the thin folds of silk. His breath deepens, as does mine, and I stop him when he leans in.

"We can't," I say, voice breathy and wanting.

"Why not?"

"You'll ruin my makeup and we have to leave in under five minutes," I say, pouting as he stands straight again.

"Rain check?" he asks, offering me an arm. I hook my arm through his and huff out a laugh.

I let him go down the stairs before me because it takes a very specific focus to walk downstairs in these heels. As I turn on the landing to descend the last eight steps, Creed stops and stares. I can't help but return the look.

He looks devilishly handsome in an all black three-piece suit, his hands in his pants pockets. His hair is styled in that old time-y way that Hollywood actors used to do, and dammit if he doesn't wear that style better than any Hollywood actor I've ever seen.

"Damn, Izzy," Joel booms, stepping around the kitchen counter. "I honestly didn't know you could look so good cleaned up like this."

"Gee, thanks," I scoff, smiling at him as I finally make my way down the stairs.

When I look back at Creed, he's on his phone, paying me no mind.

"I'd say you look nice, too, but this is almost exactly how you look for work," I say, shrugging to add emphasis.

Joel scoffs and squeezes my shoulder.

"Thank you for this, Iz. You didn't have to pick such an expensive place. You know I'm happy being taken to a McDonald's."

"I know, but you just opened your home to three vampires and your best friend just because I asked. You didn't even hesitate. That means a lot, and I want you to know how much I appreciate that."

I pull him into a side hug and squeeze his ribs. "Besides, maybe I wanted an excuse to get dressed up."

We all walk outside, and Creed heads straight for his car, turning toward me as I head for the SUV Joel pulled out of the garage.

"You're coming with me, *princesa*," he demands.

I stop, my heel slipping a little in the gravel. Logan catches my elbow.

"And if I don't want to?" I retort.

He marches toward us.

"That's too fucking bad. You're coming with me," he says, a bored look on his face.

"Okay," I say, pulling away from Logan, who is the picture of concern. "It's fine. We'll see you guys there."

Once we're in the car, I turn on him with a curled upper lip and scrunched brows.

"What the hell, Creed?"

"Is it really so hard to believe that I just want some time with you?" he drawls. "Alone."

"Actually, yeah. It is. You've been avoiding me like the plague all week."

He puts the car in drive and starts following the SUV.

"I didn't think you wanted to talk," he says.

"Actually, I told you we could talk once your heart thawed out. Because clearly, it must have been frozen when you stranded us last week."

Trees flash by us in shadowy blurs as we speed down the road toward the city.

"My shoes and clothes were covered in mud. I needed a shower."

"You're joking, right? Tell me you're joking." I stare at him, anger simmering beneath my skin.

"You actually left us there, also covered in mud, might I add, because you wanted to take a shower?"

He doesn't say anything this time. Instead, he focuses on the road ahead.

"Unbelievable." I throw my hands up, slapping them on top of my thighs. "You know, I don't think I have ever met anyone so selfish in my twenty-five years of life. Because I would *never* leave the people I care about stranded in the middle of nowhere at night just because my shoes got ruined."

"What makes you think I care about you sorry ass lot?"

"Don't do that." I shake my head. "Don't act like some emotionally detached asshole, because I know better. You wouldn't have come to

Joel's place or agreed to dinner or bought me this gorgeous dress if you didn't care."

"Maybe I don't. Maybe I just suffer through your company because of the stupid fucking mating bond woven into my brain. Ever consider that?" he throws at me, his eyes still focused ahead.

"You don't."

"Maybe I bought you that fucking dress because it settled the ache I have in my chest to take care of you."

"You didn't."

Finally, he looks at me.

"What makes you so sure?"

"This," I say, placing my hand over the clenched fist he's resting on the center console. "You don't have to fight your feelings, Creed. I'm not saying you have to be buddy-buddy with us all, but you can at least stop pretending to hate our guts."

As if out of instinct rather than conscious thought, his fingers curl around mine, caressing them on top of the console.

"You don't understand, *princesa*."

"What?" He says nothing. "What don't I understand?"

He brings my hand to his lips and kisses my knuckles. Over and over again. Butterflies erupt in my stomach, and I want to curse them for appearing. I want to have a serious conversation with the man and he goes and does this to me. I know he knows it, too.

"Mmm," he groans, taking a deep breath of the air in the car. "You know, I don't know that I can wait for the restaurant. I'm *starved*."

"Mm-hmm," I hum.

His lips kiss from my knuckles to my palm to my wrist, where he stops and licks the sensitive skin there. The veins beneath thrum as my heartbeat picks up. I remember the high from when Vincent fed off me and heat pools at my core. I want that feeling again so desperately I might beg if he doesn't start feeding in the next five seconds.

"You miss it, don't you?" he asks, his voice deep. "You miss the feeling his venom gave you."

He kisses and licks my wrist again.

I can't take it any longer.

"Bite me," I beg.

"Ask nicely, like the good girl you are."

"*Please,* Creed. Bite me."

The most devilish smile crosses his face before he bites down, a sharp pain shooting up my arm. Unlike with Vincent, the pain doesn't go away altogether while the pleasure takes over. Instead, the pain stays and aches as the ecstasy of the bite intertwines with it. Like the two sensations are dancing a waltz in my veins.

My mouth drops open as the feeling spreads throughout my entire body. My toes curl within the confines of my heels, and my free hand grips the seat as he drains the blood from my body. Who knew having your literal life sucked out of you could be so intoxicating.

City lights flash by the window as we near the restaurant, Joel's SUV still in front of us.

He adjusts his grip on my wrist, and at last, release takes over my body. A loud moan leaves my mouth as he comes up for air, licking my blood off his lips.

"You taste so fucking good, *princesa*. It's never tasted that good."

I relish that thought as I come down from my orgasm. I want to enjoy this, soak in this moment between us, but reality comes crashing back in.

"Shit," I gasp. "I don't have sleeves. They're going to see."

I find a towel in the glove box and hold it to the bite shaped wound.

"Here," he says, holding out his hand.

"I don't think this is the time for dessert, Creed."

"Will you stop worrying and give me your goddamn hand?"

I huff out a breath and let him take my hand. He bites into his palm and squeezes his own blood into the wound.

"Oh my god!" I exclaim as a sickening burn spreads through my wrist. "What are you doing?"

He wipes the blood—mine and his—away with the towel to reveal completely healed skin. His blood healed me.

"That's..." I'm at a loss for words.

"A parlor trick."

"I thought you had to drink vampire blood for it to heal you?" Albeit, my knowledge on that subject is based on corny teen romance shows.

"You can. It's just faster to drip it into an open wound."

I tuck that bit of knowledge away for a rainy day.

"Thank you," I say.

Pulling the mirror down, I give myself a once over to make sure everything is still in place and that there are no visible signs of what just took place.

"You look fine. But," he pauses and grabs the material of my dress, folding it over my lap so my black thong is on full display, "here."

He pushes the lacy material to the side and gently wipes me down with the towel.

I blush. Hard.

"I didn't know you could be so gentlemanly," I snark.

"Only for you."

Logan immediately comes to my side and tucks me into him when we get out for the valet to take the cars. I can tell that the car ride separated was nerve-wracking for him. He's practically buzzing with pent up worry.

"I told you, it was fine. You don't need to worry about me." I pat his arm, and we all walk into the restaurant.

The hostess finds our reservation and escorts us to a table in the middle of the red and white decorated restaurant. Everything is all marbled surfaces and velvet. It is definitely a place that exudes money, and I'm suddenly very nervous about the bill before we've even ordered.

I swear a sweat breaks out on my forehead when I open the menu to see that there are no prices listed for any of the items.

"This place is *nice* nice," Logan says as he browses his own menu.

"Did you think we all wore these tight fucking suits to go to a Hooters?" Creed jeers.

Joel chuckles, and I smother a laugh as I try my best to glare at Creed.

"Don't worry, old man, I'll take you to one. You'll love it," he says to Vincent, who is clueless as to what the promiscuous restaurant is.

Part of me likes his utter lack of modern knowledge; it's refreshing.

"I'm not sure he could handle Hooters," Joel butts in.

Logan snorts, and Creed nods like he knows Vincent couldn't handle all that excitement.

"They had brothels back in his day, didn't they?" Creed asks, a genuine smile on his face.

"Is that what this Hooters place is?" Vince asks.

"God, no," I interject, nearly choking on my water. "Please stop, you guys. Someone's going to overhear us."

We all make it through dinner without a single hiccup. The boys throw disses at each other and joke at each other's expenses. Occasionally, Logan breaks from the group conversation to watch me. It doesn't bother me because I know he can't help it. It's kind of sweet, in a possessive way, like he has to check to make sure I'm still there every once in a while out of fear that I might vanish.

When it's time to pay the bill, it takes every ounce of control in my body not to actually gasp at the total. I hurriedly write out a tip and get us out of the restaurant so none of them have time to look at the bill.

"Thank you again, Iz," Joel says while we wait for the cars.

"Yeah. I'm *stuffed*." Creed looks directly at me and heat spreads over my cheeks.

Vincent and Logan say their thanks, unaware of the innuendo Creed just made.

"Can you ride with us, Izzy?" Logan asks.

He's got that lost puppy look about him again, and I know he's needing some proximity to calm down. It's like the mating bond thing acts up every so often, reminding him that I'm his reason for breathing. That alone is unsettling, yet I wish I could understand that feeling on their level. To feel like your entire existence revolves around one person sounds oddly cathartic.

"You can have her, kid. She's been delicious company," Creed says.

I immediately look down at my feet and pray that nobody catches on. In my heart of hearts, I know they wouldn't catch on that quick. But at the moment, my brain isn't thinking logically, so there is a very high probability—in my brain—that they will figure out what he's saying.

"You two lovebirds take the backseat," Joel says, climbing into the driver's seat.

I roll my eyes, and Logan nudges my arm, flashing me that boyish smile. I constantly have to remind myself that it's not him that feels that way for me—it's his adjustment to being a vampire and immediately finding his mate. It would be so easy to believe that he's in love with me, and even easier to love him back. Sometimes, I wonder if I'll even know when the mate haze wears off. Will it be any different? The way I see it, there are only two options. One, the haze goes away and I'm left with a Logan who still can't keep his eyes off of me. Two, it wears off and Logan detests me for being the reason his emotions weren't his own.

I don't know which I prefer.

He holds the door for me to get in the car, and I have to hike up my dress so I don't trip over it and land face first on the black leather seats. Logan climbs in after me, not bothering to buckle.

"Buckle your seatbelt," I whisper-shout.

He chuckles and leans closer to me. "What's the point of being immortal if I can't do reckless shit like this?"

"By all means," I start, crossing my arms over my chest, "be as reckless as you want. Just save it for when you aren't around me."

"You worried about me, beautiful?" His smile is intoxicating. Like a straight shot of sunlight directly to my soul.

"Put it this way: I'd rather live the rest of my life without seeing anyone projectiled out of the windshield and squished into a bloody mess on the pavement."

"Too late for that," he quips.

"You did not fly through your windshield, Logan. Your skull was probably crushed in the rollover or something," I retort, cocking my head.

"If that's what it takes to find you, I'd let that truck crush my skull all over again," he says, lips dangerously close to mine.

"Tone it down a little," Joel interrupts from the driver's seat. "I'd rather not have a black light worthy vehicle, thank you very much."

Ignoring him, my eyes drop and I say, my voice coming out as a whisper, "That's just your mating bond saying that."

He chucks my chin so I'm looking directly at him.

"Baby, that stopped messing with my head days ago."

"W-what?"

"The only thing I don't have control over anymore is my desire to be near you. Everything else—every word I'm saying, every thought I'm thinking, every action I make—that's all me."

"Logan," I breathe, unsure what else to say.

"Tell her, Vince," he says while never taking his eyes off me.

"He is telling the truth. The emotional strings of the bond wear off much quicker than the need for proximity," Vincent says.

His voice snaps me out of my Logan-induced trance for a brief moment. How must he feel about this? He knows that Creed and I had a moment in the bathroom, and now he's witnessing my undoing at Logan's confession. Yet, I've shown no affection toward him. He doesn't act possessive or wanting like Creed and Logan do, but that doesn't mean he doesn't feel the mating bond just as strongly as they do.

Sensing my shift in mood, Logan sits back in his seat and simply rests a hand on my thigh.

Vincent looks over his shoulder at me, first locking eyes with mine, then looking down at Logan's hand.

How am I supposed to do this? I don't feel deeply connected to each of them. At least, not like they do. How can I make them happy when I don't even know exactly what it is they need? I don't know if I want all three of them. I don't even know if I want just one of them. Things with Creed are rocky, to say the least, but when he touches me, I swear I could spontaneously combust. Logan is such a good person, and I get to see more of that every day. He is content to do what makes me comfortable, rather than follow his own whims. And Vincent... Well, Vincent is complicated. When I'm around him, I feel intoxicated by his presence alone, yet there's a distance there that I can't push past. It's like a block keeping us from exploring anything further than this weird sort of friendship we have now.

"Don't feel that you have to do anything you don't want to, Isobelle. Take your time and breathe," Vincent says just to me.

"Can you read minds, too?" I ask, my brows scrunching together.

"No," he chuckles. "I've just gotten very good at reading *you.*"

What is it about these men that makes me speechless so often? It's like it's some superpower they wield against me frequently.

I can't help but think how unfair that is. He can read me so easily, yet I can't read him at all. He's so guarded, and he rarely divulges anything about himself.

Logan squeezes my thigh, and I'm suddenly anchored there in the car. Vincent is a grown—very grown, considering he's over three centuries old—man. I don't need to worry about his feelings if he's unwilling to express them.

If only it were that easy.

The car comes to a stop, and Joel announces that we're back. I rush out of the car, still careful to not rip my dress, and go straight inside. Before anyone comes in, I have a moment to myself. Gripping the counter, I take four deep breaths, counting each one, struggling to fill my lungs. All of this is so much to wrap my head around.

A firm hand brushes against the small of my back, resting there and covering me in warmth.

"Are you well?" Vincent asks, his voice causing butterflies to erupt in my stomach.

Who knew I had a thing for accents?

"I'm fine. I think I was just getting a little claustrophobic is all," I say, shaking my hair out of my face as I steel my spine.

Just then, Augie brushes against the inside of my ankles, purring and looking up at me. Poor baby needs to be fed. In retrospect, I should have fed him prior to leaving for dinner.

"Do I need to speak to Logan?" he whispers.

"No, Vince, I promise. I'm fine," I say, perking up with a smile just to make my point.

I pick up August and let him perch on my shoulder while I prepare his food. He nuzzles my neck and breathes out a heavy breath like he can finally relax.

With everything going on lately, he hasn't been getting much love. He used to be my main companion in my day-to-day life. Now, there's three vampires and Joel filling his slot. It doesn't help that Creed dislikes him, grimacing every time Augie comes into a room.

"There you go, honey. Eat up," I say, setting the metal bowl and cat on the floor.

"Almost thought you were talking to me," Creed says, winking at me as he strolls toward the stairs.

"In your dreams, Martinez," Logan throws at him as he walks through the door.

"Trust me, kid, I don't need to dream to taste her." With that, he slinks up the stairs.

Lovely.

Logan sidles up next to me, his pace matching mine as I also head for the stairs.

"I want to ask you something, and I want you to know it's coming from me," he says.

Immediately, I'm nervous.

"Okay," I respond, drawing out the 'O'.

He brushes a hand through his golden hair. "Can I possibly stay with you tonight?"

"Logan Jenkins," I giggle. "Are you asking to share a bed with me?"

"Maybe. Okay, yes. That's exactly what I'm asking."

I stop in the middle of the stairs, focusing on a speck on the wall. He does make me smile. Often. And he's so easy to talk to. Besides, he's dead. He hasn't complained once, at least not to me. He deserves this. He deserves something that might make him happy. If I happen to be that something, I'm more than obliged to give it to him.

"Let me think about it," I say, then continue walking up the stairs to take a long, hot shower.

I emerge from the bathroom, steam billowing out behind me, with my hair wrapped in a towel and another wrapped around my body. Logan is sitting in the rocking chair, scrolling through movies on the TV. He's no longer in his suit, and his hair looks damp where it sticks to his temples.

"What are you doing?" I ask, clutching the towel covering my body in a tight fist.

"I thought I'd wait for you to think in here," he says, then as he turns to face me, his eyes widen. "Oh, sorry."

Except the way his eyes devour my bare legs says that, on a deeper level, he is most definitely not sorry. His tongue darts out to moisten his lip as his gaze travels, taking in every inch of exposed skin.

I clear my throat.

"Yeah, okay. I'm gonna face this way," he turns toward the wall, "while you put something on that's not a towel."

I keep an eye on him while I rummage through drawers and pull out an oversized sweater and boxer shorts. I've never understood the girls that sleep in matching silk sets. I feel like my choice in sleepwear is far more comfortable.

"Okay, you can turn around now."

"Hell, Izzy," he chokes. "That's better?"

I'll admit, the shorts are a little short. A lot short. But they are the most comfortable pair I have, so they're here to stay.

"I think you have a little something right there," I say, pointing to the corner of my lip. He scoffs and wipes a cautionary hand over his mouth. He isn't drooling, but his reaction makes me giggle.

He pushes off the chair and stands in front of me, twitching a little before deciding to shove his hands in his pockets.

"So?" he prompts.

"Did you pick out a movie?" I ask, closing the distance between us.

He makes a strangled sound before gritting, "Are you gonna torture me like this all night?"

I turn toward the bed and perch myself on top of the comforter.

"I don't know what you mean."

Patting the bed beside me, I pull a pillow into my lap and make myself comfortable. He hops over my legs and settles in, propping himself up on an elbow. He scrolls through the movies on the screen and stops on one that I've already seen.

"I've watched this," I say.

"Well, it's my favorite, so suck it up because you're watching it again."

He clicks play, and the opening credits for *White Chicks* start playing.

"*This* is your favorite movie?" I snort.

He smiles, rolling his eyes, and scoots a smidge closer. The movie starts, and Logan's focus is locked on the screen, but I can't look anywhere but at him. His elbow is slightly pressed against my thigh and a few strands of his hair fall over where his head is propped up on his hand, tickling my leg. His confession in the car has me thinking about the last week. If everything has been completely him, then I'm not sure where we stand.

He has been so respectful of my space, and yet, when he's around, I catch myself smiling the whole time I'm in his proximity. I've been doing everything to keep him at arm's length, and he hasn't tried to challenge that. Maybe I need to get out of my own head and stop thinking about the fact that they are mated to me. I need to start thinking of their actions and feelings as those of any other man. The mating bond doesn't control their every whim. Clearly, Vincent isn't affected by it.

My hand drifts to his hair, wrapping the sunlight strands around my fingers. It's a subconscious action, coming to me as naturally as breathing. Logan freezes, his chest no longer rising and falling, his feet no longer fidgeting at the end of the bed.

"I—Sorry," I mumble, retracting my hand.

He looks up at me, something glimmering in his eyes. He looks undeniably handsome in the bluish light emanating from the TV screen. Shadows dancing across his features in the otherwise dark room.

"I didn't say you had to stop," he says.

My brows knit together. Smiling down at him, I bring my hand to comb through the hair at the nape of his neck. He leans into the touch before flipping onto his belly and pinning me between his arms, one elbow propping him up on either side of my hips. The way he looks up at me through thick lashes sets my body on fire.

The movie is completely forgotten as his left hand traces the curve of my waist.

"Can I say something honest?" he asks.

I nod, my hand still in his hair.

"I want you so badly, Isobelle." His finger comes up to trace the outline of my breast along my ribs. "I want you so badly, I physically ache."

"A-are you sure?" I ask, my voice a whisper.

"As sure as I've ever been of anything."

He leans down, his head angled over my thigh, pausing to look up and ask, "May I?"

I swallow hard and find myself nodding before I have time to really think about it. I think I want this just as badly as he does.

Tenderly, he presses a single kiss to my upper thigh. The skin beneath his lips tingles with his touch. He kisses me again, this time edging closer to the soft skin of my inner thigh. His hands fall to my hips, where he pushes up the cotton fabric of my boxers. He runs his palms over the sides of my ass and groans.

"I knew these shorts would drive me crazy," he says against my creamy skin.

I look down at him between my thighs and nearly pass out from the sight of it.

"All I have to do is move this over," he says, hooking a finger inside the strip of fabric covering my intimate bits until I'm fully exposed. "And I have all the access I need."

His breath tickles the sensitive skin there.

"Is this okay, beautiful?"

I'm not sure where my voice went, because all I can manage is another nod.

"I need to hear you, baby. I need you to tell me that this is okay."

I swallow as if doing so will magically give me the conviction I need to say this.

"I want this, too," I manage.

He flashes me that boyish smile before pressing his tongue flat against my clit and licking up my slit agonizingly slow. My body was already prepared for him, and the sensational shock of finally having his tongue against me makes me gasp. He works his tongue over my clit, occasionally sucking on the sensitive bud. My body is ablaze with the pleasure of it in mere seconds, his grip on my thighs firm so I don't squeeze the fuck out of his skull.

His tongue darts inside me, in and out, before lapping at my inner walls, searching for that spot that will be my entire undoing. My chest is tight with how hard I'm trying not to moan. Somehow, I find the remote and manage enough dexterity to turn the volume up on the TV, hoping the sound of it might mask the eruption building beneath my skin.

I'm riding the ecstasy of my orgasm in no time at all, my hips twitching with his tongue still inside me. He comes up, panting, and kisses me, so I can taste myself all over his mouth.

I move to sit on my knees once control over my muscles comes back to me. He effortlessly moves with me, our lips never coming apart. Pushing my hands beneath the hem of his shirt, I trace his abs. Everything about this man is unbelievable. I pull his shirt over his head and throw it somewhere into the unknown, my hands resting on his hard pecs. He fists the bottom of my sweater and smoothly pulls it over my head, my hair falling in a mess over my face as he tosses it. He ducks to kiss the swell of my breasts, sucking my skin lightly enough not to leave any marks.

"Fucking beautiful," he says as he continues exploring my body.

I tug on his cotton sleep pants, silently asking permission to pull them down. He obliges by pulling them off himself and moving to tug my boxers down my legs so that it's just the two of us, naked and vulnerable, pressed against each other in the dim TV light.

"Lie back for me, beautiful," he says, his hand coming up between my shoulder blades for support.

Slowly, he lowers me until I'm flat against the bed. He brushes the hair from my face and starts kissing my jaw.

"Do you have a condom?" he asks, voice breathy.

"You don't need one," I answer.

"Oh, right," he says, laughing a bit at the end. "One of the perks of dying, I guess."

He smiles against my jaw before pulling away to line himself up at my entrance.

"Are you sure this is what you w—" His voice morphs into a strangled groan as I grab his hips and drive him into me.

"I'm sure," I say as I moan. He's bigger than I thought, his dick filling me so completely I feel like one of those jelly finger toys I had as a kid. My insides stretch and move with him as he draws back and pushes himself in to the hilt.

His muscles flex as he pulls my ass into his lap, taking complete control. He grips my hips and moves them for me, his hips moving in unison to pull back and pump himself into me over and over. I press my hands against the headboard to keep myself from hitting my head, our movements becoming more and more violent.

The sound of my ass smacking against his thighs is so loud it nearly drowns out the movie in the background. I'm not even trying to be quiet at this point, moaning as my pussy stretches around him with every thrust.

I feel my orgasm building in my core, my belly tightening and my pussy clenching around his hard length.

"I'm so close," I say, my throat tight.

"Hold on just a little longer, baby." He thrusts into me hard and slow. Taking his time to draw back and thrust in again.

I grip the pillow beneath my head as we orgasm together, my cries overpowering every other sound in the room. I cry his name as waves of ecstasy crash through me. He stays inside of me as he falls over, his head landing on my chest.

Both of us are panting messes as we come down from our highs. When he eventually pulls out, I feel too empty, like one of my own organs just fell out of my body. Before I can dwell on the feeling for long, he rolls onto his side and pulls me into him, pressing a kiss to the top of my head.

"That was fucking everything, Izzy. Everything."

I don't say anything back, nuzzling into him. I shut my eyes, letting the rise and fall of his chest lull me to a state of sleepiness. He falls asleep within a few minutes, and I carefully wiggle out of his grasp to use the bathroom. When I get back, my phone lights up with a notification. There's a missed call and a brand new text from Erika on the screen.

> Erika: I need your help. Now. Please come by yourself.

Without hesitation, I pull on a pair of leggings and a sweater and leave Logan sleeping peacefully in the bed.

# Chapter 14

*Izzy*

The apartment is eerily quiet when I get there; all the lights are off and there's a steaming mug sitting on the counter, but no sign of Erika.

"Erika?" I call out. No response.

Her bedroom is the first place I think to look. The cream curtains flap out as a gust of wind comes in through the window, immediately making the hairs on my neck stand up. Erika never opens her window; she says her dad scared her with too many stories of arriving at crime scenes where the criminal snuck in through an open window. Her silver and crystal lamp is knocked over on the floor, the white lampshade lying crookedly on the other side of the room.

There was a struggle here. My breath catches in my throat when I see it. The wet smears of crimson decorating her cream-colored wall. Like she was dragged across the wall, bleeding out all over the paint.

What the hell happened?

Why did she send me that text? If she was in trouble, she should have called 9-1-1, not me. God, if only I had answered that call. I didn't even hear my phone ring, probably too distracted by Logan fucking me to notice it.

Had I answered, would she be okay?

Something thuds in the living room, causing me to jump. Before rushing out thoughtlessly, like every girl in every horror movie ever, I reach my hand under Erika's mattress and grab her twenty-gauge shotgun. Her dad gifted it to her when she moved in here. I thought it was a weird thing to give your daughter, but it made sense, seeing as her dad's a cop. If only he were here now, I'd thank him for it.

I check to make sure it's loaded, turn the safety off, and prepare to charge the living room. The fact that the gun hadn't been moved is another testament to how bad whatever happened was. She would have gone straight for it the moment she suspected danger.

The apartment is lit only by the stream of moonlight coming through the windows. From what I remember of her dad explaining the perks of having a shotgun, I don't need perfect aim to hit whoever is out here. The spray will be wide enough that I'm almost guaranteed to hit them.

As I come out of the hallway, I see a man standing at the counter with their back facing me. He's tall, and dressed completely in black, from what I can see.

"Hello, Isobelle," a deep voice says. The man doesn't bother turning around.

I point the barrel of the gun directly at him.

"Who the hell are you, and where is Erika?" I demand.

"Put the gun down. You and I both know it won't hurt me."

I don't give him the chance to say or do anything else before my finger is pulling the trigger. The butt of the gun jolts against my shoulder and my ears ring from the sound.

The man flexes on impact, every muscle in his body tensing as the pellets shred through his flesh.

I cock the shotgun, another round finding its place in the chamber.

"Don't make me ask again," I bite out.

A pained groan sounds from him, and before I can process what's happening, he tears the gun from my hands.

"You won't have to," he says.

I feel an impact at the back of my head and everything goes black.

## Monday, 0300

I blink against the light as I wake up. Everything is blurry, and my ears are ringing so loudly I can't hear anything else. I move to rub my eyes, but my hands won't budge from where they're bound behind me. My ankles are also bound, either one secured to a leg of the chair I'm strapped to. My face twists in response to my pounding head. I think I hear someone's voice, but it's muffled by the ringing.

Eventually, the words filter through to the point that I can understand them.

"Are you awake?" a girl asks. Her voice is hoarse and strangled, like she's been crying. "Izzy, fuck, please. Please tell me you're awake."

"Erika?" I try to ask, but my voice doesn't come. I swallow, wincing at the soreness there.

Looking up, I see her full head of honey blond hair and nearly start sobbing. She, too, is bound to a chair. I glance over her body, noticing that her hand is soaked in blood.

"Oh my god, what did they do to you?" I ask.

"That psycho fucking bit me," she wails.

The guy in our apartment. I shot him and he barely flinched. He *bit* her.

"Holy shit," I mutter.

"What? What's wrong?"

"They're vampires."

"Isobelle, this isn't funny! We were attacked and kidnapped. This isn't time for your stupid occult nonsense!"

"No, Erika, I'm serious. You need to listen to me very carefully. The man who attacked you, he's an actual vampire. I know this because Logan, Creed, and Vincent are also vampires. He's more dangerous than you think, okay? We need to get the hell out of here. Now."

Just then, a door shuts behind me. Erika's eyes snap to whoever just entered the room, and all the color drains from her face.

"Funny you should mention that," the man from the apartment's voice cuts through the silence like a knife. My gut drops instantly as he comes into view. His black curly hair compliments his olive-toned skin. Even in this light, I can see the green of his eyes, almost a sage color, as he looks directly at me. He's wearing a suit, sans a tie, and the top two buttons of his shirt are undone. "Where is Vincent, Isobelle?"

"What?" I ask, voice cracking. Is all of this to get to him?

"I don't need to repeat myself, Miss Axford." He slides his hand into his pocket, pulling out cigarettes and a lighter. Behind him, Erika is trembling in the chair. I can tell she's trying to put on a brave face, but she can't help the terrified shivering wracking her body.

He puts a cigarette in his mouth, lights it, and offers one to me.

"Fuck you," I spit.

He shrugs and puts the cigarettes back in his pocket. The lighter is still in his hand.

"Just remember, I tried to do this the nice way. Now things are going to have to get messy."

Smoke puffs out of his mouth as he turns around. Erika looks up at him with determination not to show him how scared she is painted on her face. When he snaps the lid of the lighter back and holds the flame near her face, she breaks.

"No. No, please! Please!" she screams.

"Want to give me an answer now, little vixen?"

My chin trembles, but I do my best to steel myself. "I don't know where he is."

Hell would have to freeze over for me to tell him where any of them are right now. Not because I think they need the protection, but because telling him where they are puts Joel in immediate danger. I could never do that.

"Liar," he chuckles.

"Dammit, Isobelle! Just tell him! He's going to fucking burn me!"

"I'm telling you the truth. I don't know where he is."

He holds the flame to Erika's cheek and her skin sizzles. Her screams fill the room, and I have to shut my eyes just so I don't have to see her agony. When he pulls away, there's a bright red spot on her face. She sobs, her whole body slumping in the chair.

"Why are you doing this? Why do you want him?" I shout.

"This is clearly your first kidnapping, because if you'd done this before, you'd understand that *we* ask the questions," another man says as he enters the room, a thick Australian accent wrapped around his words. "I'm disappointed, Ren. Thought this one would be bleedin' by now." He points his chin at me.

"If she doesn't start giving me answers, she will be," the first man—Ren—says.

"Oi, look at this pretty thing," the man says, chucking Erika under the chin, though she doesn't look up at him. He's got dark wavy hair and too-bright blue eyes. I catch a glimpse of a strange tattoo on the side of his neck as he turns to face her, squatting to her level. It looks like the letter V—or the Roman numeral for five—with the Egyptian ankh behind it.

"Get away from her," I bark, forcing my composure.

The man whips around to face me, a stomach-churning grin on his face.

"What have we here? A brave little thing," he says, standing to approach me.

"Cam," Ren warns. "You can't kill her."

"Don't worry, I won't."

My eyes dart back and forth between the two men, one standing with his arms crossed as he puffs on his cigarette, and the other taking deliberately slow steps toward me. Erika is still trembling, eyes wide as she watches Cam advance on me.

"Do you know what happens to brave little things in your situation?" he asks, eyes wild.

I grit my teeth and prepare myself for whatever is about to happen to me. Whatever he's going to do, I can take it. I have to. To protect Erika, Joel, Vincent. Erika doesn't deserve to be here. Her only mistake was being my roommate.

"They get humbled. Frightened. And they eventually," he grips my leg at my ankle and knee, "break."

My tibia and fibula snap in unison, the sickening pain of my bones breaking causing me to shout. It takes everything in me to look at my now broken leg, thankfully seeing no bone protruding from the thin material of my leggings.

"Still feeling brave?" Cam asks, his face mere inches from mine.

Looking directly into his eyes, rage and disgust twisting on my face, I spit on him. He blinks back slowly, bringing his hand up to wipe the spit from his cheek.

"You little cunt," he bites, as he lunges for me.

Something stops him, and when I look up, I find Ren with a firm grip on Cam's arm, holding him back.

"That's enough for tonight, Cameron. Leave," he orders.

Ren oozes authority. He has an aura of darkness enveloping him, Erebus made flesh and bone. He towers over us like we're rats in a lab, being observed for results, whether wanted or not. Unluckily for him, I won't break. Erika doesn't know anything, and I can't risk exposing Joel just to keep her from more suffering.

Just like the "train debate" in college, I will need to decide if I will save Erika on the one track or Joel and my boys on the other. Ren is the train, and I am the unfortunate one forced to pull the lever.

"I'll leave you to rethink your answer," Ren says, a picture of calm composure, while I clench my teeth in pain and Erika sobs across from me. He turns on his heel and walks through the door, slamming it behind him. The distinguishable scent of salt water and brine drifts in through the shutting door.

We're somewhere along the coast, the water close enough to smell, even in this creepy ass room.

In fact, it's humid in here, now that I can take the time to notice. My skin feels sticky with it, and my hair is already starting to frizz. Erika's has a slight wave to it, her natural curls coming out to play in the moist air.

"A-are you okay?" she stutters, sniffling.

"I think so," I grit out, grimacing as I attempt to move my leg. I can still wiggle my toes; I think that's a good sign. "Are you?"

She shakes her head, sniffling and crying again.

"Hey," I say. "We're going to get through this. They'll find us. They have to find us."

For once, I'm glad for the mating bond connecting the guys to me. If it's so strong that it led Creed and Logan straight to me, shouldn't they be able to find me now?

"Your cousin and friends?" she scoffs. "How? We're probably in the middle of butt fuck nowhere."

"He's not my cousin. Since we're stuck in this together, you should probably hear the whole truth," I say.

"I fucking knew it. There was no resemblance."

I cough a laugh and shake my head.

"This is going to sound complicated, but I'm going to do my best to explain what's been going on, okay?"

She looks me directly in the eyes, her aquamarines glimmering with wetness, and nods.

# Chapter 15



**Monday**

Crickets chirp outside, a symphony in the darkness of the night. The bright lights shut off about an hour ago, if I could guess, leaving only a dim bulb hanging in the corner of the barn to light up our surroundings. It flickers every once in a while as it swings back and forth in small movements. And it buzzes. The buzzing would normally drive me crazy, but thankfully, the throbbing in my leg, paired with the occasional whimper from Erika, is enough of a distraction.

In that flickering light, I try to find something within these four weathered-wood walls that might help us get out of here. I wouldn't be much help in getting away, but if I can get Erika out, she can find help. There's nothing but hay on the dirt floor, a rusty shovel resting against the wall, and an old trough. The same things I found the last seven times I scanned the room.

Erika hasn't stopped crying since Ren left. Part of me wonders how her body produces so many tears, the other part is concerned she's rapidly dehydrating herself. I've never been kidnapped, but I feel that my years surviving on my own as a teen and listening to true crime podcasts are what have given me the ability to remain calm in this situation.

Besides, I can't run anywhere on my leg, and I don't think Erika is capable of getting it together enough to orchestrate an escape. I can't do anything about it, so why should I cry and feel bad for myself?

I know they're going to find me. Creed, Logan, and Vincent all have a built-in GPS that's set to only find me. If Logan could manage to wander to my doorstep as a less than twenty-four-hour old vamp, he can find me here. Wherever here is.

Erika's crying suddenly stops, and I think she may have sobbed herself to sleep until she speaks, her head slumped in front of her with her hair still spilling over her head.

"What did you do?" she asks, voice hoarse.

"What?" I croak.

"What. Did. You. Do?" she repeats. "You got mixed up in something, didn't you? That's why they want us."

"No, Erika, I swear. From the sound of it, they want Vincent. I don't know why, considering he was entombed for three centuries. I promise you, I wouldn't do anything to put you in danger. That's why we left, why I took the guys and went somewhere else. I didn't want them at the apartment with you. I mean, Creed is a wildcard, and Logan doesn't have the best handle on his control."

"Creed may be a wildcard, but he wouldn't hurt me."

She sounds so sure of that it makes me question where she gets the confidence.

"You don't know him. Not like I do."

"You don't know him, either, don't lie. That night you came home covered in dirt, he let me talk and he listened. And when he came to bed with me, he was anything but dangerous."

For a moment, I forget about the throbbing. I forget about the ache in my ass from sitting in this chair. I forget about the imminent threat just outside the door.

He *slept* with her that night?

"What do you mean, he went to bed with you?" I ask, my voice doing nothing to hide the shock and disbelief that is broiling inside.

"Well, you know, when two people get beneath the covers and kiss each other and that leads to—"

"Okay," I rush out, stopping her from fanning the flames writhing in my chest. "I get it."

"You seemed mad at him, anyway, Iz."

How can she be so nonchalant about this? For all she knew, he could be my boyfriend. For all she knew, she could have aided him in cheating on me. Why is that what this feels like? It feels like I just walked in on my boyfriend fucking my roommate under my own roof.

Fuck this. Fuck Creed. He's not mine; I have no claim on him. I don't have the grounds to hate him for this. Sure, he's given me more orgasms than I care to admit, but I did sleep with Logan.

*Logan.*

Just last night, he was holding me in his arms while *White Chicks* played in the background.

What I wouldn't give to be back there, his cock buried inside of me, his delicious lips caressing my skin.

For the first time all day, a tear falls down my cheek.

I shut my eyes against Erika, against the dim light, against the world. Just as a deep, shaky breath leaves my chest, the door swings open, and Cameron strides in wearing sweats and a hoodie. I swallow back the fist in my throat.

"Bedtime for the big bad vampire?" I sneer. Erika's eyes damn near pop out of her head.

"Boss has a new question for you," he says, eyes sweeping the dank barn.

My head falls back, accompanying a mirthless laugh.

"How did you convince Vincent Buchanan to go with you when you found him?" he asks, rank breath fanning my face as he leans on the arms of the chair.

"I didn't. He just came with me."

"He just *came* with you?" He leans closer, a crude sneer on his face. "Was someone crying?"

"Actually, that's just a product of smelling your breath," I say coolly.

I don't know where this confident facade is coming from, or why I'm allowing myself to piss him off, when he holds every ounce of power in this situation, but it straightens my spine and fuels my rage, drowning out any self pity I felt a few minutes ago. I let it.

He leans so close that his nose tickles the skin over my carotid artery. He takes a deep inhale, crude sounds reverberating off of him.

"Such a pity he left you so vulnerable," he speaks against the hollow where my neck meets my shoulder. "He should have known better than to leave a delicious thing like you human."

"Go ahead, have a taste. I hope it's bitter," I bite.

"W-what?" Erika croaks. "What are you doing?"

"Shut the fuck up before I decide I want a chunk out of you, too, bitch."

His hand comes up to cover my mouth, and I instinctively bite it. He pulls away, shaking his hand, and scowls at me.

"Cute," he bites. "But when I do it, it'll be much harder than that."

Then he lunges forward and my entire neck spasms in throat-clenching agony. There's a distinct, sharp pain where his teeth are actually tearing through my skin, but emanating from that is nothing but burning that wraps itself around my throat and constricts my airway. This is nothing like when Vincent or Creed fed from me, and I don't know which I'd prefer. On one hand, there's the agony that I am currently in, yet on the other, I would have to suffer the pains of Cameron being the one to make my body worship his bite.

That would be worse.

He bites harder as he draws blood out of me, a strangled, raspy scream ripping out of my throat. Erika is shouting and sobbing in protest while Cameron has his way with me. After a while, the pain starts to fade, as does my energy. My eyes become droopy and my limbs feel like lead.

"That's enough." The words are muffled and unclear, but I'm sure that's what the voice says.

I open my eyes to see who it is, but they won't open more than a crack, and what I can see is too blurry to make sense of. Someone's palm presses against my forehead and cheeks.

"She's two pints short of dying, Cameron," he says. More words follow, but I can't tell one from the other anymore. Everything around me blends into one big jumble in my head.

There's an ache behind my eyes that spreads throughout my skull and down the back of my neck. The spot where he bit me is throbbing but numb, so all I feel is the pressure of my heartbeat against my flesh. The burning comes back on the side of my throat, scorching through my veins, until eventually, everything goes black.

# CHAPTER 16

*Logan*

## Monday morning

The morning sun beams in through the window, waking me up like a warm embrace. The covers are pulled around me, tucking me in like a burrito, and my face is buried in the soft pillow. I smile against it as Izzy's scent infiltrates my senses. A happy groan escapes me as last night's events come into my mind, a play-by-play of exactly how close she and I got.

When I turn around to kiss her good morning, I'm met with an empty bed. I swing an arm out as if my eyes might be lying to me and she actually is lying right beside me. As I'm met with nothing but empty sheets, I haul myself out of bed and throw on my pants from last night that were tossed across the room. The wonderful aroma of coffee hits me as I open the door, and I inhale it deeply. I head to my room to freshen up before joining Izzy and, likely, Joel downstairs.

"Morning, stud," Joel says as I shuffle into the kitchen. He pours me a mug of coffee, and I sweep it into my palms, immediately taking a sip of life's nectar.

"Morning," I chirp.

"I'd ask how your night went, but I heard the answer to that circa ten p.m."

I don't even try to deny the shit-eating grin on my face.

"Speaking of, where is your lover girl?" he asks, looking over my shoulder as if she'll pop out behind me any minute.

"I thought she was down here with you," I say, setting my coffee on the countertop. "You haven't seen her this morning?"

"No, I figured she was sleeping off the effects of last night."

The time it takes me to get back to the bedroom doesn't allow for another thought to filter through my head. I sweep the bathroom, closet, and bedroom again for good measure. Then I barge into Vincent's room. Then Creed's. She isn't in either of their rooms. She's not even in Joel's, wallowing in her own thoughts, maybe regretting last night. She isn't here.

"What the fuck is going on, kid? Someone better be dying," Creed rasps as he comes out of his room, rubbing his eyes with his palm heels.

"She's gone," I mumble.

I sweep her bedroom again, this time followed by a slightly more awake Creed and a disgruntled Vincent.

"The fuck did you just say?" Creed asks, staring at me with an intensity that either suggests I have two heads or I just stabbed him.

"She isn't here. Her phone's gone, too."

"Where did she go?" Vincent asks, stretching his arms over his head.

"Would I be panicking like this if I knew that?" I nearly shout.

"Damn, you must be a *really* shitty lay," Creed sneers, and I clench my fists to keep from tearing his chest in two.

"What's going on?" Joel asks, pushing past Vince to get into the room.

"Izzy is gone." Saying it for the second time makes everything feel so heavy.

"What do you mean, gone? Where did she go?" he asks.

If someone asks me that again, I'm going to kill them. I push through the three of them and run outside to find her car is missing as well. She went somewhere and didn't tell any of us.

What if she really does regret last night? She couldn't even bear to stay with me until morning.

"Take a breath, Logan. I have her location. We can just check to see where she is," Joel says.

He looks at his phone for a moment, nodding and saying, "See? She's at her apartment."

"I'm going there. I want to make sure she's okay."

"She's fine, kid. Ease up on the puppy dog behavior, would you?" Creed sneers as he turns back toward the house.

"She left without saying anything. That's weird."

"I'll come with you," Vince says, walking to the car. I don't bother putting a shirt on before getting in the driver's seat of the BMW that Joel lent me.

Vince is quiet until we hit a half mile from the house.

"What do you feel?" he asks, breaking the silence.

"It feels like when you jump off a cliff and your stomach flips. Like I think I'm about to die, but my body hasn't caught up."

His lips press into a line, and he just looks out the windshield. He stays silent the entire ride to the apartment.

When we get there, I haphazardly park and have to force myself to run at a normal human pace to get to her door. With a shaky hand, I open the already unlocked door. The scent hits me first.

Blood.

Then I notice the mug of chilled tea on the counter. Following the scent, I'm led to Erika's room, where I'm met with the horror of the state of everything. There was a struggle.

"You can smell her, can't you?" Vincent asks as he follows me in.

"Yeah. Like she was just here."

"That's not her blood," he adds, gesturing to the red streaked wall.

If it's not her blood, then what happened to *her*? Did she have to fight? Was she the one who tried to throw that lamp? Was it her that tried to grab the bed sheets to keep from being dragged away?

"Should we call the cops?" I ask, voice shaky.

"We shouldn't involve a third party; it's too risky. This was a vampire."

I sniff the air but don't pick up on anything other than the blood. The vise grip of thirst takes hold around my throat.

"What the hell happened to her?" I croak, trying to maintain my sanity as the thirst grapples with it in my mind.

"She was attacked. And she was taken."

My throat tightens like a vise until I can no longer breathe. Everything at the edges of my vision turns fuzzy, and my muscles are frozen solid.

*Taken.*

Someone took her. They attacked Erika and then took her.

"Logan, you're shaking, lad. Are you well?"

My eyes sting, there's a ringing in my ears, and every part of me feels hot. All I can do is shake my head, an animalistic sound rumbling through my throat.

I could kill someone for this.

I *will* kill someone for this.

"Logan, take a breath." He looks around, stopping at the blood streaks on the wall. "Actually, hold your breath."

"I can't," I choke out.

Keys jingle somewhere nearby, catching my attention. My legs move of their own volition when the fresh scent of salt and iron hits me. There's a woman carrying grocery totes fidgeting with the lock of her door out in the hall. She's young, pretty for someone her age, with brown hair tied in a knot atop her head. I notice everything about her. Her delicate scent of vanilla. Her breath leaving her lungs in short, frustrated bursts. The thrum of her blood pumping through her veins, beating against the walls of her arteries.

Most importantly, I notice that she's helpless.

She jumps as I approach, her heart rate escalating as she takes me in. Then she does exactly what I want her to do. She smiles.

"Oh my gosh, I didn't see you," she rushes out. "Um, I hate to ask, but do you think you can help me with these while I find my house key? I swear I'd lose my head if it weren't attached to me."

I take the bags, looking around at all the doors holding potential witnesses behind them, and wait for her to open the door. She steps inside, gesturing for me to come in and thanking me for the help.

Slamming the door behind me, I lunge at her. My teeth sink into the delicate flesh at the crux of her neck, the delicious taste of her thick, warm blood coating my tongue instantly. She struggles against my grip, trying to fight me off, unaware of the impossibility. At this moment, I feel more alive than I have since the day I died. I'm in power, and this silly woman can't do anything to stop me from taking what I want. What I *need*.

"Logan," a deep voice scolds from behind me, filled with authority.

I don't care. I just want to keep feeding. To keep giving my body what it craves so badly.

She stops fighting.

"*Logan.*"

With strong distaste for the man I know is standing behind me, I remove my teeth from the woman's neck, rolling my head back to look at him over my shoulder. Vincent is standing there, one arm outstretched for me, an all too serious, yet sad, glint in his eyes.

"Let her go," he coaxes, gesturing for me to hand the woman in my arms over to him.

It only makes me grip her tighter.

"Let her go, Logan."

Her head falls against my chest, and the scent of peach wafts from beneath her blood. I'm reminded of the woman we came here for. She smells like pomegranates and sweet dark chocolate. I love that smell. This woman doesn't smell like that. This woman isn't Izzy.

Like a veil lifting from me, I snap back into my body, becoming aware of what I've just done.

Hands trembling, my grip loosens, and the woman slumps to the ground.

*Thud.*

That's the sound her head makes when it hits the hardwood floor.

That sound reverberates through my body and rattles the heart in my chest.

My eyes lock with Vincent's, that glint of sadness in his eyes deepening as he takes in the panic in mine. The whole world tilts on its axis in that moment, between looking at Vince and dropping to my knees. My fingers tangle with the now bloodied locks of her hair where it came loose from the bun, cradling her head in my hands.

"I'm sorry," I sob, my voice cracking.

Tears I hadn't realized were building roll off my cheeks and land on her blanched cheeks.

"I'm... so... so-sorry," I stutter, rocking her lifeless body in my arms as I haul her torso into my lap.

"Lad?" Vincent squats, hands resting on his knees as he gives me the most pathetic look anyone ever has.

"H-how could I? I mean—She was just—Why?" I can't form any other coherent sentence. Why did I do this? *How* could I do this?

I didn't want to...

I can't even think it. If I so much as think about what I've done, I fear I won't be able to leave this apartment.

"This isn't your fault," he says, eyes searching for mine.

"Y-you tried to stop me." *Sniffle.* "You tried, and I-I-I..."

I hiccup, my body still trying to cling to oxygen, even after death.

Her body stopped trying. It'll never try again. Because of me.

"I don't even know her name," I mutter, almost unintelligible, through my agonized sobbing.

"Listen to me," he says, clapping a hand over my shoulder. "This. Is. Not. Your. Fault."

At last, I look up at him, the few longer strands of my hair falling over my forehead, to find him watching me. I thought he was looking at me with pity or contempt, but now I see I was wrong. The look he gives me is one of shared pain. His eyes say that he's been in my shoes before.

"Let her go," he repeats, this time softly, rather than demanding.

I gently let her body rest against the floor and struggle to stand. It's like what's left of her soul is begging me to stay. To suffer, as I look into her still open baby blue eyes.

My throat is strangled by the vise grip of my pain as Vincent takes a step forward and does the last thing I expected, but the one thing I need. He pulls me into a firm hug.

I start crying again; this time my sobs are muffled in his shoulder. We're about the same height, if not exactly the same. I never realized that before.

"It'll be okay. You'll be okay."

Pulling away, I ask the only thing I can bring myself to ask, "Why did I do this?"

"It'll make sense in time, but you need to hear me when I say this isn't your fault."

He keeps repeating that phrase, but I can't bring myself to believe it's true. These were my actions. My vicious thoughts. I didn't even know my own mind in those moments when my thirst was so powerful it burned my throat. Will it always be like this?

"What the fuck happened?"

With bloodshot eyes, I look toward the doorway to find Creed stepping over the threshold.

The last person I hoped to see.

"I, uh, I—"

"*You* killed her?" he scoffs. "The golden boy got his squeaky clean hands a little dirty? I'm shocked." He lays a hand over his chest.

"Fuck you," I mumble. He smirks at me as he saunters over to the bloody pile that is the woman from the hallway.

The asshole pokes her. Like some random roadkill.

"Don't—"

"The lad doesn't need this right now," Vincent says, tone stern.

"Hey," Creed says, throwing his hands up in the air, "I'm trying to help. You did make quite the mess, didn't you, kid?"

He abruptly stands and runs through the house.

"Good news: no indoor cameras. Bad news: looks like she has a roommate."

My head snaps up to find him holding a framed picture of her and a scruffy bearded man lounging on the same couch sitting three feet to my right.

Someone's going to miss her.

Who am I kidding? Of course, *someone* would miss her. But seeing the face of one of those people sends a new pain through my chest. Everything feels heavy. The air around me even weighs down on me, pushing me into the floor.

"Get him out of here," Creed says.

It's hard to focus on him when I can barely breathe. This is all too much. Fuck, I haven't felt even remotely like this since my parent's divorce. Even then, I was well enough to have the ability to breathe air into my lungs. Now, my lungs feel tight, begging me for oxygen that I can't give them.

Vincent claps a hand on my back and pushes me toward the door. Whatever fragments of the woman's soul that are left call after me. She wants me to stay, if only for my pain to last longer.

Little does she know, I'll be feeling this for the rest of my life. Which, apparently, is forever.

# CHAPTER 17



**Wednesday**

I groan as my eyes struggle to stay open. My head is resting on my shoulder, since I'm barely strong enough to hold it up. I think, based on the light that filters through the cracks in the walls, that two days have passed. I'm pretty sure that makes today Wednesday.

Cameron has made a habit of using me as a human body bag since Monday night. He comes in here at least three times a day. Half the time, someone follows after him and makes me burn again, which I've since figured out is somebody healing me. I'm never conscious enough to see who it is that's healing Cam's bites, but Erika says it's Ren.

Cam just left from grabbing a midday snack from my neck, but this time, Ren didn't follow after him to heal me. He's gotten better, I think, at not taking too much blood. I don't feel like I'm about to pass out, just exhausted and aching everywhere. My leg is so swollen I barely recognize it as my own whenever I look at it now. Every time I move it, it hurts. I'm seriously hoping that it heals on its own, since no one has thought to set it with something. What I wouldn't give just to have a splint and an Ace bandage.

We have been given water, but so far, we've had nothing to eat. Yesterday, Cameron came in here and ate a piece of toast in front of us just to watch us salivate. He hasn't bothered breaking any more of my bones, and he has barely touched a hair on Erika's head, so, as long as that doesn't change, he can eat as much toast as he wants.

Despite what Erika revealed to me, I'm not mad at her. I know she said it to hurt me, and I can't blame her for that. After all, I'm the entire reason she's here. If I hadn't gone off to find a vampire in the middle of fucking Germany, none of this would be happening.

Nope, I can't think like that. If I start thinking like that, I'll spiral. I can't afford to spiral. Not now. Not until we get out of here.

"Are you okay?" she asks.

She's been quiet all day, her voice would have startled me if I wasn't beyond tired and just trying to cling on to consciousness.

"Fine," I say, my voice coming out as a raspy whisper.

I've found over the last day that it's become more painful to even speak, my voice grating the surface of my throat when it tries to come out.

"When do you think he'll come back to ask you more questions? He only came yesterday to bleed on you," she asks.

"I don't know." *And I don't care.* The latter goes unsaid. Ren can ask me as many stupid, repetitive questions as he wants. He won't get anything useful out of me. Mainly because I don't know anything he wants me to tell him. Aside from Vincent's location, which he very likely could have moved on from, since I'm no longer there, I can't provide him any answers. He seems hellbent on knowing how I tricked Vincent into following me back to Boston after I found him. He isn't satisfied with my answer, even though it's the truth, so it seems I can't please him at all.

Though, with him, I'm sure he'd be unhappy if I told him the sky was blue.

As if he were summoned by the mere thought of him, Ren strolls through the barn door. His sleeves are rolled up to his elbows, a tattoo identical to Cameron's on his forearm. He looks different today, less put together. His hair is tousled like he tossed and turned in his sleep and didn't bother combing it. There are faint bags under his eyes, too. Maybe he didn't get much sleep.

I couldn't care less, since I'm not exactly tucked into a bed at the Ritz. Actually, I hope he's losing sleep. I hope he's exhausted.

"Where the fuck is he, Isobelle?" he asks by way of greeting. He crosses his arms and huffs out a breath, doing nothing to hide how tired he is. Tired due to lack of sleep or something else, I don't know.

"I don't know." I force my head up so that it's in its proper place between my shoulders.

"Fucking Cameron. He came in here *again?*" He shakes his head, frustration and annoyance oozing from him, and bites into his palm. He presses it to my neck, and I bite my cheek to keep from shouting out as the burning takes over.

Rolling my neck to work out the soreness, I watch him pace before he stops right beside Erika. The look in his eyes promises nothing good, and I send a silent prayer to whoever is listening that he doesn't hurt her. I can take it if it's happening to me. I'm not so sure I'd do too well if anything else happens to her. He burned her once, and I won't let that happen again.

Erika's chin trembles, and her hands shake where they're strapped to the arms of the chair. He hasn't even threatened to touch her, and yet, she's terrified.

"I'm done with these games of yours, little vixen," he drawls. A muscle in his jaw feathers as he rolls his head to one side, then the other, cracking his neck. "Just give me *something*. Where he is. Why he trusts you. Why he followed you. *Something*."

"What? Is your boss not happy with what you've gotten out of me so far?"

His jaw ticks again, and he shuts his eyes for a few long seconds.

"Don't make me do it. You don't want this," he says, clenching his jaw.

"Don't make you do what?" I ask, straining a little against my restraints.

"Give me something worth my time and I won't snap your neck like a fucking twig."

Erika gasps, her body stills. I, on the other hand, bark out a laugh. "Do it," I challenge.

I look him dead in the eyes as I say, "I dare you."

"Are you crazy?" Erika shrieks.

I pray that he's stupid enough to kill me. With the amount of vampire blood he's put into my system in the last three days, I'd come back stronger and faster and angry enough to kick his ass.

*Hell hath no fury like a woman scorned.*

Imagine if she were a vampire with superhuman abilities.

Ren chuckles, his Adam's apple bobbing with each deep boom. Then he looks at me, eyes dark, and smirks.

"You'll wish I was the one to turn you when the time comes, vixen. It's my blood your heart will sing for. My blood your body will crave in its most depraved moments. Mark my words."

With whatever bravery I still have embedded in my bones, I spit at his feet. He looks down, a bored expression on his face, then looks back up at me.

"I'm going to draw all of that courage out of you, little vixen. Until you've got nothing left to fight me with."

For the first time in three days, he unties me and removes me from the chair. A loud gasp rips through me as weight is put on my broken leg. Hot pain radiates from it throughout my entire body.

"Stop! Stop! Please!" I shout.

He grips my arm tighter and pulls me close to him. Into my ear, he whispers, "This is just the beginning. Now walk."

With me in tow, he marches out of the barn and toward the house a couple of yards away. It's tall, at least two stories, with wood plank walls that have severely chipped white paint over them. There are very few windows, only one on each floor on the side of the house that faces the barn. There are no other buildings as far as the eye can see. Waves crash against a cliff to my right. To my left is just wild grass for miles.

I shout as my foot catches on a rock in the grass, sending me falling forward and pain searing through my leg. Ren catches me and keeps pushing for the house, not slowing a single step. He takes me up three steps onto a barely held together porch and into the house through the splintering front door. I don't have any time to take in what the house looks like before he throws a second door open and we're descending another set of steps. Each step down the stairs sends flares of pain through my leg, and it takes everything in me to not scream, cry, anything.

I try to think of a time where I was happy to ease the pain, but every single step snaps me out of it. I can't focus on anything. Not Joel, or August, or Creed, or Vincent. Not even Logan. I was with him the last time I was happy.

Ren throws me to the ground like a sack of meat and flesh, rather than the human that I am. I look around me to find horror after horror surrounding me. There's a thick wooden table in the center of the basement, five leather straps attached to it where someone's arms, legs, and head would lay.

Dried blood is crusted to its splintering surface and the ground beneath it.

On the walls, there are racks of knives and tools.

I'm glad Erika doesn't have to see this. She doesn't have the stomach for what's about to happen to me. Neither do I, but as long as he doesn't have any of my boys, I can take it.

I can take it all and more if it means keeping them safe. Even if it means I don't make it out of this basement.

# CHAPTER 18

## *Creed*

**Thursday**

I walk into the living room to find Jenkins sitting on the couch, staring straight ahead at the wall. Buchanan is standing behind the couch, arms crossed, with a book in his hands. Joel is sitting at the kitchen island on his computer, trying to find where the hell Isobelle might be.

"What's up with the kid?" I ask, stepping up next to Vincent. Ever since he killed that lady at Isobelle's apartment, he's been an incredibly annoying mess. All he does now is sulk in her room, or in the living room, or while he rummages through Joel's liquor cabinet.

He's been a fucking shell of himself all week.

"I can't smell her anymore." It's Logan who answers me. He turns half toward me, just enough to see his bloodshot eyes, framed by dark circles.

"Fucking Christ, kid. Have you eaten at all since Monday?" I ask.

"Can't."

I walk to the kitchen and grab him a bag of A negative. He lets it drop into his lap without so much as a glance.

"Her scent isn't here anymore. Haven't you noticed?" His voice is hoarse and monotone, likely the result of hours' worth of crying alone in her bedroom.

"You need to eat," I demand.

"Not until we get her back."

"For fuck's sake, Logan. Drink the goddamn blood bag. You won't be of any use getting her back if you're weaker than a thirteen-year-old girl." My voice raises to a shout.

What the fuck are we all doing? Vincent has had his nose stuck in books all week, Jenkins has been basically catatonic, and I've been driving around the city and along every back road, trying to find her. Joel is the only one of us doing anything actually productive. Since Iz went missing, he's been scouring databases to find something that might point to her location. He's sifted through security and traffic camera footage, looked up recent foreclosures, and recently purchased homes.

So far, he hasn't found anything substantial, and I'm getting fucking tired. Every day she's gone, the pit in my stomach grows, and I don't fucking know how to stop it. If anything, it's a pain in my ass to have to think about her every minute of every hour of every goddamn day.

Not only that, but any blood that isn't hers tastes like dog shit now. Buchanan says the same thing. It's like, since we've had a taste, she's the only thing we actually want. When she's around, it's not as bad. Blood doesn't taste as good as hers, but it doesn't make me actually fucking want to regurgitate. Her proximity just makes everything in my body chill out, since at least my mate is near me. Now that she isn't, my body wants to reject everything it needs until I get her back.

Sometimes, I really fucking wish she had never let Buchanan feed from her. At least, then, none of this would have happened. The mating bond never would have been triggered, and I wouldn't give a shit about some random woman who'd gone missing.

Instead, I'm plagued with nightmares of a beautiful brown-eyed woman with dimples I would gladly die again for and long brunette hair that frames her face and falls over her shoulders like running water. Whenever I close my eyes, I see her angelic fucking face.

She haunts me.

I still taste her phantom skin on my tongue, the sweet pure taste of her blood gushing for me as I pierced her wrist. I can smell her arousal as if her ghost is standing next to me, waiting and wanting for me.

That smells a shit ton better than the stench Logan is giving off lately. Whatever he's feeling isn't something I'm familiar with. It's deep, and even the smell of it makes my bones ache. It's like he's dead.

He needs Izzy more than any of us. Even August isn't a ghost of himself like Logan is. He likes to frequent my bedroom now, for some godforsaken reason. I left the closet door open once this week and came back to find my shit completely covered in black cat hair.

I look over Joel's shoulder and watch him work. He's gone back to scouring camera footage, as if he hasn't done that twice already.

"Still nothing?" I ask.

"No," he sighs, dropping his head into his palm. "It's like she just vanished. She hasn't been picked up on a single camera from here to Maine."

"Shit, Anderson, you've looked over footage for the whole week from here to fucking *Maine*?"

"More than that, actually. We need to find her."

I reach into my pocket for a pack of cigarettes, loosing a deep breath. "Yeah. I know."

I glance back at the kid. He's still staring at the same damn spot on the wall.

Shaking my head, I make my exit and head for the back door. I can't take this depressing shit for much longer; I might spontaneously combust.

The chill of the evening breeze cools me as I step onto the back porch. The house overlooks a small lake surrounded by pines and aspens. The leaves are just beginning to change color as autumn gets its claws in summer and slowly drags it, and all the heat and greenness, beneath its orange and pumpkin-filled corpse. Summer is when the world is alive, autumn is when it's dead but not decayed, winter is when it's just bones left, and spring is life climbing its way from the depths of the earth.

Persephone escaping the Underworld.

My Persephone was taken. I plan to burn the entire world until there's nothing left but rubble and ash to get her back. She might be an annoying little *cucaracha*, but she's mine.

Holding the cigarette between my lips, I flick open my lighter and bring the flame to the end of it. That first drag of smoke feels like life in my lungs. The tendrils of it wrapping my throat and coating my lungs in sickening bliss.

In life, my mother would slap a cigarette out of my hand and stomp it out herself if she even saw me with one. She hated the smell of them and swore that smoking was of the devil. In death, I feel closer to the devil than God. If smoking really is a vise gifted to me by the ruler of Hell, I guess I'm going there when this eternal life of mine ends, anyway.

I think she was the reason I quit so long ago. When she passed, I couldn't bring myself to light another one. The old pack that Izzy spotted in my car was the last pack I'd ever bought before my mom died. It hasn't left my dash.

Until four days ago.

Four days ago, my heart was ripped from my chest and my internal organs stopped giving a shit about my wellbeing. Four days ago, my heart was taken by Isobelle Axford and remains painfully beating only for her. Until we get her back, it's her fist wrapped around the vital muscle. Her fist forcing it to beat.

Like it's read my thoughts, a sharp tug pulls at my chest. It's forceful enough to cause me to take a step forward. I grab my chest and catch my breath after it was ripped from me with the tug.

Stunning me even further, Logan appears at my side. His eyes look a little less... *dead*.

"Did you feel that?" he asks, rushing his words.

I swallow back the tension in my throat and nod. "Yeah."

"It's her. It's Izzy. Something happened that's letting us feel her again," he says. This is the first time in days that I've seen an actual expression on his face that wasn't depressing. Before, he was walking around like an extra in a Tim Burton movie.

I open my mouth to say something, but come up short of words.

"He's right. It's her, Creed." Vincent steps out onto the porch, his hands shoved in his pants' pockets.

I meet his stare, soaking in everything he's not saying in front of the kid. If we're feeling a pull this strong, something's wrong. Something, or some*one,* is threatening her life in a way that has all of our Izzy-sized radars set to ultra sensitive.

"Will someone explain what the hell is happening?" Joel asks, appearing in the doorway. "Logan just moved from the couch to out here faster than he's moved since Monday, and Vincent actually went so still, I thought he was having some weird supernatural stroke."

"We can find Izzy," Logan announces. The monotone has left his voice, and I've never felt worse for him. Don't get me wrong, I didn't like seeing him in his depressed state, but now he has the only thing more dangerous than our kind.

He has hope.

"Right. We all felt one tug toward her and suddenly we've got her location? We'll need more than that, kid. A lot more," I bite, clenching my teeth as the hurt sets into his features.

"It'll happen again. I can still feel something. We're going to find her." His voice cracks. "We have to."

He goes back inside, disappearing behind Joel as he goes to find somewhere to mope again. I can feel Vincent's glare burning holes in my head as I watch Joel's face twist with disgust.

"What is wrong with you?" Joel asks, a sneer pointed directly at me on his face.

"A lot, or so I'm told." I take another drag of the cigarette.

He steps forward, closing some of the distance between us in an attempt to intimidate me. My brows raise in faux amusement as I wait to hear what else he has to say.

"Of all the people that sweet girl could have been fated by the universe to be with, you're a disappointment. She deserves a lot more than an asshole with a vendetta against the entire world. Including her, for some godforsaken reason.

"I don't care that your soul is tied to hers, or whatever, for the rest of your miserable existence. Until the day I die, I will feel sorry for her because she is forced to deal with you for the rest of her life. I know better than to think she'd remove you from the situation, because she has a heart, unlike you. Take your bullshit out on whoever you want, but you hurt her, and I will find a way to end your life, Creed. That means hurting her through other people. So, you take it easy on Logan and keep your vile mouth shut unless you have something helpful to say. Got it?"

I don't bother saying anything. Instead, I exhale smoke directly into his face and watch him get flustered and stomp back inside, where he can put himself to good use.

"You got anything to add to that?" I turn toward Vincent, where he's standing with his arms crossed over his chest.

Slowly, he shakes his head and sighs.

"You don't have to be the bad guy to protect people. It's not worth the hurt you inflict upon them."

I scoff at him and turn back to face the lake. His footsteps fade into the distance behind me as he leaves to clean up my mess.

*I'd rather it be me doing the hurting.*

I'm sitting in my car in the driveway of Joel's house as I contemplate why I came out here in the first place. The sun has set, but there are no stars in the sky tonight. They're hidden beneath a thick layer of storm clouds. Lightning dances in the sky as it begins to sprinkle. I'm watching as a raindrop races from the top of my windshield to the wipers, when another, stronger tug pulls at my chest.

That's it. That's seven since this afternoon.

Turning the key in the ignition, I listen to the sweet purr of the engine turning on and steel myself, shaking my head. I honk the horn repeatedly until Joel opens the front door.

"Get the prude and the kid; we're going to get our girl back," I shout through the rolled-down window.

He doesn't hesitate before turning his back to me and promptly returning with Buchanan and Jenkins. When he moves to climb into the backseat, I turn to him and shake my head.

"You'll only slow us down when we get there. Stay here and get shit ready for her," I say.

"Like what?" He's not protesting my direction, only trying to understand what he can do. I get it. He feels more helpless than the rest of us in this situation.

"Start a fire. Make some hot tea. I don't know, stuff to comfort her. I'm sure she'll need it."

Before another minute passes, we're speeding out of the driveway and down the road.

# Chapter 19



**Thursday**

Pain. Hot. Searing. Pain.

I've endured so much of it that I don't think it registers every time that his teeth pierce my skin or every time he slices pieces of me open with one of his many blades.

Ren keeps asking me the same questions, sometimes worded differently, and every time I don't give him a satisfactory answer, he inflicts more torture upon my body. I've been strapped to this medieval table for hours, I think, being bitten and cut and maimed.

I think I'm screaming, but my throat is too worn to realize it, and my ears are ringing too loudly to hear it. He hasn't let Cameron down here, at least not that I've noticed. That's either a blessing or a curse; I'm undecided. On the one hand, it's nice to know exactly what to expect from Ren, as long as he stays here. On the other, Cameron might be stupid enough to actually kill me. That would at least end my suffering. I'm sure I've bled the vampire blood from my system at this point, so if I died, I'd more than likely stay that way.

I wouldn't mind that. I'd get to see my parents if he stupidly ended my life.

But what would they do to Erika? If I'm gone, there's no reason she should keep breathing, in their eyes. At this point, she's only here because, sooner or later, they're going to use her to get me to talk.

"How did you get Vincent to choose you over her?" Ren asks. Another new way to ask the same question.

I open my eyes to stare into the blinding white light hanging above me. Every time he asks me one of these questions, he mentions *her*.

*"There was one woman. I loved her with my entire heart."*

Vincent's words filter back through my memory as, piece by piece, I put this together.

*"I loved her, but she was just using me. She was no longer capable of love when she met me. I was naïve and couldn't see that."*

This woman was using him. The journal entry that led me to him comes to mind. The anger and betrayal in the writer's words. What did he say her name was? I dig through my head, trying to remember the one piece of information he's given me that could be vital to me right now.

*"Vivienne. Her name was Vivienne."*

"I know who she is," I mutter. My voice doesn't sound like my own. It's raspy and quiet as it leaves my throat.

"What did you say?" Ren asks, his tone biting.

"I know who's making you do this. Who's making you ask these questions over and over again." I blink tears out of my eyes as a strange sense of victory washes through me. "It's Vivienne. It has been this whole time."

Everything is silent, the only sound to be heard is the beating of rain against the roof upstairs. The longer he stays mute, the more my senses filter back into me. The smell of my blood is strong; I'm almost scared to see what damage he's done. He hasn't healed me once since he brought me down here. I'm not even sure I'll survive at this rate. Forget about Cameron, Ren might be just as likely to kill me. The only difference is that he'll draw out the process so that I feel every agonizing moment until I draw my last breath.

He unstraps me from the chair, jostling me as he haphazardly releases me from the bindings. He lifts me into his arms, my body going limp as I'm lifted from the splintered table. So much of my strength has been siphoned from my body that I don't even care to lift my head.

Death doesn't scare me anymore. It did, for a long while. I don't want to die, but there's only so much a body can take before it subconsciously begs for mercy of any kind.

Death would be a great mercy compared to what I've had to endure. For all the pain to end. All the haunting thoughts of what might happen to the people I care about wouldn't be an issue anymore, either. If I were to die tonight, then eventually, I would be reunited with them all, anyway. First, I would run into my mother's arms in heaven. Then my dad's. Then I'd wait for everyone else so that I could wrap my arms around them again. Joel, Logan, Vincent, Erika. Even Creed.

The thought of never getting to feel them while their hearts still beat and their skin is still warm moistens my eyes. I might never see them again. I might never laugh with them or argue with them or even cry over them. I might never get a chance to love them. I want so badly to love them the way they want me to. Especially Logan. I know I don't love him yet, but I could.

Rain cascades over my skin as Ren carries me back across the way to the barn. I close my eyes against the cool drops and let my tears fall. He won't be able to see me crying if I do it in the rain.

Erika cries out for me when we enter, my body still limp in Ren's arms. He ties me back to the chair, and I simply let my head fall. If Erika can still shout and cry, then she's okay. They didn't hurt her while I was away.

Ren says something, but I don't pay attention. Instead, I focus on the dark stains in my leggings that encircle the places where he cut into me. He never cut me deep, but it was still enough to inflict the pain he wanted. My head feels light, and my body is buzzing and hot.

He shouts my name, but again, I don't pay him any mind.

Then he stabs me. Right in my thigh. My head snaps up, and another guttural scream pierces the quiet space around us. The crickets even stop chirping.

He removes the knife just as quickly as he put it in, and drawls, "Now have I got your attention?"

He takes the knife and walks over to Erika, who is quivering so hard her chair is shaking.

"No? Maybe this will," he sneers.

"No, no, no, no. Please," she cries.

"No! Ren, stop!" I scream.

He has Erika's chin in his hand, her body writhing to get away from him. I struggle against my restraints, but I don't even have the strength on a good day to break them.

He takes the knife he just pulled out of my thigh and stabs Erika's shoulder. The blood-curdling scream that fills the room, bouncing off the walls, rips the breath from my lungs. Blood gushes from the wound as he pulls it out, twisting it and cracking a bone.

"Please!" I sob. "I don't know anything! I swear to God, I don't know anything!"

"Keep spewing lies out of that pretty little mouth of yours, little vixen. So long as you do, I get to keep having my fun."

"Fuck you," I say, choking on the words as a sob wracks my body.

He takes the knife and slices his hand open, not even a flinch registering on his face. Holding his hand over Erika's shoulder, he lets his blood heal her. She's audibly relieved after the burning subsides. I want to be, too, but I know better.

"Ren, no! No, please! Ask me anything I can actually answer, and I swear I'll tell you! Just don't do *that*!"

"How did you get Vincent to betray her?" he asks again. The same question he keeps asking.

Erika hangs her head, crying because she knows as much as I do that I can't answer that.

"I didn't! Maybe you should ask Vivienne what she did that was so terrible it drove him to lock himself in a tomb for three hundred years!"

He *tsks*, slowly shaking his head and stepping behind Erika. He strokes her hair and slides both his hands down her cheeks to cup her face. She's still shaking, and I want more than anything to make this stop.

There's a terrible cracking sound.

Then Erika is dead.

Her body goes limp, slumped over in the chair she's been tied to for days.

I scream.

"No! What did you do?" I turn to watch as he steps around her. "What did you do?"

Utter defeat floods my body. Everything I've done to protect them, Erika included, was for nothing. I left because I didn't want her in any danger. I packed my things and left the home I worked so hard to create for myself in that apartment. For her.

She's dead, despite everything, because of me.

"You feel like being honest now?"

"Fuck you," I spit at him. He chuckles, squatting in front of me with a hand on either of my knees.

He shoves two fingers into the stab wound in my thigh.

Gritting my teeth, I hold back a scream. I don't want to give him the satisfaction. When he removes his fingers and sucks my blood off of them, bile burns my throat. I want to fucking kill him. I want my blood to be the last he tastes while on this earth.

"You taste so," he pauses as though his brain actually functions and he's not just some militant robot controlled by that bitch, "*sweet.*"

"I hope she wakes up soon and breaks out of those ropes. I hope she rips your fucking head off."

"Strong words from such a weak girl. Pity she won't be able to follow through." He stands, towering over me. "All she'll be able to think about when she wakes up is the terrible hunger she's in.

"She won't rip my head off, little vixen, because she'll be too busy biting into yours."

He plunges the knife into my other leg. This time, I do scream; the sound turning into full body sobs, because not only does he stab me, but he starts carving toward my inner thigh.

"I'll need you bleeding, no hard feelings. I simply can't take any chances of her ignoring you and escaping to find civilization. Just a little further," he grunts the last part, "and I'll hit your artery."

As much as I want to move, to fight back, I stay deathly still. I'm afraid that if I move my legs, I'll make my situation even worse. He won't slice the artery clean open; I'd bleed out in minutes. No, he has to knick it just enough to get me bleeding a decent flow, but not so much that I die before Erika wakes up.

Creed once told me the femoral artery is dangerous because people forget it's there. And once the blood is flowing, there's no chance of surviving that.

God, do I wish he were here. To have Creed break me out of these ropes and just hold me until I've cried my last tear. To have his body pressed into mine, soaking me in his heat and ridding me of the bone-deep chill I feel now. I don't care that I'm pissed at him. I don't care that he's been an asshole countless times. I just want *someone*.

I know I don't have long before I die. With blood loss and hunger combined, I have maybe a day or less.

I only wish I could have done more.

All of this can't have been for nothing.

"Your vampire queen won't be very happy if her prisoner turns up dead before she gets the answers she wants," I say, looking up from the spot on the floor I've been staring at to meet his cold green eyes.

"You're not giving me anything useful," he drawls, sounding bored as he continues to carefully slice my leg open.

"Maybe you're not asking the right questions."

His dark eyebrows raise on his forehead. He nods his head, a down-turned smile on his face.

The knife comes out of my thigh and the limb gushes. He paces to where Erika is slumped over, then turns to face me. At least the pain of the knife tearing away at my muscle has stopped. Now I'm left with the searing pain of a fresh wound.

"What should I be asking, little vixen?"

I open my mouth to speak, but someone else does it for me.

"How about which one of us should get the privilege of killing you?" Creed snarks as he steps into the room. Logan rushes Ren and pins him to the wall.

I sob. They're here. My boys are here.

"This is going to hurt, love," Vincent warns as he appears, kneeling before me. He bites his hand and starts coating my major wounds in his blood. My nerves feel like they've been doused in gasoline and lit ablaze. This time, it's worse than in the past. This time, I want to scream at him to stop.

I don't. I know he's healing me, and I know the searing pain means my cells are regenerating and fusing back together.

"Erika," I say, her name coming out breathy, thanks to the scream I'm holding in my throat. "Get Erika."

I look up, and Ren is gone. Logan is clutching his chest in pain, and Creed is cursing under his breath. It's only when Logan moves his hand that I see the hole that's stitching itself back together. I lean toward him but can barely move as my body continues to heal itself, still confined by the rope. Vincent registers the panic on my face and turns around.

"What the hell happened?" he booms.

"That fucker tried to tear the kid's heart out of his goddamned chest."

"You saved him?" I ask.

Creed looks at me, a softness in his eyes that I've never seen before, and then turns toward Erika.

They've formed this strange sort of family—we all have—and I'm ashamed I didn't realize it until now. We'd all risk our lives protecting each other. Before, I thought Creed would rather let Ren kill Logan just so he could rip Ren's head off. But he didn't. He let Ren get away to help Logan.

"Shit." Creed unties Erika while Vince gets my binds. "She's turning."

He meets my eyes, likely finding the redness that comes after crying and putting the rest of the puzzle together. "You don't have to talk now, but after you rest..."

"I know, Vince. I know." My voice breaks as more tears fall. I want to lock this whole experience in a tiny box and hide it away in my mind forever. I don't want to remember any of it. But I have to live with it, I have to learn from it.

I can't let it break me. I *won't* let him break me.

"Wrap your arms around me, love," Vincent says as he encircles my waist in his arms. I hang my arms around his neck and let him pick me up, holding me in a bridal carry. I nuzzle my cheek into the warmth of his chest and let the tears I've been holding back all week fall. "It's okay. I've got you, love. And I'm not letting you go again."

In the car, I lie across the backseat, with my head in Logan's lap. He caresses my hair with one hand and holds my hand with the other.

"Where's Erika?" I croak.

"I put her in the trunk," Creed says as he slams the driver's side door.

"What?" I bark, lifting my head from Logan's lap.

"Relax, she won't wake up in there. But she can't be in here with you if she does wake up. It's safer."

"She just went through the most traumatic experience of her life, died, and now has to wake up thirsty and alone in the trunk of your car?"

"Yup," Creed says, popping the 'p'.

"It seems cruel, but it is safer this way, Isobelle," Vincent backs him up.

I've no strength to fight them on this, so I let my head fall back onto Logan's thighs and try to let the notion that they're here and they saved me settle into my mind. I feel like a part of me thinks I'm hallucinating this whole thing.

I bring a hand up to Logan's chest, where a large hole is torn out of his shirt. He's mostly healed, just redness remaining where the gaping hole used to be.

He grabs my hand and brings it to his lips, kissing my palm. "I'm okay, beautiful. I have you. How can I not be?"

This bed has never felt more comfortable than it does right now. I'm curled up under one of the fuzzy blankets that I brought here a while back with fuzzy socks on and my hair doing whatever the hell it wants to be doing. My cheek rests on Logan's chest, ever so gently moving up and down with the rise and fall of his breaths.

He stayed with me all night after we got back, carrying me to my room and vowing not to leave my side until I explicitly asked him to. He even helped me shower all the blood and gunk that was coating me off and got me dressed in pajamas. When I woke up this morning, he was ready and waiting for me with a cup of hot chocolate, waffles, and sausage links. While I was eating, I asked about how Erika was doing, and he told me that Creed and Vince have been helping her acclimate since she woke up.

Following breakfast, I asked him to draw the curtains and get back in bed with me. I turned on Twilight, and he didn't have a single complaint. We're on Eclipse now, and neither of us have left this room.

"Oh shit," he blurts as Bella punches Jacob on the screen. He fiddles with a strand of my hair and looks down at me. "Would you do that if Creed tried to kiss you?"

I bark out a laugh and look up to meet his crystal eyes.

"What is wrong with you?" I chuckle, shoving his ribs.

"You've got to admit, it would be fucking hilarious to watch his face if you did," he says, that toothy, boyish grin I love so much spread across his face.

"Would you want me to stop him if he tried?" I ask, my voice softening with my smile.

"I'd want you to do whatever *you* wanted, beautiful. If you want to lock lips with that ogre of a man, then do it. But if you wanted to slug him, I definitely wouldn't protest."

He ends his sentence by giving me a gentle kiss on the top of my head.

"And," he starts, drawing out the word like he already knows I won't like what's coming next. I groan and bury my face in his chest. "As much as I love this, you've been gone for a week, and there are things you should probably be doing."

"I'm healing. What's more important than that?" I retort, my voice muffled by his shirt.

"Maybe you can start by powering on your phone?" He strokes a hand over the back of my head. "Make sure nobody's filed a missing person's case on you."

I lift my head, a large mass of hair falling over my face, and grimace at him.

"Since when were you the reasonable one here?" I grumble.

"Since I needed to be," he says, smiling down at me as he leans over to the nightstand. "Here."

He plops my phone in my hand, cueing me to turn over and power it on. It's cracked from when I dropped it in the apartment. Logan said Vincent, of all people, found it when they went looking for me. I guess my forcing him to watch modern television has paid off, considering the one person who didn't even know phones existed a few weeks ago was the one to pick it up.

The lock screen finally appears, followed by hundreds of notifications. I scroll through the notification hub and sit up when I see the absurd amount of missed calls, all from the same number.

"What?" Logan asks, sitting up to look over my shoulder.

"Look at all of these," I say as I scroll through the missed calls.

"Who's Michael Winters?"

"Erika's dad."

If Mr. Winters has called *me* this much, I can't imagine what Erika's inbox looks like. Her dad is one of the most intense people I've ever met, for lack of better words. He's the chief of the Boston Police Department and definitely looks the part. He's a tall man, with a military haircut and muscles other men his age would weep for. And he's scary as shit.

"That's not good, is it?"

"No. No, it isn't."

I immediately plug Erika's name into my search bar and anxiously wait for the results to formulate. My heart drops into my stomach when I read the top article.

"Oh shit," Logan curses.

The headline reads: *Erika Winters, daughter of BPD Chief, Michael Winters, missing.* Her face is plastered all over the internet. My name and picture are sprinkled into a few articles here and there, but a missing orphaned college occult professor isn't nearly as important in the public eye as the only daughter of the city police chief.

"How's Erika doing?" I ask.

"Not good enough to deal with this right now."

"Well, I don't exactly feel good enough to leave this room, but sometimes, we have to deal with things we aren't ready for. I'm going to get dressed. Can you please tell Joel not to say anything until I'm down there?"

I head for the bathroom to freshen up and brush my hair. When I emerge, he's still in the room, just standing by the door, staring at the knob.

"Logan?" As I get closer to him, I realize his hands are shaking. "Hey, are you okay?"

"I-I need to tell you something before we go out there," he stutters. Even his voice is shaky.

I reach out and grab his hand in both of mine. "What is it?"

He's still staring at the door. It's almost like he can't bring himself to look at me. His pulse is thrumming like a hummingbird under my thumb, and his hands continue to shake.

"Logan," I whisper. "Look at me."

Slowly, his head turns until he's half facing me.

"Whatever it is, you can tell me."

"I don't know if I can." His voice is hushed, and his lip quivers ever so slightly.

I squeeze his hand and look up at him so our eyes meet. I try to portray everything he needs to hear in that look. That I won't judge him and that he's safe. Whatever it is he needs to say, it's enough to make him switch from happy and comforting to shaking and nearly mute in less than five minutes.

"I killed someone," he says so quietly that I almost miss it.

"You what?" I ask. I know I heard him right, but I need to hear it once more because in no world could I imagine this sweet, loving, gentle man killing somebody.

"It was when we were at your apartment. I was so... angry. And Erika's blood was all over the walls, and I just got so hungry. I didn't even know who I was when I did it, but I did. Next thing I knew, Vincent was coaxing me away from her body."

Tears start streaming down his face and his voice cracks. My own chin trembles at seeing him like this.

"Did you think I was going to judge you for that?" I ask.

"How could you not?"

He looks away from me again.

"That wasn't your fault, Logan. You were hurting and vulnerable. You couldn't control the bloodlust, and nobody expects you to. You're so new to this, and I'm sorry."

I'm sorry because I feel like, in all of this mess, I forgot that his entire life was flipped upside down. Not only did he die, but he came back with a whole new set of abilities and cravings that he can't even begin to understand.

"Hey," I say, voice breathy and quiet. I bring a hand to his face and gently push his head so that he's looking at me, stroking my thumb along his cheekbone. Rising to my tiptoes, I kiss him. I kiss him like the very act might erase some of his pain. I kiss him as if my lips and tongue are enough to heal all of his broken pieces.

I want to be able to do that because, more than anyone else under this roof, he deserves it.

I kiss him until I'm lightheaded, because every second that we're locked together like this is a mercy for the both of us. A break from the mess of a world we're forced to live in. An escape from every reminder outside this door that our lives aren't perfect.

The longer I kiss him, the longer we can pretend that we're the only two that exist in this messed up world we live in.

When our lips do part, I stay hanging on him, arms firmly wrapped around his neck.

"I don't want to leave this room, either. Opening that door means bursting this perfect bubble we've been in all day. But we can't stay."

"I know, baby," he says, his breath dancing along my skin. "God, what did I ever do to deserve you?"

I press one more chaste kiss to his lips before letting him go. He takes a deep breath and opens the door, bursting our bubble.

"Careful on your leg," he says on his way out. "Creed said it'd be sore for a few days."

I nod, smiling at him, and wait for the door to close to let that smile fall.

Getting dressed and walking downstairs means I have to face what happened to me. I promised Vince that I'd tell him everything that Ren and Cam did.

I slip a lightweight black sweater over my head.

How am I supposed to tell him everything without breaking?

I step into a pair of dark wash jeans.

How do I recount the entire week without losing the brave facade I've been keeping up this whole time?

I step into my old sneakers.

I'm afraid.

I'm afraid, and I feel like curling up right here on the floor and never talking to anyone again. Since Monday, I've put on a brave face. I've compartmentalized every moment of the last week because, if I hadn't, I would have caved in on myself. If I open up about it now, what's going to happen to me? Will I be able to handle the words that have to come out of my mouth? Can I relive my own memories?

"Izzy?" Creed appears in front of me. "What's wrong?"

He throws his arm over my body and pushes me behind him as he looks around the room.

"I could smell fear from the kitchen," he says, searching my eyes now that he knows the room is empty.

Chin quivering and eyes watery, I look into his hazel eyes.

"I am scared," I say, my voice cracking.

"Of what?"

"Of confronting what happened. I'm scared of opening the little jar I've stowed everything away in, in my head. I'm scared I'll break."

He grabs both of my shoulders and leans over until we're at eye level.

"Listen to me, Isobelle." He squeezes my shoulders. "You will not break. You've been through a lot, nobody doubts that, but you are too strong to break."

Tears trickle down my cheeks as I become a sniffling mess in his hands.

"If you can put up with my bullshit, you can get through anything. Most people would run the other way after the shit I've pulled on you, but you don't. You look me in the face and soldier on."

His hands move from my shoulders to my face.

"So, open that jar, *princesa*. And when it feels like it's too much for you to handle, look it in the eyes and prove that it will not break you."

The tears rush out of me now, rather than trickle.

"Better yet, break the fucking jar."

A laugh rattles my chest, and a genuine smile blossoms on my face.

"I'm gonna shatter that damn jar," I say.

"That's my girl."

He brushes my tears away and squeezes my shoulder one last time before turning for the door.

He waits for me at the threshold, so I take a deep breath, exhaling slowly, and follow him out.

My phone vibrates rapidly in my hand as we make our way down the hallway. I still when I see Mr. Winters' name lighting up my screen. He's calling me. Right now.

"Who is it?" Creed asks, sensing my sudden stop before even turning around.

I give him a deflated look before finally answering the phone.

"Hello, Mr. Winters."

"Isobelle? You're alright?" he booms through the speaker. I can hear the urgency in his voice.

"Y-yes, I'm alright. I'm sorry I've missed your calls. I—"

"Where's Erika? Is she with you? Why the hell have I not heard from her in a week, and why was nobody at your apartment when I stopped by?"

My eyes flick up to Creed, who shrugs in response to the questioning glance.

"We came to stay with a friend of mine. Erika was having a rough time at work, and I convinced her to take an off-the-grid vacation." The lie falls off my tongue easily. I hadn't necessarily planned that response, but it made enough sense. Hopefully he feels that way. "Listen, I'm really sorry neither of us said anything. I promise we're both okay."

"If you took a vacation, why were neither of your workplaces notified, Isobelle?"

He's got me there. Creed must see the panic in my eyes because he starts mouthing something at me. I make out what he's saying and repeat it into the phone.

"We tried to email, but I think our internet got disconnected, so they didn't go through. My friend's place is pretty much in the middle of nowhere."

"Is that right? What's this friend's name?"

"Uh, Creed. He's got a cabin that he let us stay at."

Creed's eyes widen, and he jerks his head at me.

*I'm sorry,* I mouth at him.

"Where is my daughter?" he asks, all the panicked urgency from earlier leached from his voice, leaving only firmness.

"She's not here right now, but I can tell her to call you as soon as she gets back."

"Where did she go?" The cool calmness in his tone is enough to make me shiver. He has a way about him that makes it hard not to submit to his every whim.

He's grilling me, and I'm about to pop like a Cracker Jack.

"The store."

He *hmphs* and lets out a deep breath.

"Right. How about, rather than having her call me, you both come over for dinner tonight? You can stay here."

"That... sounds," I pause to take a breath, "great!"

"And bring that *friend* of yours. Creed. You know how much Gale loves guests."

Creed shakes his head so violently I fear it falling off his shoulders.

"I'm sure he'd love to come. Thank you, Mr. Winters."

The second my thumb hits the 'end call' button, Creed is shouting at me.

"Why the hell would you say my name? I'm not going to that dinner."

"I don't know! I panicked! You *have* to go. I cannot be trusted to keep up this big of a lie around that man. Ever."

He rolls his head back and pinches the bridge of his nose.

"One time I went over there, and within three seconds, he cracked me open like an egg and had me spilling Erika's secrets all over him. She was in her party girl era, and that was not something her parents were supposed to know. She didn't talk to me for a week after that, but I'm telling you, there was no hope for my mouth staying shut with the way he asks questions."

Rubbing a hand down his face, he looks at me plainly.

"What should I wear to this thing?"

"Casual clothes. Jeans and a shirt would be fine."

He nods, and I bounce on the balls of my feet.

"Thank you, thank you, thank you," I rush out. As I pass him to head downstairs, I brush a hand over his arm.

Now to tell Erika about the plans we've been hooked into.

I would gladly choose any of the things I thought I would have to do today over going to this dinner. Vince gave me a pass on recounting my week of torture and mental damage since he didn't want me to have to show up to the Winters' house with tears streaking my face. I suppose that's very thoughtful; I'm just glad I got to keep the jar shut for another day.

I'm sifting through my things, putting myself together as much as humanly possible. It's chilly outside in the evenings now, so he shouldn't question my choice in attire. It would be weird not to take my jacket off inside their house, especially since Mrs. Winters keeps it like a furnace once it hits September, so I have to wear a long sleeve under it.

I hadn't seen them earlier. The bite marks. They're littered across my body like macabre freckles. I don't know why they haven't healed, and I'm not ready to ask about it. Logan either hasn't noticed them, or just assumed they were taking longer to heal than the rest of my wounds. When I looked at them in the mirror, critically scrutinizing the bite marks, I realized they won't ever go away. They've healed already, leaving four identical icy white scars on my left forearm, right tricep, right inner thigh, and my left ankle.

I remember the bite on my thigh hurting the most. Not only because of the sensitivity in the area, but because of the violation I felt as Ren tore into my most intimate skin. He bit so high up that even shorts would cover the majority of the scar. He tore my leggings apart at the seam, widening the hole so he could sink his teeth into my pale, fragile skin.

A shiver crawls over my spine, and I immediately move to clutch my necklace, but it isn't there.

The necklace that I haven't taken off since I was seven isn't safely clasped around my neck.

I finish zipping and buttoning my jeans and immediately begin tearing apart the room and bathroom. I throw blankets, pillows, and towels all over the floor. Until my drawers and cabinets are emptied, I rip apart everything.

My breathing quickens, and my chest rises and falls in short, shallow bursts. I spin, examining the mess on the floor in hopes that I'll catch sight of a gold, shiny glint amongst the chaos. But there's nothing there. I've looked everywhere I could possibly look in this room, and it's not here.

Joel keeps the house too meticulously clean not to have found it if it were in the kitchen or living room or something. It *has* to be here. If it's not here, then...

Images of that place flash through my memory. The splintering wood. The windowless walls.

Even the smell of old hay.

I don't realize I've collapsed until pain shoots through my knees as they hit the floor. I dig through the clothes lying around me, holding back the tears threatening to ruin my makeup like my life depends on it. As much as I'm hurting, I need Mr. Winters to believe that we just got back from a relaxing woodland vacation. People don't typically cry after those.

My breath hitches in my throat, and it becomes hard to breathe. I bring my hands to my chest, clutching them there to stop the shaking.

"Izzy?" His voice enters the space before he does. Without missing a beat, Logan is on the floor in front of me, knees resting on a pair of pajama pants. "What's wrong?"

If no one ever asks me that question again, it'll be too soon.

*What's wrong? Are you alright?*

I can't take it.

"Isobelle." His voice is more stern now, an attempt to claim my attention. "Talk to me."

He reaches out and places his hands over mine. I shove them away and instantly feel bad. He looks at me strangely, like he can see my soul cracking with his own eyes.

"Don't."

"Izzy..."

"Just stop, please." My voice is a quivering, shaky sound. "I lost it."

"Lost what?"

"It's gone, Logan. I can't get it back." I won't go back to that place. I can't. Even if that means losing my necklace to it forever.

A sob rips through me, the tears finally falling.

"I'm going to hold you now," Logan says. He's not asking for permission. He knows I need him, but I pushed him away, and he's making sure I won't do it again.

He wraps his strong arms around me and pulls me into him. I turn my head so I don't ruin my makeup by smudging it all over his shirt. The thin layers of product are the only things making me look rested tonight. I honestly think the dark circles ringing my eyes are permanently stuck there.

"Great, she's a mess," I hear Erika grumble. "You need to get it together, Isobelle. We have to go, so can you fix your mascara and take a goddamn breath? *Please.*"

I raise my head, grimacing at her over Logan's shoulder. Creed is leaning against the doorframe behind her, taking in the state of my room. He lets out a low whistle as his eyes sweep over the mess. Her burn mark is gone; it must have healed when she turned. She looks... good. Like nothing happened at all.

"Are you sure she has her thirst under control enough for this?" Logan asks as he helps me up.

"I'm sure, cowboy. Not all of us are as easily controlled by our cravings as I hear you are," she quips.

I whip my head around to gawk at her.

"What the hell is wrong with you?" I snap.

"What's wrong with me? Take a look around. I'm not the one standing in a pile of my own pants."

I have no words. She's no stranger to being blunt, but now she's being vile.

"We're all going through things, Izzy. Learn to get a grip before we get to my parents', would you?"

She rolls her eyes and strolls out of the room, heels click-clacking on the hardwood floor as she goes.

"I'm going to kill her," I mutter.

"Too late for that, Iz. Come on, let's go," Creed says, turning around and walking down the hall.

"I might kill him, too."

"I would pay to see that," Logan chuckles as he comes up behind me, rubbing comforting hands down my arms. "But I think putting shoes on and getting in the car should take priority. Are you sure I can't come?"

"Yes," I sigh. I'd much rather him come than Creed, but it wasn't Logan's name I had said on the phone. If I thought Creed would let me get away with taking Logan in his place, I'd jump on the opportunity faster than a snake pouncing at a threat. "I'll be fine. Just know that if either of them is missing in the morning, their body is buried in a shallow grave in the woods."

"I'll gladly be an accessory to murder if they were killed by your hands," he whispers in my ear, followed by a chaste kiss on the cheek.

I smile, leaning into him for a fleeting moment. If only I could stay here forever.

Wiping the tears from my cheeks, I walk to the bathroom to fix my mascara and the streaks of it running down my face. I steel myself and head for the bedroom door.

Vincent is waiting at the bottom of the stairs, Creed and Erika nowhere in sight.

"Erika won't be a problem. She's had enough blood to fill an elephant," Vince says as I reach him.

"That doesn't stop her from pissing me off," I groan.

"No, that, it doesn't. I trust that you'll be able to take her father's suspicion off of the both of you, and off of Creed. When you get back tomorrow, we need to talk."

My shoulders slump, and I shut my eyes.

"I know."

"I understand how difficult it is, Isobelle, but we need to know what happened to you. It will put all our minds at ease once our questions are answered."

He'd told me earlier that not knowing what happened is taking a toll on them. The bond makes their bodies, minds, and souls stress over the unknown. Once they know what happened, they'll be able to focus on other things. Until then, the unanswered questions eat away at them.

"I know. I'll tell you everything tomorrow."

He nods once before turning to open the door. He holds it open for me, and I stride out, head high, and make my way to the car. We take Erika's, since Creed's still has bloodstains in the back, and I don't want to drive with my sore leg. I slide into the backseat and buckle up.

"You're better now?" Erika asks, looking at me over her shoulder from the driver's seat.

"Yeah."

"Good. Keep it that way. You can go back to being a mess tomorrow."

With that, she takes the car out of park, and we're on our way.

*Izzy*

T he Winters live in a two story home in Burlington that I have always loved. It's much nicer than the house I grew up in, but the warmth that surrounds it reminds me of my childhood home.

Mr. Winters' truck is parked in the driveway, right next to his take-home police car. Mrs. Winters parks her car in the garage. We walk up the brick pathway to their front door and I try to flatten out any wrinkles in my shirt thanks to sitting for so long.

Gale opens the door, a welcoming smile on her face as she comes out with open arms to hug her daughter, then me. Her sunken eyes don't go amiss as she passes from one of us to the other. She looks like she hasn't slept in a very long time. But I guess that's only natural, considering her daughter was a missing person for a week.

"Oh, honey, you look incredible," she says as she places her hands on Erika's cheeks. She looks much better than I do, thanks to her vampiric rejuvenation. "That time out in nature must have done wonders for you."

"Yeah, it's like I'm a brand new person," Erika replies, smiling at her mother.

"And you," she coos as she brushes a thumb over the hollow of my cheek. "You look tired, my dear."

I do my best to fake a smile for her, unsure of what to say to that. She looks at me more intensely, scrutinizing every minor imperfection on my face.

"That's my fault," Creed chimes in from beside me. "She *loves* spending sleepless nights at my place."

Her smile turns into a thin line, and her eyes go wide.

I blink rapidly, as if it will erase the words that just left Creed's mouth.

"Oh, to be young and in love," she chuckles, waving her hands at us. "Come on, kiddos. I've got lasagna in the oven."

She ushers us inside, and I take the opportunity with her back to us to glare daggers at Creed, to which he flashes me a cheeky smile. Bastard.

"Daddy," Erika says excitedly as we round the corner into the living room. Her dad is standing at the fireplace, leaning on the mantle, with a glass of amber liquid in his hand. Unlike her mother's calming presence, with her short brown hair and deep blue eyes, Mr. Winters is an inherently intimidating man. He's tall, with a strong jaw, salt and pepper hair cropped short on his head, and a handlebar mustache to match.

"Hey, pumpkin," he says as he squeezes Erika in a one-armed hug. "Isobelle," he greets me, with a curt nod.

My stomach churns, and it's all I can do not to sweat. He normally gives me a hug and asks how I've been.

"Mr. Winters," Creed says, sticking his hand out.

Michael takes his hand and looks Creed up and down as he shakes it.

"You must be Creed."

He looks anything but thrilled to meet him.

"Isn't he handsome, dear? He and Izzy are dating! Isn't that nice?" Gale chimes in from the kitchen. Over the counter, I can see her working on a salad and checking the timer on the oven every so often.

"Hm," he grunts.

If I had a knife, I'd cut the tension in the room. Erika is the only one seemingly relaxed at the moment. Creed looks relaxed, but I can feel how tense his muscles are where he's brushed up against my back. He slowly drags his hand across my tailbone and hooks his hand around the curve of my waist, pulling me into him. I just *know* he's enjoying this way too much.

I'd be lying if I said I didn't enjoy it a little.

I need to change this man's ringtone to Hot N Cold by Katy Perry. Despite how comforting he's been today, I haven't forgotten what Erika told me in the barn. She was so sure that he wouldn't do anything to hurt her. It makes me wonder if she thinks something more of that night they shared. Based on the sideways stare and clenched jaw she's got going on, as she takes in Creed's hand on my waist, I'd say she definitely does.

I can't help but wonder how Creed feels.

"Dinner's ready!" Gale sing-songs from the kitchen.

"Saved by the lasagna," Creed says, smirking at Mr. Winters. I hadn't realized until now that they'd been in some weird kind of stare off.

Once Mr. Winters is out of earshot, I break away from him and grumble under my breath, "You are *so* chaotic, you know that?"

"Comes with the package, sweetheart."

We make our way to the dining table and take our seats. Mr. Winters sits at the head of the table, Gale is next to him and across from Erika. I decide to sit next to Erika, thinking Creed would take the seat across from me since all the others are taken. Instead of doing that—because that would have been the sane thing to do—he pulls out the chair at the other end of the table, directly across from Mr. Winters, and happily plants his ass in it.

A muscle in Mr. Winters' jaw ticks, and he pops his knuckles as he leans his elbows on the table that always seemed so big until now. Mrs. Winters bows her head, her hands clasped in front of her, and silently waits for us all to follow suit. Of course, Creed and Mr. Winters are the last two to bow, another testosterone fueled stare off passing between them.

Gale starts reciting the same prayer she says every time I've been over for dinner, ending with a satisfied *amen.*

"Dig in while it's hot." She smiles at me, then at Creed.

I'm not sure whether she's just utterly oblivious to the thick tension between her husband and my... Creed, or she's choosing to ignore it in the name of having a peaceful dinner. She is doing a great job on her part of making this dinner feel normal, either way.

"So," Mr. Winters says after plating himself a piece of lasagna, "you've got a cabin, is that right?"

"Yes, sir. It's a real beauty," Creed answers.

"Daddy, you and Mom ought to look into getting a cabin. It'd be a nice getaway for you both," Erika says.

"What makes you think we need a getaway, pumpkin?" He turns to his daughter.

"For starters, the tick that's been permanently in your jaw since we got here."

I nearly shoot meat sauce out of my nose as I choke on pure disbelief. I had the impression that the feud going on between the two men was going to be an unspoken thing, not something we brought attention to.

"There's no tick in my jaw," he deadpans.

"I know you better than you know yourself. You haven't relaxed since we walked into the house."

Erika daintily takes a bite of her lasagna, using her fork to point at her father.

"Can you blame me? My daughter and her roommate both go missing for a week, then come back without a single issue in the world! I had the entire police force looking for you, Erika Anne!" He slams his fist down on the table, the force of it shaking our plates.

"Oh," Gale chimes in. "I forgot to bring over the salad."

She gets up and dusts off her dress before walking to the kitchen. Her blatant dismissal of her husband's outburst has me feeling very uneasy. If Logan, or even Creed, did something like that, I'd at least try to get them to cool off.

"Well, I was fine, Dad. We both were. I needed a break to clear my head and relax, so that's what we did. We took a break from everything and stayed at Creed's wonderful cabin in the middle of the goddamned woods. Will you *please* stop acting like we committed a crime and eat the rest of your meal without glaring at anybody?"

I purse my lips, my muscles tense as I wait for some kind of violent response from Mr. Winters. Creed's shoulders tense up and he sits up straighter, his hand clamping over my wrist like he's ready to pull me away from whatever he expects is about to happen.

"Do you want balsamic or Italian, dear?" Mrs. Winters asks, waiting for his response behind the counter. From here, I can see the shaking in her hands.

I know well enough that Mr. Winters isn't abusive. He would never hit his wife or his daughter, but that doesn't mean he doesn't have these outbursts often enough to cause his wife to shake at the raise of his voice. My dad was never very aggressive. He was the type to talk things out to get to the root of any problems we had. His approach gave me this intense fear of disappointing him, all because I never felt like he was truly angry with me. The thought of his disappointment was enough to have me in tears if I did something I knew he wouldn't approve of.

"Just bring them both, honey," he replies, grinding his teeth as he takes a few deep breaths.

"I'm glad you're okay, Erika. You, too, Isobelle. But next time you feel like taking a week-long, internet-free retreat, tell us," he says with clenched fists.

"Of course, Daddy. I'm sorry we worried you."

The way that Erika handled that entire interaction makes me think that she's no stranger to his outbursts, either. She only ever speaks highly of her dad; I never thought he had this side to him. She must have had to learn to face him on her own growing up since her mother clearly has never done anything to calm him down. She's stronger than I thought. If only that side of her came out while we were held captive in that barn.

The rest of dinner goes smoothly. Mr. Winters asks Creed normal questions about his life, like what he does for a living and where he's from. He tells him that he owns a bar in Jersey and that he's from Florida. I'm frustrated that I don't know if either of those facts is true.

After dinner, Gale brings out a tray of mini eclairs and starts asking Erika and me how our vacation was. We deserve an Oscar for our performance. As the evening went on, we all talked and laughed and acted totally civil with each other.

"I'll show you two to the guest room," Mrs. Winters says as we all get up from their huge L-shaped couch. "There's a bathroom just across the hall, and there should be towels and soaps in there already for you."

"I'm sorry, we're sharing a room?" I clarify.

"Yes, dear. I haven't had a chance to wash Carter's sheets. He just stayed with us a few days ago, but now that I know you're dating, it's all good and dandy. I was so worried one of you would have to take the couch."

"That's very thoughtful of you, Mrs. Winters," Creed croons. His deep tone tells me all I need to know about how *he* feels about this situation.

"Here you are," she says as she opens the door to the guest bedroom.

Inside is a king-sized bed, covered in cream sheets and a red duvet. There are ranch style nightstands on either side and a dresser across from the foot of the bed. The back of the dresser is a big mirror that reflects the exact place we'll be sleeping.

"Let me know if you need anything." She smiles at us and disappears down the hallway. The master bedroom and Erika's room are both on the first floor, while the guest room and Carter's room are upstairs.

I haven't seen Carter, Erika's younger brother, in a very long time. I think he's taking pre-med classes in New York.

"Rock, paper, scissors for who gets to shower first?" Creed asks, turning to me with a sly grin on his face.

"I kick in my sleep, fair warning." I level a glare at him as I set my bag on the bed and fish out my pajamas.

"I don't hear Logan complaining."

"Yeah, I *like* Logan. I *tolerate* you."

"So, your sleep spasms respond to your feelings toward someone? Tell me, did those spasms make you moan his name in the middle of the night last week?"

I spin around so fast my own hair slaps me in the face.

"Excuse me?" I gawk.

"Please, even if I didn't have vampire hearing, I wouldn't have been able to tune you two out."

He pushes off the door frame and comes up behind me. "*Oh, Logan. Yes. Logan.*"

"Shut up, or I swear to god I'll shove a sock in your mouth. I'm not playing," I threaten, gripping a pair of socks in my fist.

"Oo, can you do panties instead?"

Gripping my pjs, I push against him and head for the door. Once I'm in the bathroom, I lock the door and immediately start the water. As it heats up, I send up a silent prayer that I'll survive the night without attempting to strangle him.

When Creed comes back into the bedroom wrapped in a towel, I pretend to be asleep. I can see a fuzzy picture of him before me as I squint, his back facing my direction. I couldn't actually fall asleep, like I hoped I'd be able to, the nerves twisting my gut far too much to get comfortable. I debated making him sleep on the floor, but I know he'd never agree to that.

He slides on a pair of basketball shorts, his glorious bare ass on display between the moment he drops the towel and when the shorts cover him, and turns toward the bed. I shut my eyes and focus on taking deep breaths. The bed shifts as he gets under the covers at my side. I'm lying so that my back is to him and I'm facing a wall.

"I know you're not sleeping, *princesa,*" he whispers in my ear, his breath tickling my neck. When I continue to fake slumber, he leans in closer and says, "I can hear your heartbeat. It's beating much faster than when you *are* asleep."

"I'm *trying* to sleep. You're not helping," I say.

"If you need to relax, you just have to ask. Trust me, in that realm, I can be very, *very* helpful."

I huff out a breath and pull the covers up to my chin. He shifts his weight around until he stills, and I think he might be falling asleep. I only realize how wrong I am when the warmth of his body presses against my back and his hand caresses my midriff.

"What are you doing?" I ask, my breath hitching in my throat.

"Remember when you called me chaotic?" His hand trails lower, his fingers tracing loops just above the waistband of my sweats.

"Mmhmm," I moan and bite my lip as his teeth tug on my earlobe.

"Let me show you a little chaos." His lips brush my neck as he speaks.

He sucks my sensitive skin, then presses his tongue flat over the spot and kisses it.

"Creed," I breathe. A warning. A prompt.

"Shh, *princesa*, give me tonight."

"Creed, we are in Erika's parents' guest room. We shouldn't," I say, a feeble attempt to stop something I'm not sure I want to.

"Then I guess you'll just have to be quiet for me."

He lifts his head and flashes me a devilish grin. Every thought to protest exits my brain as he moves his lips to the swell of my breast. He pushes my shirt up to my throat so that my entire torso is exposed to him, and I can't help but blush as his eyes hungrily roam over my body. I know he's seen me before—much more of me—but this feels strangely more intimate than our moment in my bathroom.

He moves so that his body is positioned on top of me and slowly sinks lower on the bed, sucking, licking, and kissing down my stomach. When he reaches my waistband, I stop him.

"Don't," I rush out. "I'm on my period."

He looks up at me, over my abdomen and breasts, and meets my eyes. There's a darkness to them that I haven't seen before, and he grins up at me.

"You think I didn't already know that?" he quips. When my eyes widen to the size of saucers, he scoffs and continues to say, "*Please*, Izzy. The second you started bleeding this afternoon, I scented it. Why do you think I'm trying so hard to get in your panties?"

My lips move as if to say something back to that, but in all honesty, I'm not sure whether that information is profoundly disturbing or makes total sense. Then, without warning, he slowly drags my waistband to my ankles.

"*Ohmygod*," I whisper, debating whether I should stop him before this becomes borderline weird. But I think better of it. At the end of the day, I'd be crazy to be the girl who turned down period sex with an actual vampire. "At least put a towel down."

"That's the attitude," he praises.

He lifts himself off the bed and grabs his discarded towel. I thank God it's black. He folds it in half then brings it over to where I'm lying in my underwear.

"Lift your hips, baby," he commands.

I do so, and he tucks the towel beneath me. He pulls my sweatpants the rest of the way off, and I do the same with my shirt. He reaches for my underwear, but I stop him. Subconsciously, some part of me knows this is abnormal. I push that part of me to the side and tell her to shut the hell up for the rest of the night.

He smirks, pushing my hands away, and hooks two fingers under the waistband at either hip. Then he exposes me in the most vulnerable way I could imagine. The cool air against my center sends chills through my body, but is soon replaced by the warmth of Creed's tongue as he licks from the bottom of my slit to the top, lapping up the blood already there. A satisfied moan rumbles from deep in his chest, and he dips his head back down.

"You're fucking delicious, *princesa*," he says with his head between my thighs.

My body instantly reacts to his mouth on my clit, sucking and licking my most sensitive bud. My teeth bite into my bottom lip, every ounce of focus I have in this moment going into staying quiet while his mouth works magic on me.

"Tell me I'm the only one to get to taste you like this." The sultry look in his eyes, combined with his tongue flicking over my clit, renders my mouth useless. "Say I'm the only one."

My hips buck when he removes his mouth from me, staring at me darkly, waiting for a response.

"Creed, *please*," I beg.

"Say it."

"Yes. You're the only one."

He grins that dangerous grin I'm becoming addicted to and wraps his hands around my thighs, spreading them wider.

"You'll do well to remember that."

Then he's diving back into his feast with animalistic ferocity. He pushes his tongue into my bleeding opening, slowly circling my inner walls. Quiet, breathy moans escape him as he does this. The actions and sounds he's making have my head falling back.

My hands find his hair, and I anchor myself there, gripping his deep brown locks and pushing him further into me. Without my permission, a moan leaves my mouth. A loud moan.

Rather than stopping to remind me to stay quiet, he deepens his strokes and picks up the pace. Within seconds, I'm a panting mess, gripping his hair tighter, as if holding on to it will keep my body on this plane of existence.

As if sensing my imminent release, he releases one of my thighs and begins circling my clit with his fingers while simultaneously driving me to the edge with his vicious tongue. I can feel the fiery promise of an orgasm building in my core with every passing second.

How a man who can be so vile is capable of creating this kind of ecstasy is beyond me, but I thank every deity known to man for gracing him with that gift. If Hades was as skilled with his tongue and hands as Creed is, Persephone never would have wanted to leave. If this man is so proficient with this, I'm almost frightened to find out how well-versed he is with his larger extremity.

"I'm coming," I whisper-shout into the room. My ability to see was taken about ten seconds ago, so I don't bother lifting my head to see him.

I clench around his tongue in spasms, and he continues to dart in and out of me, hitting my G-spot like he's got a map with a big ass 'X marks the spot' painted over it. The waves of my orgasm crash over me, stealing my focus as I begin to shout his name. With preternatural speed, he covers my mouth with his hand until the only noise I'm making is breathing. Once I'm a panting, jelly-boned mess, I lift my head to look at the man who just gave me one of the best orgasms of my life.

He is a dark god between my thighs.

He lifts his head from my center, his chest rising and falling fast and deep as he settles on his knees. His eyes are full of seductive shadows, and his nostrils flare with carnal satisfaction. His lips, chin, and the tip of his nose are covered in my blood, streaking down onto his neck. I can do nothing but breathlessly stare, in awe with the vampiric god looming over me.

His tongue darts out and slowly licks the perimeter of his mouth. He sucks air through his teeth, his fangs protruding from his gums in the sexiest way I could ever imagine fangs being.

"Fuck, Izzy," he groans. "After getting a taste of you, I know I'll never have better blood than yours."

He pulls the towel out from under me and cleans his face, then he cleans between my thighs. Once I have control of my muscles again, I find my underwear, the pad still in them, and my sweats on the floor, and pull them on.

"That was... an incredible experience," I say, crawling back into bed.

He shifts back under the covers and crosses his arms behind his head. As his eyes close, he looses a deep breath and settles into his spot.

"You better remember what you said, *princesa*. I'm the only one who will ever get to taste you like that. That's a promise."

M r. Winters was gone by the time Creed and I went downstairs for breakfast. Gale said something about him needing to clear something up at work. After eating more cinnamon rolls than any human should ever consume, we thanked Mrs. Winters for her hospitality and got on the road. Erika has been uncharacteristically quiet this morning, and I'm too happy about it to ask why.

I made Creed wash his face twice this morning, faded streaks of red staining his skin when we woke up. He, of course, made a stupid comment about saving it for later and needing to go back for seconds, since I made him wash it off. That did not, and will not, happen. As much as I want to deny what we did last night, the image of him kneeling between my thighs with darkened eyes and my blood dripping down his chin continues to awaken the butterflies in my stomach.

"What are you thinking about?" Creed asks, turning around to face me in the front seat. He's got that damn grin directed right at me again.

"Nothing," I say, meeting his eyes with a look that says 'keep your mouth shut'.

"You sure?" He wiggles his eyebrows, then deliberately licks his bottom lip.

"Positive."

Erika reaches for the volume dial and turns the music all the way up. I purse my lips, and Creed bites back a laugh.

"What's your problem, blondie?" he asks.

She aggressively turns the volume back down and takes her eyes off the road to look at him.

"The next time you two decide to get *freaky,* can you do it somewhere that isn't directly above my childhood bedroom? I've got vampire hearing now, remember? Or did you forget that I was tortured and killed less than forty-eight hours ago?" she bites, venom lacing her words.

"I was there, too, Erika. You weren't alone."

"God, are you really trying to make this about you?" she scoffs. "Ever since your knights in shining armor rescued us, everything has been about poor Izzy. *I* woke up in a trunk after being murdered. *I* had to drink actual blood after being told my entire life has changed. Not you. You got a nice little nap and a cozy morning in with your new boyfriend. Don't try to act like we experienced the same thing."

I shake my head, disbelief flooding through me as she spits absolute bullshit at me.

"Watch it," Creed snaps, his teeth clenched tight as he glares daggers at Erika.

"No, you know what? You're right. We didn't experience the same thing. You sat in a chair, practically untouched for an entire week, crying nonstop, while I was being fed on, day in and day out. You watched as I was bled nearly to death. Then, when I was taken into that house—" My voice cracks, and I nearly can't continue. My chin starts to quiver and tears fill my eyes. I go on, trying to strengthen my trembling voice,

"While I was being sliced into, bitten, and played with like a slab of meat, you were left in that chair. You were unscathed while I was being carved until my will to keep going left me completely.

"So, I'm *sorry* that you were turned into a vampire. I really am. But at least you're still alive and the worst memories you have to deal with are of *me* being tortured."

She looks back at the road without saying another word. I hate to make it sound like I'm discrediting what she's been through; I'm not. I know what she's suffered has taken a toll on her, too, but for her to try to act like she's been through so much worse than me immediately puts me on the defensive. I protected her in that place, in the only way I could. I knew that if I kept running my mouth, they'd put all their efforts into me, not her. And it worked, for a while, at least.

Recounting just that little bit makes my hands shake and my vision blur at the edges. It was a small mercy that Creed didn't seem to see my scars in the dark last night. Had he asked me about them, I would have come undone. Undeniable terror floods through me at the thought of having to relive every gruesome detail in order to tell Vincent, Logan, and Creed what happened today.

Part of me wants to turn around and go back to the Winters'. At least there, I could pretend like nothing happened. It was nice to live a lie for a night.

The rest of the car ride to Joel's is silent, aside from the music whispering out of the speakers. Creed stares out at the road, jaw tense and muscles locked, the whole way. The furious glare on his face when he snapped at Erika almost had me thinking he would kill her if she said anything else.

She parks the car right in front of the porch, where Vincent and Logan are already standing in wait. Vincent is as clean looking as ever, clad in a collared button-up shirt, with the sleeves rolled up to his elbows, tucked into a pair of slacks. Logan, on the other hand, looks like he didn't get a wink of sleep last night.

"Morning, sunshine," Creed remarks to him, slamming the passenger door.

Logan meets me at the bottom of the steps and wraps me in the warmest hug. He holds me to him, like he's afraid I might vanish.

"How was dinner?" he asks.

"Eventful," I say, deciding to leave it at that.

He pulls away and cocks a brow. Rather than get into the mess that was the Winters family dinner, I press a quick kiss to his cheek and move past him to climb the three steps up to the porch. "Good morning, Vincent," I say.

The corners of his mouth lift, creating the smallest of smiles, and he nods at me in greeting. A warm bundle of fur brushes against my ankles, and I look down to find August rubbing against me, purring as he does. I bend over to pick him up, and he settles on my chest, clinging on to the fabric covering my shoulder.

"I missed you, too, buddy."

I nuzzle my cheek into his side and head inside the house. I think he likes it here, at Joel's. According to Joel, Augie's been spending a lot of time outside. He likes chasing things in the grass and laying out on the porch to sunbathe. I think we'll have to move somewhere like this when we get our own place again. Somewhere with grass and sunshine and warmth. Our little apartment was good for a while, but as new as this weird relationship with the boys is, our family has grown.

Joel squints at me from his stool at the counter when I walk in. He looks me up and down before a wicked grin spreads over his face.

"You look... *rested*."

I bark out a laugh before I can think better of it, then proceed to glare at him. I mouth at him to shut up. He smirks and slowly nods his head, turning back to his computer.

I take August to the living room and plop down on the couch, dead center on a cushion.

"Are you all coming? Let's get this over with," I say, flitting my eyes between the three of them.

Joel gets up to leave, and I hear Erika's car start again. She drives off to who knows where.

"You can stay, Joel," I say.

He stops halfway down the hall, turning to face me halfway.

"I don't think I need to. You'll tell me what you want to when you're ready."

With that, he disappears down the hall and into his room.

Logan takes a seat next to me at the end of the couch, giving me just enough space so we're not touching anywhere. Vincent takes the armchair diagonal to the couch, and Creed stays standing across from me. They all settle into silence while they watch me, waiting for me to speak. August settles on my lap, curling into a little black ball.

"Um," I start, "this is going to be hard, so just be patient, okay?"

I look at Vincent as I begin. He seems like the safest to focus on. Creed's fury in the car, after I exposed a little of what happened to me, is something I don't want to face while flaying these memories out. And Logan's already looking at me with pity and heartbreak in his eyes. If I look at him, I'll burst out crying before I can get the words out.

Vincent is a neutral place. A rock to ground myself on amidst the storm. He doesn't show much emotion on a daily basis, and that isn't changing now.

I start with the night I was taken, telling them about the text and the blood and Ren in the apartment. Then I tell them about that first night—how Erika was burned and my leg was broken. Creed curses Cam out under his breath. It's all relatively easy to tell them, up until I get to that day.

"Ren came into the barn; he was already frustrated, and I was afraid he'd hurt Erika," I start, the vivid memory of that moment playing in my head like a film. "He took me to the basement of the house. There were knives everywhere."

My chin quivers, and I set my jaw to try to stop it. I take a deep breath, trying to force myself to get through the details without my voice shaking. I'm so *tired* of my voice shaking.

"He forced me down on the table. I can still feel the splinters in my back. I didn't fight him while he tightened the straps on my body. Not even when the panic set in as he strapped my head down. Then he, um," deep breath, "h-he took down one of the knives…"

*"This one's my favorite," Ren croons, twirling the knife so the light glints off its sharp edge.*

*I can feel tears well in my eyes and my chin starts to tremble with dread, because I know what he's going to do. I know he's going to hurt me, draw out my screams with each cut he makes.*

*"This might hurt," he says.*

*Then he presses the tip into the hollow at the base of my throat and slices my skin just deep enough to bleed from the top to the bottom of my sternum.*

*"You might want to think about opening that pretty mouth of yours and saying something useful, or this is going to get so much worse for you, little vixen."*

*"I told you," I bite, "I don't know why Vincent stayed, just that he did. I don't know where he is. So, carve away, because my answers aren't going to change."*

*"As you wish," he says, then the knife bites into my side.*

*He keeps cutting and slicing, sometimes carving out bits of my skin and holding it up for me to see as he licks the blood off it. He uses my body like a canvas and the knife is his paintbrush.*

*He's an artist creating a gruesome masterpiece.*

*I can't see what he's doing most of the time, my head firmly strapped down to the table, but I know he has something in store for me when I hear the knife clink when he sets it down.*

*"Enough with the child's play," he says. "I think I want another taste."*

*His teeth sink into my ankle, white hot pain shooting up my leg and burning into my foot. He releases me, then moves up to my thigh, tearing open my leggings and biting into the creamy flesh at the apex of my thigh.*

*I scream so loudly it drowns out the rain and the faint hum of the TV upstairs.*

I recount the rest of that day to them. I tell them about the rest of what he put me through in the basement, about Ren working for Vivienne, and about him taking me back to the barn.

"I-I thought I'd n-never see you again," I stutter, the vise grip of threatening sobs clutching my throat. "After that, he killed Erika, and then you guys showed up."

Vincent's expression has remained the same this entire time, a blank slate purely there to absorb this information. I finally break away from looking at him to take in the others' expressions.

Creed's nostrils are flared and his jaw flexes. I can see that he's grinding his teeth to keep from saying whatever it is on his tongue. His hazel eyes burn with rage that he and I both know he can't act on unless we find Ren.

Slowly, I turn to face Logan. His jaw is set, but rather than the furious way Creed's is, his is set to keep from trembling. His eyes are glistening with unshed tears that he's blinked back, and the sorrowful look in his eyes causes me to look away, down at my hands as I pet my cat.

"You guys can say something," I mumble.

Logan's weight shifts on the couch, and his hand covers my knee. He squeezes and I lay my hand over his, gripping his fingers.

"I'll kill them," Creed says, voice low and filled with dark promise. "I'll find them and fucking kill them."

"They want me; they'll be back. Vivienne's wanted me punished since I locked myself in that tomb," Vincent says. "I have to leave."

My head snaps up.

"What? No!" The words leave my mouth too fast, but I don't care. "None of you are leaving. Unless that's what you want, but I think it's obvious that the place I'm safest is with the three of you."

"It's not safe for you if I stay."

His ocean blue eyes pierce mine. He's set in his conviction, but I won't have it.

"It's not safe for *you* if you go," I retort.

"My safety isn't the priority here."

"If you leave, what's to say Vivienne won't send someone after Izzy just to punish you? If she finds out you've found your mate, Izzy is target number one for that crazy bitch," Creed snaps. "You're staying, old man. Whether you want to or not. We need a solidified line of defense, and I can't be the only one here to do that."

"He's right," Logan starts. "Without you, Izzy is vulnerable. I can hold my own in a bar fight, but against centuries old vampires hellbent on hurting us, I doubt I'd be much help."

Vince huffs out a breath, pinching the bridge of his nose.

"Alright, but if I'm staying, you two are getting training," he says with every ounce of severity as an exhausted dad.

"Training?" I repeat.

"Starting tomorrow. You need to learn to defend yourself long enough for us to help you," he says to me, then turns to Logan. "And you need to learn to fight. You're going to need to if you want to survive in this new world you're in."

I nod, meeting Vincent's eyes. Looking into them now, I find determination and worry mixing in the deep pools of blue.

"Hey, how about we all eat some lunch and watch a movie? I think we could all use something to boost our spirits after *that* conversation," Logan suggests.

"Fuck no," Creed snorts before I have time to register the suggestion.

"Why not?" I ask, turning to him with my glistening eyes.

He grits his teeth, shaking his head and closing his eyes for a moment.

"Vince, will you watch with us?" I ask, turning to the stoic man in the corner.

"I don't see myself having anything better to occupy my time," he says.

"Great. Goddamnit, Buchanan." Creed rolls his eyes, then looks at me, giving me the fakest smile he can muster. "What movie?"

We all sit on the back porch, enjoying the cool autumn day, while we eat the grilled cheeses I made for everyone. Logan grimaced at me in the kitchen when I added pickles to mine, layering them between the cheese and bread. I told him to try it, but he refused to put 'that abomination' in his mouth.

He's sitting next to me on the step as I peer out at the lake. My mom would have loved this place. Admittedly, she's the one who used to make me grilled cheese sandwiches with pickles in them when I was a kid. The first time I stayed over with Joel, I made one for him. He instantly fell in love with it.

"You pick a movie yet?" Creed asks around his last mouthful.

"You ate that so fast," I remark, gawking at his now empty hands.

"I was hungry, and it's not like you were offering," he says.

I roll my eyes at him and turn back to the lake.

"Come get me when you figure it out. Until then, I'll be repeatedly banging my head against a wall."

He retreats into the house, and Vincent follows soon after to shower before we get comfy.

"It's eleven in the morning. What the hell does he have to shower for?" Logan tuts.

He takes another bite of his sandwich, finishing it, and shrugs it off. His hand finds its place on my knee and everything suddenly stills. The air around us thickens, and I can feel a ball building in my throat when he asks me that single question.

"Are you alright?"

I hate that question. I hate it so much I wish I could turn back time to the first person who ever asked it and drive a dagger through their heart.

But right now, it feels like the gravity of my world lies within that question.

His warm brown eyes bore into my own as my hands, still holding on to my sandwich, slowly fall into my lap.

"You just had to relive every traumatizing moment of the week you were gone. It's okay not to be okay," he says, his voice soft and filled with tenderness.

The breeze blows wisps of my hair in my face as I try to figure out an answer that isn't a lie. Normally, I'd look at him and tell him that I'm fine and move on from the subject, but the truth is, I'm not fine. And if I tell Logan that I'm fine, that would be a lie. I don't want to lie to him.

"I'll be alright," I say. "Eventually."

He nods, squeezing my leg. He's so perfect, too perfect to deserve the crappy card that life dealt him.

"Are *you* alright?" I ask him.

"Me? Yeah, now that we have you back," he says, smiling rays of pure sunshine in my direction.

"No, Logan," I start, glancing down between us as I attempt to find words to the questions in my head. "I mean are you really alright? You've been through so much change, and you've accepted it all like none of it's a big deal. What you've experienced in the past few weeks has been life altering, and I've never taken the time to ask if you are okay."

He runs his hand up and down my thigh idly.

"Before everything happened, I wasn't exactly in the best place. My dad passed a few months ago, and please don't give me any cheesy 'I'm sorry' stuff, okay? He and I were... close. He left his ranch to me, and I thought I could handle it, but truth is, I had no idea what I was doing. That's why I came here. I was trying to make a business deal to start the ranch up again.

"The day that I died, I woke up alone and in the dark. I thought things were never going to get better. Then, after who knows how long, of scorching myself under the sun following that tug that brought me to that apartment, I found *you*."

"You remember waking up?" I ask, eyes watery with unshed tears.

"While you were gone, it started coming back to me. But, my point is, I thought my life was over, that I'd never feel anything but despair and anger and grief again, but then I found you. You showed me that I could be happy again. In the short time I've known you, I've felt more alive than I have in months. So, to answer your question, I'm better than alright. Because I have you."

My chin quivers under his warm gaze. I want nothing more than to take this sunray of a man and put him in a little jar to keep him safe from the storm clouds that threaten to block his light.

Guilt floods me, draining me of his sunshine and filling me with dark clouds. From here on out, I won't lie to him. No secrets. Not between us.

"I need to tell you something," I say, biting the inside of my cheek.

"What is it?"

He tilts his head to the side as he continues stroking my thigh.

"I, uh, slept with Creed," I get out. "It wasn't like *that*. We didn't, um, he didn't, you know, *insert* anything. Well, except for his..."

"Izzy," he interjects, stopping me from making this conversation incredibly awkward. I look up at him through the hair that's fallen over my face. "You slept with Creed?"

"Kinda?"

"Okay," he shrugs.

"Okay?"

"Okay."

My eyes flick back and forth between both of his as I wait for something else to come out of his mouth.

"Care to elaborate? What the hell does okay mean? Okay, you're pissed? Okay, you hate me?"

"I just told you that you're the reason I found to keep going, and you think that, because you slept with Creed, I could hate you?" He lifts a single brow. "You're his mate, too, Iz. Not to sound like a possessive asshole, but you belong to all three of us, not just me. So, I'm *okay* with you sleeping with Creed. Or Vincent, if that ever happens."

I blink at him, at a loss for words. This is totally new territory here. I've never considered polyamory, if that's what this even is, so I don't have a formed opinion on the subject. Though, I'll be the first to admit, the notion that I *belong* to more than one man scares me a bit.

"I am a little shocked that you slept with him in the family home of your roommate's parents," he chides.

I shove my face in my hands, groaning as he chuckles.

"I'm terrible for that, aren't I?" I mutter.

"I was thinking impressive would be more fitting. I mean, to stay that quiet in a house full of people—"

"*Logan Jenkins!*" I gasp, eyes widening at his ear to ear smile.

"I'm just saying, we might have to put that talent to the test sometime, beautiful."

He winks.

"Come on, let's go find a movie that will make Creed want to scratch his eyes out," he says, wrapping his arm over my shoulders as we both stand.

I don't know what good I've brought to this world to be granted the right to have a man like him in my life, but whatever it was, I'd do it a thousand times over to keep him forever.

# CHAPTER 23

Creed grunts, bending over and stumbling backward as Vincent demonstrates why the art of surprise is so important in a fight against someone with super speed. He's been going through topics like this for an hour and a half with Creed, while Logan and I sit on the back porch steps, watching them.

"Hit me like that one more time, old man. I'll show you the fucking art of surprise," Creed growls.

"We are teaching them combat techniques; punches come with the territory," Vincent replies, brushing off his shirt like there's dirt all over it.

"You saying you can't take it, tough guy?" I say, and Logan snickers. Creed glares at us.

"Wanna give it a try, lover boy?" he sneers, taking a step toward Logan.

He almost looks like he's about to get up, then Vincent clears his throat and Logan just rolls his eyes and refocuses. Vince and Creed show us what a vamp on vamp fight would look like in real time. They turn into a blur of fists and movement.

I have to admit, watching two of the most attractive men I've ever seen go through the motions of fighting each other turns me on a little.

Vince punches Creed in the jaw, snapping his head to the side. Creed spits blood on the ground and turns back to Vincent, smiling with chaos in his eyes.

Okay, it turns me on a lot.

"Keep trying to distract me with that scent, *princesa*, and I might have to snap both their necks just to have you to myself," Creed says as he gets Vincent in a headlock.

That's the end of their fight, because if they were really battling, Creed would have snapped Vincent's neck in that moment. I grind my teeth, glaring at him with every intent to kill him.

"Hey, Vince?"

"Yes, love?"

"Can lesson one be how to whittle?" I ask, keeping my eyes trained on Creed.

Creed's brows wiggle and Vincent chuckles deeply.

"Give me a blunt tree branch and the deed is done, beautiful," Logan says at my side.

"Try it, kid. I dare you," Creed threatens.

"Let us refocus on the lesson, shall we?" Vince redirects the conversation.

He continues lecturing us about what to expect in a vampire fight and what advantages I have as a human. He said he wanted to go through everything we should know now, so we understand why he teaches us things later, so here we are, listening to the 'how to fight the undead' handbook.

When he's done, he tells us to run a lap around the lake.

"I'm sorry, what?" I ask, eyes wide.

"Will the two of you also be running around the lake?" Logan asks.

"Yes, we will." Vince crosses his arms over his chest. "We'll need to keep up our stamina to be prepared."

"Oh, I assure you, my stamina needs no improvement," Creed scoffs. "Isn't that right, Izzy?"

My cheeks blaze with heat as those damn butterflies in my stomach flutter to life.

"I'm gonna start running now."

With that, I take off toward the lake at a steady jog. Three figures blur past me, lapping the entirety of the lake once before I'm even a quarter of the way done. My lungs ache with each painful intake as I huff and puff my way around the lake's edge.

Logan slows to a regular human pace, joining me.

"You've got this, baby. Just think of something to motivate you. Something that fuels you. Push yourself."

I don't say anything. Instead, I try to find that motivation. Could it be something I want?

Something I love? Something I hate?

I have it.

I push my limbs to their limit, ushering myself forward with new-found gasoline in my tank. I think of Ren. Of all the things he's done to me and my hatred for him. That is what fuels me to run through the pain as my limbs burn. Even as my lungs beg for a break from my heavy panting and my ribs ache, I push ahead.

"That's my girl," Logan praises, then speeds off again.

I think of every slice of that blade against my skin. Every wound he inflicted. Every scream that tore through my throat.

The burning that pulses through my entire body now is nothing—dull even—compared to that pain. I push through it, forcing my body to its limit, as I make the halfway point of my second lap. I push and I push and I push. Until I hit a wall.

I stumble back, held up by strong hands clamping my biceps. Anger paints my face as I glare daggers up at whoever just stopped me. Vincent is standing in front of me, holding my arms and staring down at me.

"What the hell?" I burst.

"That was two laps. You're done."

I struggle against his grip, to no avail.

"No, I could've kept going. Why'd you stop me?" I bite.

"Because, Isobelle, you're done. Your heart is pounding, and your entire body is flush. You keep going, and you're going to pass out. Go back up to the house and get water."

My brows knit together in a frustrated 'V' as I continue glaring at him. "*Now.*"

Finally, I rip out of his grip and huff out a breath. Logan comes to my side, walking in sync with me toward the house.

"What was that?" he asks, reaching out for my hand.

I tear my hand away, clenching my teeth as I storm up the steps.

"Izzy?"

I whip around to face him, stopping him in his tracks.

"Don't make me tell you I'm fine, Logan. I told myself I wouldn't lie to you, so just *don't.*"

He nods, defeat on his face, and lets me walk into the house alone.

"Isobelle," Vincent stops me in the doorway. "Talk to me."

"I already have."

"You told me what happened, but you left out the part about the scars you've been left with," he says.

Panic rushes through me, like pure adrenaline through my veins. Has he seen the bites? When?

Even today, I'm wearing leggings and a jacket. How could he have seen them?

"Just know that, when you are ready, you may confide in me, should you feel comfortable. Emotional scars are something I am well acquainted with."

My shoulders lose their tension and strange relief floods through me. He hasn't seen my scars.

No one has. No one but me.

"I... Thank you, Vince."

He nods curtly, patting my shoulder, his hand lingering there a bit longer than necessary, and goes into the house. The anger I felt before ebbs, but doesn't fade. I feel like I want to punch a hole in the wall, but I also feel like I want to curl into a fetal position and cry for hours until my tear ducts run dry.

Logan can't help. Neither can Joel, not right now. Right now, I need to be alone, and that clearly won't happen in this house.

I walk straight through the house to the front door, grabbing my car keys off the shelf by the door. Rain falls from the dark clouds that have been building all morning, and it drenches me on my way to the car. Erika's car is parked in the driveway, but I didn't notice her come back last night. I haven't seen her this morning, either.

Right now, I couldn't give less of a shit about her whereabouts. Not after our argument yesterday. Not with the ebbing rage still coursing through my veins.

I start the car and start pulling out of the driveway. I'm almost on the road when Creed appears in front of the hood, dripping with rain. I stare at him, shouting for him to move, but he doesn't budge. His hands are cemented to the hood of my car. Even if I tried to drive through him, I think more damage would be inflicted on my car than on him. In a last ditch effort to get out of this driveway, I honk at him. "Move, Creed!"

He just stands there, blocking my exit and staring me down.

*Alright, Izzy, you can get around him. He's not a brick wall. Just back up and back out of the driveway.*

I reverse, then slam on the brakes, as the car starts to rock. Rain cascades over the back window as I turn around to find Creed firmly planted at my bumper. Throwing the car in park, I get out into the now pouring rain.

"I swear to God, Creed, if you dented my car, I'm gonna—"

"You're going to what? Scream at me? Hit me? Threaten me? Go right ahead. But the one thing you aren't going to do is leave this goddamn house. Not without one of us with you."

Water drips off his hair that is now curling down his forehead. Drops of rain cling to his eyelashes and run down his face. His shirt is completely drenched, clinging on to his skin as if it's molded to him.

"I need space," I say, desperate to just get out of here.

"You need to be safe. Space isn't an option. If you're too emotionally damaged to function, go lock yourself in your room. Take your love struck puppy with you for all I care, but you will not be leaving this house alone, Isobelle."

He crosses his arms over his chest, his muscles flexing as the chill of the autumn breeze sweeps over us. The rain is cold as it is.

"Creed," I beg, "*please.*"

A muscle in his jaw feathers and he rolls out his shoulders. If I run, he's ready to catch me. He might drag me into the house kicking and screaming.

"No. That's final. You want to leave, let's go. But you'll be accompanied by Vincent or myself."

"What about Logan?" I rebut.

"He's a good kid, but he's not prepared to do what it takes to keep you safe if Ren comes after you again. He'd die trying, and we can't risk that."

"This is ridiculous! I'm not a prisoner," I whine.

The rain beats down on us, the wind picking up more intensely. Creed is a statue in the storm, unmovable and ever strong.

"Go inside, Izzy."

His eyes stare into mine, exposing my soul within. He sets his jaw and waits for me to move, but I cross my arms and meet his gaze instead.

"Isobelle, get your ass inside."

"No."

"Now."

"You'll have to make me, Creed. Make me your prisoner. I am not required to go willingly."

He growls and his nostrils flare. I can actually see the hazel in his eyes burning yellow with the growing anger within him. His jaw feathers once more before he takes another step forward and throws me over his shoulder with ease. I screech as my stomach hits his shoulder.

"Creed! What are you doing?" I shout.

"Making you my prisoner, *princesa*. Like you asked."

He starts walking to the porch with me struggling against his grip.

"My car, Creed! It's still running!"

We get through the door where Logan, Vincent, and Joel are all standing in wait, watching this scene unravel.

"Kid, park her car," Creed says.

He carries me upstairs and practically throws me down on my bed.

"Get comfy. I'm sure Logan will be joining you in your cell shortly."

He turns around and walks out the door, slamming it behind him.

After the sun set, I texted Joel. He came up to talk with me for a while, and I ended up telling him the majority of what happened to me, and he opened a bottle of wine after I cried enough tears to fill a small trough. He stayed for a glass before going back downstairs to sleep.

Logan brought me dinner about an hour ago—a luxurious peanut butter and honey sandwich—and sat in the rocking chair in my room while I ate it. I've been binge watching my favorite show since Creed locked me in here. Okay, locked is exaggerated. He never actually locked the door, he just closed it. But I'm pissed at him, anyway, so I'm going to keep saying he locked me in.

Now, I'm soaking in the perfect temperature bubble bath, sipping on my third glass of wine, listening to an audiobook.

I've decided to get out after I finish this glass, slowly sipping from it and letting the warm feeling it causes wash over my senses. Logan waits for me on the other side of the door, giving me some space, while I relax in the tub, but after thirty minutes, I've started to miss him. It's weird. Sometimes, it feels like I crave him just as much as he craves me.

I emerge from the bathroom, wrapped in a towel, with my hair wrapped in a bun atop my head.

Logan is sitting on the bed, legs kicked out in front of him, wearing only a pair of sweatpants. Wordlessly, I crawl onto the bed and wrap myself around his body, nuzzling my face into the crook of his neck.

"Hello again to you, too, beautiful," he says, wrapping his arms around my torso.

He presses a kiss to the top of my head and tightens his arms around me. The lights are turned off, aside from the Tiffany lamp on the nightstand on his side of the bed. It lights the whole room in a warm, purplish aura.

"Make me feel better," I whisper into his neck.

I kiss him there, over and over, kissing and tasting the supple, tan skin where his neck meets his collarbone. He groans happily as one of his hands slides down to cup my ass.

"Anything you want, baby. You want me to make you feel better? I'll make you feel so good that you forget about everything else for the night."

He kisses me, taking my lips with his. He commands my entire body with just that kiss. The towel slides off me as I straddle him, my spine curved so as to not separate from him. His hands roam my body, tracing over every dimple, every curve, every single detail of me. He kisses my jaw, trailing down my neck and collarbone.

"Take off your pants," I breathe, frantic and needy for him.

His sweats are off in a matter of seconds, thrown into the abyss of the room. I raise myself up, reaching down to hold him where I need him. He grunts as my fingers curl around his cock.

I sink down onto him, taking his entire length in one excruciatingly amazing move. All of him fits inside of me like I was made for him, my body giving and flexing where it needs him.

His hands grip my hips, and my hands flatten over his abs. The satisfying noises he makes as I rock my hips over him, sliding his cock out, then back in, over and over, are enough to make me never want to stop. I love that I can make him so dumbfoundedly happy with just my body.

His mouth falls open as he moans, the sound of it mingling with my own in the space around us. I can feel the waves of my orgasm building as I continue to rock against him, quickening my pace ever so slightly. My clit rubs against his body as I rock back and forth on his cock.

As our shared orgasm tears through us, I scream out with the immense pleasure we've created. He holds my hips down with enough force that I know I'll bruise tomorrow, not letting me come off him as he spills into me. The feeling of total fulfillment floods me as I sit on top of him, panting and sweaty.

When he lets go of my hips, I fall into him, letting his cock slide out of me, leaving me empty and wanting all over again. We lay there, breathing heavily and coming down from the high that is each other for a while before either of us speaks again.

"Can I try something?" he asks.

I lift my head from his chest and look at him, cocking a brow.

"It's just... I don't know," he starts, laying his head back, all coy and nervous.

"What is it?" I prompt.

"Could I feed on you?"

Of all of them, he's the only one who hasn't tasted me. That must drive him crazy.

"Sure," I breathe, bending my neck to the side, exposing myself to him. I brush my hair out of the way and wait for the piercing pain I know is coming.

He hesitantly puts his mouth on my throat, then he bites down. As he does, I'm reminded of the scars marring my body. I'm glad he hadn't noticed them in the dim light, but I feel like it wouldn't be the end of the world if he had. Maybe I'll show him in the morning. I think I'd like that.

Toe-curling pleasure takes over as he figures out how to direct his venom. I moan, rolling back my eyes as he drinks from me. I'm lost in the symphony of sensation inside my body as he takes what he wants. What he *needs*.

"What the fuck is going on in here?" Creed shouts as he throws the door open. My eyes fly open to find him standing in the doorway, Vince's form coming in behind him.

I want to tell Logan to stop, that he needs to take his mouth off of my neck, but I can't. The small prick of pain I felt when he bit me is long gone, replaced by a type of euphoria my body has learned to crave. It's like my entire body is on fire, burning for him.

"Get the fuck off of her, Jenkins!"

Logan snaps out of whatever blood-induced trance he was in and releases me, rushing to cover us up with a sheet. I want to scream at him. I need his mouth on my neck, his tongue pressed against my delicate skin.

Instead, Vince comes around the bed and pulls me further away from him, tucking me into his chest. He's gentle and warm and exactly what I needed to pull me out of that haze.

"What the hell were you thinking, kid? Huh? Do you *want* to kill her?" Creed steps closer to Logan's side of the bed.

"Stop," I attempt to tell him, but it comes out in a whisper.

"No, Isobelle. He's still new. Do you know how dangerous that was? He doesn't have a grasp on his control yet! He could have fucking killed you!"

"Ease up, Creed," Vince says sternly.

"Stay out of this, old man."

I tilt my chin up to see Vincent glaring daggers at Creed. Vince gives me a lot more leeway than I deserve, and even I wouldn't snap at him like that.

"Oh, did I strike a nerve? Self-conscious of our age, are we?"

"My age just means I'm more than capable of teaching you some respect."

"Try me. I dare you."

"Stop! Creed, just… go," I interject, not liking the turn the conversation is taking.

He looks at me like I've stabbed his dog, but eventually huffs and storms out.

"You too, Logan. Go get cleaned up. We'll discuss this later." Vince is soft in his directions.

"Is she…"

"She'll be fine. Go shower and get some rest."

I hear the shuffling of feet and then the door closes softly. I nuzzle myself in Vince's chest, tiredness settling over me.

"You're still bleeding, love." He pulls away and rests my head on a pillow. "Let me help you."

I nod, unable to form words at the moment, and turn my head. He climbs onto the bed, the sheets pulling toward him a little. As the fabric brushes over my nipples, I'm reminded that I'm completely naked beneath it.

His weight shifts the balance of the bed as he lies down next to me. His hands come up to brush the hair away from my neck, lingering on the skin there. He pulls me closer to him and dips his head low.

Two quiet seconds pass, and I watch him bite his tongue before the warm press of his it is against the open wound on my neck. He draws out the motion in one long pass, followed by another. "All." He kisses my neck. "Healed." Another kiss.

His head comes up, and he plants one last kiss on my forehead before lifting me from the bed and walking us to the bathroom.

"I'm going to clean you, love. You've lost quite a bit of blood, so let me do this for you."

I manage to nod, lethargy seeping into my bones.

With ease, he gets me to my feet and, to my surprise, I'm able to stand. Once the water hits, I shut my eyes, soaking in the warmth pouring over my skin. Vince lathers soap into my hair, massaging my scalp in a way that has my knees turning to Jell-O.

He's careful not to overstep any boundaries as he scrubs my body with my loofah. If only I had the energy to tell him I don't want any boundaries. Not anymore. Not with him.

After the soap is rinsed off, I linger there for a few minutes, pressing my back into his broad chest. I allow myself the selfish moment, because having him this close and this vulnerable feels like we've finally jumped over whatever hurdle was stopping us before.

I don't remember him turning the water off or dressing me in pajamas, but I drift off to sleep with my cheek tucked against his neck and his arm holding me close to him.

# CHAPTER 24



I couldn't sleep last night. Not after Creed hauled me out of Izzy's room and lectured me about how dangerous feeding on her was. He and Vince can do it because they've had centuries to learn control, apparently.

After he went into great detail about how easy it is to drain someone of so much blood there's no coming back, he reminded me of what happened to that woman in the apartment. I went to the room Joel set up for me and laid awake, staring at the ceiling for the rest of the night.

I expect to see dark circles under my eyes when I drag myself into the bathroom, but there aren't any. Come to think of it, I don't even feel tired. Mentally and emotionally, I'm exhausted. That's become a new normal for me, though. Physically, I feel ready to fight a grizzly with my bare hands. It must be Izzy's blood; it has to be. Something about drinking *her* blood revitalized me.

Guilt twists my gut, bending and squeezing it until I'm nauseous. Izzy could have died because of my recklessness, yet I can't help but remember how amazing she tasted. The woman I fed on before, the blood bags that Joel gets for us—neither even begin to compare to her blood.

The faint ache I've become accustomed to in my gums tears me from the oncoming spiral I was diving headfirst into. My reflection shocks me, even after all this time. Looking back at me is a monster, with bloodshot eyes and too long canines. He's a predator. He's an abomination.

He fiends for the girl he craves.

The girl I love.

I want to tell myself that last night was his fault. He was in control. The monster. I reach out for the mirror, my fingers pressing against the glass, and remind myself that we are one in the same. We aren't Jekyll and Hyde. He is me, and I am him.

*I* am a monster.

*He* is a man.

In the world I live in now, those two words mean the exact same thing.

A soft knock raps on my door, and I glance at my phone to check the time. Who is awake at five a.m.?

"Logan?" Her voice travels through the door to my ears in a soft whisper.

The girl willing to look past the monster and only see the man. She's here. Now. After everything.

"Logan, please let me in," she pleads.

The calming sound of her breathing draws me out of the bathroom and to the bedroom door. I press my head against the cool wood and listen to every inhale and exhale of breath coming from the other side.

"I know you're up. I heard you walking around a little bit ago," she whispers.

I sigh, closing my eyes against my own thoughts. I don't want to see her—to face her—but every fiber in my body wants her near me. Wants her tucked into my chest with my arms wrapped around her, holding her close.

I turn the knob and open the door, finding Izzy in a pair of pajama pants and a tank top, with a blanket wrapped around her shoulders. She smiles at me, the dawn rising before morning. Dawn used to be my favorite part of the day because of how peaceful it was in its beauty. Now, not even dawn could outshine that smile. Those dimples. Those earthy brown doe eyes.

"Close the door. I don't want to wake the others," she whispers.

I close the door, and when I turn back to her, she's perched on my bed with her legs criss-crossed and the blanket wrapped around her whole torso. I don't move toward her, even as she sits there expectantly. We've grown into a habit of being close, even when we aren't alone. When I sit on the couch, she lies on the other end with her feet in my lap—or her head. It's our normal.

She cocks her head, her brows scrunching, because what I'm doing right now is not our normal.

"What is it?" she asks.

"I don't want to hurt you again."

Her eyes soften for a moment before confusion warps her features.

"Hurt me?" she asks.

"Like last night," I say.

"Logan," she starts, standing from the bed. "That wasn't—You didn't—"

"Yes. I did. If Creed and Vincent hadn't come in, I-I don't know if I would have stopped. I don't know if I *could* have. You don't understand what it feels like to feed from you. Your blood was like fucking cocaine to me." I step back when she takes a step toward me, and she freezes. "Izzy, I'm so sorry."

I can't bear to look at her, to see the hurt on her face, so I look down instead. I can hear her footsteps as she comes closer. Her palm flattens against my chest as she comes toe-to-toe with me.

"Logan, you didn't hurt me. Hey, look at me." She tilts my face up with her other hand, pressing it against my cheek. "I'm fine. See? I'm *fine*. I don't regret a single thing about last night, and it might break my heart if you did. Feeding off me might have been an amazing experience for you, but being fed on by you was just as amazing for *me*. I let you do that because I wanted to experience that with you."

Her eyes search mine, waiting for a response I don't have.

"And I would let you do it a thousand times over if it meant making you as happy as you were last night."

"No, Iz. We can't do that again."

She smiles up at me, warmth glowing in her eyes.

What I wouldn't give to take this girl back to California and wrap her in blankets around the fire pit at the ranch. She'd love it there; I'm sure of it.

Just then, my phone rings in my pocket. I pull it out and stare at the name on my screen.

"Who is it?" she asks.

"My brother," I sigh.

When Joel brought me this phone yesterday, I powered it on and got it set up with my old data, thanks to his help. No one had realized I lost my phone to the lake when the truck was pushed in until Joel noticed I was never on it.

I'd received about a hundred texts from JJ, each one increasingly more worried than the last. I texted him back with a simple *I'm fine, I'll talk to you later.* Guess that didn't suffice.

"Oh. I didn't know you had a brother," Izzy says, glancing down at the phone. "Answer it."

I take a deep breath to prepare myself for whatever slew of threats my older brother is about to throw at me, then I answer the phone.

"JJ," I say by way of greeting.

"What the fuck is wrong with you, Logan? You better have one hell of a story to explain you ghosting Mom and me for *weeks*. I'm talking a you-were-in-a-coma kind of story."

I hadn't realized until now how much I missed my brother's voice. He and I have always been close. He was my best friend growing up—until the divorce. I favored time with our dad, while he preferred being with Mom. We still made time to see each other, even if that meant making a run for burgers after one of his football games or my baseball games.

"I had one text from Mom, Jake. I doubt she was missing me."

"God, Logan," he scoffs. "That is so not the point. If you hadn't texted me yesterday, I was seriously about to buy a ticket to Boston myself to track you down. Or at least file a missing persons report. Jesus Christ. I thought you were lying dead in a ditch somewhere!"

"Relax. I'm fine, okay?"

Izzy chews on her lip while JJ and I hash things out. She's the picture of perfection, standing in front of me, waiting patiently.

"That's great, man. You're *fine*. When are you coming home?"

"I... don't know."

"You don't know? Right, then I guess I'll just tell you over the phone, then." My muscles tense up and I imagine the worst. Something happened to Mom.

"What?" I ask, afraid to hear the answer.

"The ranch is gone, Logan. The bank took it."

Everything stops around me. The ranch is... gone? How can it be gone? I've done everything to keep that place. That's the reason I came here. The reason I died. Had I not come to Boston to make that deal, I never would have been so stressed that I took that drive. No. That ranch is everything I have.

Had.

Fuck.

My thoughts are spiraling. All the while, my vision turns blurry, and it gets harder to breathe regularly.

"I'm sorry. I tried to keep it a little while longer, but they wouldn't cooperate. I don't know what they're going to do with it, but it's not ours anymore."

"Flash?" I ask, only able to speak the name of my favorite horse as my entire world comes crashing down around me.

"I..." There's a long pause on the other line. "I'm sorry."

I remove the phone from my ear and hang up, slipping it back into my pocket. My eyes are unfocused when I hear Izzy's voice filter through my turmoil.

"What's wrong? What happened?" she asks.

I swallow back the onslaught of emotions trying to bring me to my knees and do my best to refocus on her. My light in the dark. Although, right now, even she can't make everything go away.

"The bank took my dad's ranch."

I choke on the words. I can't believe them, but I know Jake wouldn't lie to me. Not about that.

"Oh my god, Logan," she breathes, stepping toward me. "I'm so sorry."

She wraps her arms around me, pressing her cheek against my chest and just holding me. My arms are limp at my sides.

"That ranch was *everything* to me. I gave *everything* for it."

"I know," she whispers. "I know."

She tightens her arms around my waist and holds me for as long as I need. I rest my chin against her head, inhaling the scent of her shampoo and letting it anchor me to her. When I finally wrap my arms around her, I hold her like she's the only thing I have.

Maybe that's because she is. She's everything I have left.

"Can we fix this?" she asks.

I shake my head, closing my eyes and letting myself bask in her touch. "No, baby. We can't."

She gets up on her tiptoes, still hugging me tight, and kisses my cheek. She rests her head on my collarbone and lets me hold her there in the middle of the room.

"We should get out today. We can all go to Mateo's and get gelato. It won't undo what happened, but it might help you feel a little better for a while."

I brush my hand through her long brown hair, enjoying the softness of it against my fingers.

"That sounds like a great idea, beautiful. But for now, just let me hold you like this a little longer."

She nods and nuzzles into me, our bodies melting together in the chilly room.

I sit in the back of the car with Izzy while Creed drives the four of us into the city. There's been an odd amount of awkward silence between everyone this morning, but I don't think I'm the cause. Izzy steals glances every now and again at Vincent, whose focus is trained at the road ahead.

I look between the two of them, trying to figure out what on earth happened last night.

"Okay," I start, not bothering to try to whisper privately to Izzy, because we're in a car with vampires who would hear it, anyway, "did you two bump nasties or something?"

Isobelle's eyes widen to the size of baseballs, and Vincent clears his throat.

"What? No! I—Why would you—What?" Izzy stutters, shaking her head as she stares at me like I've grown a second head.

"It's bumping *uglies*, Logan," Creed says. I can see his sly smile in the mirror.

"There was no bumping anything! What are you on?" Izzy exclaims.

"You haven't spoken all morning. I mean, that's not exactly out of the ordinary for you two, but you also haven't made eye contact all morning. Something's up," I say.

"There's nothing going on. I don't know what you mean," Izzy says defensively, crossing her arms over the seatbelt.

"Creed, back me up here. They're acting weird."

Creed shrugs and glances back at Izzy in the rearview mirror.

"The kid's right. You're both acting like awkward college kids. Look, I'd understand if you told me Buchanan slipped and happened to fall into your pussy, Iz. If that's the lie you need to tell to justify sleeping with Count Dracula," Creed says.

"Oh my god! Will you both stop it? Vince, a little backup here?"

Creed grins out at the road, and I snicker. Her frustration is entertaining in so many ways.

"We did not have any relations last night. The two of you are reading into things that are insignificant," Vincent says.

"So, that's why you've got her scent all over you today?" Creed jeers.

"He stayed with me last night. Does that satisfy you? He slept in my bed. Fully clothed. After I showered," Izzy explains.

She looks between Creed and me, both taking way too much joy from this conversation, and huffs out a breath.

"You couldn't have stood on your feet alone if you tried, Izzy. That why the old man is so quiet today? Thinking about what our sexy little mate looked like naked and dripping with water last night?" Creed says, smirking and wiggling his brows at Vincent.

Izzy gives up, covering her face with her hands, and I chuckle. Vincent just shakes his head wordlessly, that look of fatherly disappointment he seems to have mastered on his face.

"You two are awful," Izzy groans. "So what if we *had* slept together—which, again, we did not. We're both full-grown adults."

"You're really making your way through the group, Iz. If Joel didn't bat for the other team, I'd start to get worried," Creed says. He winks at her in the mirror. "You know what? I actually might be jealous of Jenkins. He's the only one of us to know what it feels like to be inside of you."

Izzy's jaw drops, and she stares holes into the back of Creed's head.

"I think that's enough, man. Don't take it too far," I warn.

Creed scoffs, rolling his eyes.

"So, you two get to bone as loud as you'd like, and I can't say anything about it? Hard to see how that's fair," he pouts.

"It's not like you're a stranger to her body, Creed," Vincent mumbles.

"Okay," Izzy interjects. "New rule. There will be no more talking about mine, Logan's, Creed's, or anybody's sex life for the rest of the day. I'd love to say forever, but I know you too well to have that high of hopes." She throws a judgmental glance at Creed.

Creed responds by placing a pair of all-black aviators on his face and turning up the stereo. Hard rock blasts from the speakers as we drive into the city. Izzy is watching buildings pass out the window, and I'm watching her.

I fear I will be eternally mesmerized by her. Her long dark brown hair that curls softly around her face. Her big, beautiful brown eyes. Her dimples. Her supple curves. Her soft olive skin. All of her.

"I can feel your eyes, Logan," she says, still watching the world outside the window.

I smile at her, smothering a laugh, and lean my head back on the seat.

Mateo's is packed when we arrive, the lunch rush filling the restaurant so much that there's a line going out the door. I step out of the car, onto the curb, and hold the door open for Izzy to scoot across the seat and follow me out. She stumbles getting out, the toe of her shoe catching on the curb, and falls into me. I shuffle back a step but grasp her arms to keep her upright.

"You know," she starts, "I've had a lot fewer scabs and bruises since I've met you all."

I decide not to remind her of the condition she was in when we found her in that barn, shoving down the furious feeling that bubbles up my throat at the imagery.

"Fall on me as many times as you'd like, beautiful. I'm okay with anything that keeps your hands on me." I wink.

She blushes, shoving me away playfully and walking toward the restaurant. Instead of walking past the line of people and finding Gianni directly, she waits in the long line of people. Vincent and I fall in line with her while Creed grumbles about the wait.

"You haven't tasted the food Mateo and Gianni can make. Trust me, it's worth the line," Izzy says. "Just ask Logan and Vince."

"Right, because I'm going to trust the palette of a centuries old corpse whose food knowledge doesn't extend further than roasted pig."

"The food of my time extended much further than the simplicity of a roasted pig. But I will say, the food here tops most of the cuisine back then," Vincent says.

"Iz, you've got to work on the way he talks. He opens his mouth and I can practically hear the eighteenth century trying to crawl out of it," Creed says, leaning against the brick wall that frames the door.

"It's not *that* bad," she says, her voice pitching up as she speaks.

"I don't want this to sound mean—you know I respect you, man." I grimace. "But it is pretty bad. You talk like you're in a period movie."

"I don't know what you speak of. My dialect is fine."

Izzy cringes and shakes her head at him.

"It's a work in progress, that's all," she assures him, rubbing a hand down his sweater-donned arm.

Finally, we move inside the restaurant. The smell of oregano and other spices wafts into our faces, and I can't help but stop to sniff the air. When I open my eyes, Izzy is doing the same thing with her eyes closed and her nose tipped up.

"Is that my lil Isobelle?" an older man with a Mario Bros' mustache asks as he walks up to us.

"Mateo!" Izzy exclaims, breaking away from us to throw her arms around the gray-haired Italian restaurant owner. "I missed you last time I was in. How are you?"

"How am I? How are you? Look at you, *cara mia*. You're glowing! A little tired around the eyes, however," he says. His accent is even thicker than his sons, a hybrid of Italian and Boston.

"Thanks," Izzy scoffs, smiling at Mateo with warmth in her eyes. "How's the missus?"

"Angelina is just fine. You shoulda called; she'd love to see you." He glances from her to the three of us, his wrinkled eyes scanning each of us. "Who are your friends?"

"Oh, right." Izzy steps back, so she's situated in the middle of us. "Mateo, meet Logan, Creed, and Vincent. They're friends from school."

"Uh huh," he squints at us. "Handsome shits, ain't they?"

"I certainly like to think so," Creed says.

Izzy subtly rolls her eyes and forces a laugh.

"Just friends, eh? 'Cause that one's looking at ya like he wants to eat ya," Mateo says, looking Creed up and down. Then his eyes meet mine.

For some reason, I want to prove myself to this man. As if winning his approval grants me full permission to call Isobelle mine.

I step forward and extend my hand. "It's nice to meet you, sir."

He looks me up and down, then throws his head back, laughing.

"Oh, please, son. A friend of my lil Isobelle's is a friend to the whole family."

He swats my hand to the side and comes in for a hug. To my enjoyment, he shakes Creed's hand. Vincent bows his head at Mateo before he has a chance to hug him. The dirty look Creed gives him when Mateo turns his back has Izzy smothering a laugh. I'd be lying if I said I didn't want to give him hell for not getting a hug.

"Grab a table, sweetheart. I'll tell Gianni to whip up four 'Izzy's'."

"Thank you, Mateo."

We follow Izzy to a booth in the corner of the restaurant and slide into our seats. I, of course, sit next to her, while Creed and Vince occupy the bench across from us.

"What the hell is an *Izzy*?" Creed asks.

"Heaven in sandwich form," I say.

Izzy giggles, then points at me and says, "What he said."

After lunch, we took Izzy shopping, or more accurately, she took us shopping. She bought an absurd amount of sweaters and form-fitting jackets. She also made all of us buy workout clothes, then convinced me that I needed to get clothes for myself. Now, as the sun is beginning to set, we are all in line at an ice cream shop, looking over the flavor options.

After several minutes of tasting flavors with wide and wonder-filled eyes, Vincent orders plain vanilla. Izzy gets double chocolate, Creed gets rocky road, and I get mint chocolate chip.

"Of all the flavors you tried, you decided to get the most boring one?" I ask Vincent.

"Boring does not equate to bad tasting," he rebuts.

"Touché."

"I think vanilla is a great choice," Izzy says.

Creed scoffs. "Please. There is nothing about you that is vanilla. Not anymore, at least."

"Wow. I'm impressed. You went a whole five hours before making any sexual innuendos," Izzy remarks.

Creed wiggles his brows and slowly licks his spoon. Absolutely disgusting. Does his flirt mode ever turn off? Seriously, there has to be a switch or something.

Izzy, on the other hand, tries to hide the fact that she is staring at the motion like she's imagining his tongue somewhere else. I nudge her with my elbow and snicker when she snaps out of her fantasy, looking at me with wide eyes. Silently, I make a gesture like I'm zipping my lips shut, and she laughs.

The sun has fallen by the time we're halfway to Joel's place—home, I guess. Calling his house home feels wrong, like deep down, I know that's not what it is. Whether I associate that term with California—with my dad's ranch—or someplace I know I'll be in the future, I'm not sure. What I do know is that, from now until I breathe my last breath, *home* is wherever Izzy is.

I look at her as I think about the notion, watching as her eyes drift along the treeline out the window. Her cheeks and nose are pink due to the chill of the night and Creed's refusal to turn the heater on. I listen to each one of her heartbeats, pumping with her own blood and keeping her vital organs alive. My heart beats because of the blood of others that I've consumed. She and I are not the same.

It is easy to remember that she's human and I'm not. She's breakable, fragile even. At least compared to me. Perhaps it won't be *my* last breath that ends it for us. It's more likely to be hers. She has a stopwatch on her life, ticking until someone presses the stem. I don't. My stopwatch stopped ticking three and a half weeks ago, when my truck spiraled off the road.

"I didn't know the carnival was in town," she says, perking up as she examines the bright lights emanating from the trees.

"I wouldn't call that *in town*, Iz," I say.

"I love the carnival. I go every year with Joel. Last year, we brought Erika, too. We should go this week! It'll be fun," she rushes out, excitement building in her voice.

"Negative, *princesa*," Creed says.

"Oh, come on, Creed. You'd enjoy *something* there."

"No, Izzy. There would be too many chances for you to be vulnerable to attack. Ren is still out there," he says, a bite to his tone.

She frowns out the window, trying to hide her face from me, but doesn't argue. Her safety is our priority, no matter the differences the three of us have. I just wish her happiness was as important in their eyes as it is in mine.

# CHAPTER 25

## Vincent

Creed, Logan, and I wait by the house as Isobelle completes her lap around the lake. Each of us has already completed five laps. She jogs up to us, breathless and sweat-soaked.

"So," she says between deep breaths, "what's the lesson plan today, Vince?"

"Today, I want to see what you are already capable of. Logan will be with Creed while I work with you."

She and Logan share a look that I don't quite understand. They've seemed to form a deeper bond than she shares with myself; many an unspoken word has passed between them in the past weeks.

"I'm not sure who you think I am, but I'm not really *capable* of more than punching. And even in that field, I'm no Rocky."

I tilt my head, and she waves her hands at me. I see, that was another modern reference I don't understand.

Creed and Logan begin a decent distance away from us while I help Isobelle improve her fighting stance. She sets her feet shoulder length apart and squares her shoulders in my direction. Once she's ready, we begin.

"I want you to fight me. Pretend that I am an attacker and you need to fight me off."

She huffs out a breath and shakes out her tense muscles, resetting her stance. Aiming a punch directly at my face, her knuckles slam into my nose. Immediately, she retracts her fist and gawks in horror.

"Ohmygod, Vincent! Why didn't you do anything?" she exclaims frantically. "You're bleeding."

I raise my hand to my face and feel the warm drips of blood coming from my nose.

"That was a strong hit," I commend her.

"Gee, thanks," she says, her eyes still wide as she examines my face. "Why didn't you block me? Or dodge, for Christ's sake?"

"I need to see how strong you are."

"So you let me break your nose? Unbelievable."

She presses her palms into her temples and takes a step back.

"Again," I say.

"Will you dodge this time?" she asks.

I shrug in response and hunch into a fighting stance. She mimics me and prepares to hit me again. This time, she aims for my jaw. Her right hook snaps my head to the side.

I can sense her pulling back again, so I prompt her, "Keep going."

She keeps punching me, grunting and breathing heavily the longer she goes. I take every hit as though her fists are pebbles being thrown by a child. She is inflicting damage, but my body is fast to heal itself. The pain she causes is nothing compared to the cruel blows of the guards who raised me.

When she stops, letting her fists fall to her sides all red and bloody, she watches me. I stand tall in front of her, looking down into her brown eyes.

"That was easy, wasn't it?"

"Well, yeah," she says as she continues to huff and puff.

"Good. Compose yourself and go again."

She nods, gulping as she catches her breaths. She bounces on the balls of her feet and falls back into her stance.

This time, when she swings at me, I dodge her at my speed. She tries again and misses.

Punch.

Miss.

Punch.

Miss.

Punch.

Miss.

She starts furiously throwing her fists at me, trying to simply land something. She does not.

After a while, I lunge at her and pin her to the earth. The breath gets knocked out of her, and she looks up at me, panicked, while her lungs beg for breath. Her cheeks redden and she struggles against my grip on her wrists.

Looking at her now, beneath me with her dark hair splayed around her face like a halo, her mouth slightly open and her eyes on me, she is the most beautiful being I've ever laid eyes on. Even as her body writhes for air and freedom, her beauty strikes me.

Finally, she inhales deeply, filling her lungs with much needed oxygen.

"What the hell?" she gasps.

"It is not as easy when your opponent is a vampire with enhanced speed and strength, is it?"

"No," she huffs. "How the hell am I supposed to do this?"

Her head falls back against the ground. She shuts her eyes and takes a frustrated breath. I stand and reach my hand out for her.

"I'm going to show you," I say.

She takes my hand and lets me pull her to her feet.

For the following hour, I show her how to use her abilities to her advantage. She's human. No vampire would expect her to have a chance against them. She can use that. We go through the motions of using the element of surprise and how she can use subtlety to best an opponent.

I am no fool. This will not be an easy task when it comes time for her to use these skills, but my heartbeat slows, knowing that she *has* the skills. She has much learning to do, but that is what I am here for. Every morning, until the day her body isn't able to handle it any longer, I will be here, ready and willing to train her.

There is shouting nearby, and I am reminded that we are not alone out here in the moist morning air. My focus was so intent on Isobelle, I had forgotten the other two were training as well.

A dull aching arises in my chest when I look in their direction, an ache that is not my own. Glancing at Isobelle, I can see how torn she is when she watches them. Realization knocks the breath from my lungs, forcing me to stand straighter to keep from falling to my knees in front of this frail human girl.

The bond is growing.

The other two don't seem to notice the same feeling as I do. If they do, they're not thinking anything of it. The aching—the aching that isn't my own—is Isobelle's. I am feeling what she is, a dulled version of it, at least. She feels so strongly for Creed and Logan—whether it is love or other—that watching them fight hurts her.

Why do they not feel it?

Isobelle is much closer to them, emotionally and in every other sense. Why is it that only I am feeling this ache? Her body is practically screaming at mine.

"That's enough," I bark, nearly choking on the words.

Her pain, even in this small amount, is suffocating.

They don't hear me, so I march over to them and separate them myself. I thought that would stop this insufferable aching, but it amplifies.

I look back at her and see that she isn't focused on us any longer. Her gaze has drifted to the house. To Erika, stepping into view.

The engine of her vehicle is still running, so she is not here to stay long. Creed stiffens. He must have scented the change in our mate's emotions. It makes sense that he didn't catch a shift in scent before; his talents extend to strong emotions. Dull and weak feelings don't catch in the air the way the strong ones do. Vivienne had the same talent.

"Both of you, go inside."

Creed glares at me, his eyes flitting between Isobelle and myself. Logan stares at me as though I've grown a third eye.

"Inside."

Logan notices the bite in my tone and goes inside without any further questions. Creed sets his jaw and squares his shoulders. I meet his eyes, finding the hidden glimmer of concern in them and doing my best to reassure him without saying anything. Eventually, he huffs out a breath and begrudgingly goes inside.

I turn back to Isobelle and find her staring out at the lake. Walking over to her, I stop a breath away. Her scent infiltrates my senses, and the aching persists. We stand there together in silence for a decent duration, her staring at the lake and me staring at her.

She is the first to speak.

"She didn't deserve this. I left her there. Alone. She didn't deserve it. Any of it."

"Neither did you," I say.

"She wasn't involved in any of this. Her only crime was being my roommate. I should have known not to leave her alone. I-I didn't know she'd be in danger."

"What happened to you both is no fault of yours. Vivienne did this because she wants me. You cannot blame yourself."

She wraps her arms around herself, the breeze blowing loose strands of hair into her face.

"I should've never left her. I just... I didn't know."

The crack in her voice sends another sharp pain through my chest, but this time, I am unsure who it belongs to.

After that night that I slept in her bed, things have changed. Before, I was happy standing idly by and keeping a close eye on her. Now, I cannot fathom letting her feel this way on her own. I want to hold her, to allow her to feel whatever she chooses to feel with me as her shield. I want her to feel safe while she wallows.

A strong gust of wind blows up from the water and forces her jacket to fall down her shoulder. My eyes catch on a patch of skin that is a contrasting shade of white to her olive skin. She quickly pulls the jacket back into place, and I am just as quick to pull it back down.

"Vince, don't," she says, trying to tug the fabric from my grip.

It's too late to cover it up. The scar marring her perfect skin. Fury rages within me as the image of it sears itself into my mind.

"*He* did this to you?" I say through clenched teeth.

"Yes."

"Why did you not say anything?"

"I wasn't ready."

My jaw clenches, and I cover her arm back up with her sleeve.

"Are you ready now?" I ask.

"No."

I nod and look out at the lake. The clouds covering the sky make the water's reflection a pale gray color that dampens the colors of the nature around it. The grass even seems dull where it rings the lake.

I stumble when Isobelle's arms wrap around me forcefully. She nuzzles into me, tears streaming down her face.

"It's alright," I say, wrapping one arm around her waist while using the other to stroke her hair.

"Thank you," she whispers.

"Always," I reply.

Today has been up and down. My adrenaline was high this morning when I thought I was beating the crap out of Vincent, then everything crashed when I saw Erika and he saw my scar. Since that, I've pretty much been walking around like an emotional bomb, ready to go off any minute.

Erika was gone again by the time Vince and I went inside after I soaked his shirt with tears for fifteen minutes. Creed left soon after that and didn't come back until after we'd all eaten dinner. Logan asked if I wanted to go on a hike with him, since the weather was so nice, but I wasn't feeling up for that, either. Joel watched a couple episodes of cheesy reality TV with me before he had to go into the office for back-to-back meetings, and Vincent read in the recliner in the living room all day.

The shower I took was scorching, and my skin is still red now as I climb into bed. Vincent is already asleep on top of the covers. After my breakdown this morning, he hasn't left my side. We didn't speak about tonight's sleeping arrangement, but I wasn't going to protest. He makes me feel secure. I needed that tonight.

Shaking off all the stresses of the day, I lay my head on the pillow. My eyes just fall shut when someone's large hand gently shakes my shoulder. I'm exhausted from training today and the emotional grenade I was holding onto inside of myself and don't particularly feel like opening my eyes to see which of my household members is attempting to steal my sleep from me.

He shakes me again.

I crack my eyes open just enough to see Logan kneeling at my bedside. He raises a finger to his lips, nodding to the very asleep Vincent on my other side.

"Get up," he mouths.

When my brows scrunch together, he extends his hand to me.

"Trust me."

My eyes meet his in the darkness, and there's a glimmer there in his golden brown eyes that wasn't there this afternoon.

"I do," I mouth back, keeping this conversation absolutely silent. I take his hand and gingerly crawl out of bed. Thankfully, Vince was just as tired as me, so he doesn't stir at my absence.

Logan guides me downstairs and directs me to put on the pair of sneakers I left by the front door. Then, in an oversized t-shirt and boxers, I follow him into the night.

There's a chill in the air, but I don't mind. I can't mind when Logan is this happy. He's smiling from ear to ear, breathing in the crisp air, his hand slipping into mine.

"You know how you said you trust me?" he whispers, still aware that there are two vampires just inside the wooden door at our backs. "I'm gonna need you to remember that."

Before I can question what *that* means, he pulls me onto his back and breaks out in a full run through the thick trees surrounding the house.

The feeling of moving at vamp speed is something I don't think I'll ever get used to. The air rushing against my skin, everything moving past us in a blur of light and color. It's euphoric. Never in a million years would I have dreamt that this would be within my realm of existence—maybe when I was younger, I hoped *I* would be running this fast. Now that I have this, I couldn't imagine any better way to experience it than on one of their backs or in one of their arms.

We stop at the gates of the carnival.

"Why'd you bring me here?" It's clearly closed for the night and, if I'm being honest, being in the empty venue is kind of creepy.

"I saw how disappointed you were that we couldn't come," he says, looking at the ground instead of me. "You've been sacrificing a lot for us, and I wanted to give you this. This is one thing that I *can* do for you, Izzy."

Tears rim my eyes as I take his hands and hold them to my chest.

"Spending time training and doing what I can to keep you guys safe isn't a burden to me. I need you to know that. Sure, I would love to spend a day here and just forget about everything that's happened and everything to come. But if spending my day training until I want to puke means keeping you and me safe, Logan, I'd choose the latter every day for the rest of my life." The soft smile on his face makes my heart melt. I'd do anything for them.

"Then let me help you forget for a night," he says, finally meeting my eyes.

"Lead the way."

The fairgrounds are hauntingly pretty, with nothing but the moonlight lighting up the rides and closed food stands. He guides me straight to the massive Ferris wheel at the edge of the grounds. This thing is taller than Joel's house.

"It won't be exactly the same, it not being turned on and all, but at least the view will be nice."

He shrugs.

"I'm not going to like your means of getting up there, am I?"

He laughs, tilting his head back and saying, "No, probably not."

"Great."

"Just hold on to me and shut your eyes."

I do.

I feel the familiar rush of wind against my skin, and I hear the eerie creak of metal, then I'm sitting on my butt, rocking back and forth.

My eyes open to the most beautiful view of Boston I've ever seen. The twinkling lights of the city are like stars against the night sky. He was right. It isn't the same. It's better. There's no fear of losing this moment as the cart slowly descends. There's only peace and stillness and the assurance that this view won't leave me unless I want it to.

I lean into him, and he wraps an arm around my shoulders. I shiver a little, the brisk night air causing goosebumps to rise from my skin.

"Shit, here." He pulls his hoodie over his head and hands it to me. I put it on, enjoying the smell of him wrapped around me like this, and lay my head on his shoulder. "I should've had you grab a jacket before we left."

"I like this one a lot better than any that I own, believe me." He chuckles, his cheeks blushing.

"Except maybe my cherry red velvet trench coat."

"I bet you look amazing in that, but even if you wore it with lingerie underneath, I don't think I could like it more than the sight of you wearing my clothes."

Now I'm the one blushing.

I nuzzle into him more and stare out into the city lights. It's so peaceful up here, not a single thing to bother us. I feel completely at ease in Logan's arms.

"What do you want, Izzy?" he asks, his voice hushed as if he's afraid to speak.

"What do you mean?" I tilt my chin up so I can see him. He's perfectly comfortable; the only sign of his nerves is the feather in his jaw.

"What do you want?" he asks again.

"Now or in the future?"

"Both."

I lay my head back down, pondering an answer that actually means something and not one of my usual, very un-serious ones. Do I even know what I want?

"I don't really know what I want down the line. I guess I'd like to settle down someday."

"Do you want kids?"

I blink back surprise. He's never asked, nor has he even mentioned kids. I forget sometimes that he's my age, so recently a human. I hadn't realized that he might still have desires like having kids. He hasn't had the time to process that impossibility yet, like Vince and Creed have.

"Do *you* want kids?" I ask, finding that I'm both eager and afraid for his answer.

It's silent for several minutes before he speaks again.

"I did." I sit up so I can look at him, twisting in the seat. "I always wanted to have kids one day. Sometimes, when I was at my lowest, I would imagine taking my son out to the stables at the crack of dawn to feed our horses. Or I would imagine sitting with my daughter at a lake somewhere, teaching her how to cast a line. I wanted to be better for them. I wanted to be better than my parents and not fuck it up."

"Logan." I breathe his name as my heart breaks for him. The pain in his face breaks me a little more than his words already have. I slowly shift to straddle his lap, careful not to tip the cart and send us flying to the ground below. Only one of us would survive that. Linking my fingers behind his neck, I say, "You would have been an amazing dad."

His smile is laced with grief. Grief for the future children he'll never have. Grief for the future he's lost. Grief for himself.

"You never answered me." His voice is a mere whisper.

"No," I answer honestly. "I couldn't have a child and live the rest of my life in fear that they would lose me. I'm too scared of dying before they've lived a full life to bring a kid into this world."

"Izzy, why would you think that?" He's not being judgmental, he just doesn't understand. I haven't opened up about my past to any of them, so that's understandable.

"My parents died when I was twelve." Somehow, my voice doesn't break. "I was really close with my mom. She's the reason I'm so obsessed with vampires. I never thought I would have to face the day I'd have to lose her, at least not until I was well into adulthood, but I did. I couldn't become a mother because I couldn't leave my child behind like that."

His thumb sweeps a tear from my cheek that I wasn't aware had fallen. He cups my cheek, staring at me with a strange intensity in his eyes.

"I love you," he whispers, almost too quiet to be perceptible.

I still.

"What?"

"I love you." His voice is much stronger this time, like he's sure of what he's saying.

"Logan, I—" I start, my voice trailing off.

"I didn't say it to hear it back. I said it so you'd know."

This man. This beautiful, strong, kind, and loving man.

I lean forward, pressing my lips to his and causing the cart to rock a little. Once he's over the initial shock, he kisses me back. There's a gentleness in his kiss, but there's also passion. I want nothing more than to own all of his passion. His hands find my back, pressing me closer to him. Everything inside of me is telling me this is right.

Kissing him feels like home.

A satisfied moan leaves my throat, muffled by his mouth, as he opens up to me. Allowing me more of him. My fingers tangle in his golden hair, tugging a little to tilt his head up for me to have more access. His hands travel down my back, squeezing my ass.

"Logan," I say, my voice heady as I break the kiss for a millisecond to get the word out. "You asked me what I want."

"Tell me, baby. Whatever it is, I'll give it to you."

"I want you."

"Then have me. Have all of me."

Our lips rejoin as my hands travel downward to his jeans. I lift off of his lap so I can undo his pants and free his cock. I move on to pull my shorts down, his hands firm against my back so I don't fall.

Sinking down onto his hard cock feels like ecstasy flowing through my veins. He fills me so completely it's like finding a part of myself I didn't know was missing.

"Fuck, baby," he shudders. "You were made for me."

I bite my swollen lip as I start rocking on his lap, rolling my hips at a pace that has my breath hitched in my throat. His hands go under his hoodie on my body and my shirt to trail up my stomach and find my breasts. He rubs and squeezes my peaked nipples, driving the waves of pleasure from my core out to my entire body.

"You're so perfect," he says into my neck, where he's begun trailing kisses along my skin.

My pussy begins to clench around him, both he and I losing ourselves in a cacophony of moans.

Heat buds at my center as he takes me closer to finishing. "That's it, baby. Use me. Take what you want." I meet his brown eyes that glow gold in the moonlight.

He grunts, then smiles and says, "I love you."

My eyes roll back, and the words leave my mouth before I realize I'm saying them.

"Say it again."

He moans and obliges.

"I love you. I love you. I love you. I'll say it again and again until I can't anymore, beautiful."

My orgasm crashes through me. I have to bite his shoulder to keep myself from screaming. He easily rocks my hips on his cock a few more times before he follows me over the edge, his cum filling me beyond satisfaction.

I lie on top of him, my face buried in his neck and his cock still inside me, as the waves of pleasure work their way through me. Once I have enough control of my body to speak, I take a deep breath.

"I love you, too."

I wake up to a chill in Logan's bed with his head on my chest. After we came back from the carnival grounds, we decided it was best that we showered and slept in his room so we didn't wake up Vincent. The shower was only slightly counterproductive, given that he placed my thighs on his shoulders and gave me my second orgasm of the night while the warm water ran down his back.

I'm completely naked, and the biting cold that's in the air makes my entire body break out in goosebumps. I try to pull the covers over myself, but they're wrapped around Logan like a tortilla. He groans as I tug on them harder.

"Logan," I whisper, "I need to get up. I'm freezing."

With his arms wrapped around me, he props his chin on my chest and looks up at me with grogginess still in his eyes.

"Please?" I try.

He grumbles something, but eventually rolls off me. I hurry to his closet and steal a sweatshirt and some drawstring sweatpants. The chilly air freezes my feet from where it seeps in under the door.

With the intention of turning the thermostat up to get the heater going, I leave the room. A breeze immediately hits me, and I realize it's coming from downstairs. I descend them to find the front door wide open and muddy shoe tracks leading from the threshold into the house.

Every hair on my body stands straight, with fear this time rather than cold. Could Ren have found us? Or Cameron?

I pick up Joel's pointy umbrella from beside the door and tiptoe through the house, following the tracks. I should probably wake up the boys, but something in me tells me to follow the tracks myself.

The floorboards creak ahead, coming from the kitchen. I move forward, toward the sound, and crane my head around the corner. Standing in the dining room, looking out the window, motionless, is a blond woman drenched in blood. It is soaked into her hair and stains her hands, shoes, and clothes.

"Erika?" I gulp.

Slowly, she turns around. I gasp when her face comes into view. There is crimson coating her skin. It's smudged on her forehead and cheeks and cascades down her chin. It's mostly dry now, crusting onto her neck and chest where it is darker in color.

"What happened?" I ask. She stares past me. "Are you hurt?"

She keeps silent, her blue eyes looking into the distance, yet looking at nothing at all.

I don't want to take my eyes off of her out of fear that she might disappear. My phone is still in my bedroom, where I plugged it in before getting into bed last night, and I don't want to frighten her by shouting.

"Izzy?" Creed asks, and I risk a glance to my left to see him stepping into the foyer. "I smelled blood. What's going on?"

I nod toward Erika, and he stops short when he sees her.

"Erika," Creed says, his tone soft and his hands out in front of him like she might spook as easily as a frightened deer. "Why don't you sit down?"

She doesn't move, doesn't even look at him. She still stares past me with empty eyes.

Creed continues to inch toward her. Once he's close enough, he slowly lays a hand on her shoulder. The second his hand touches her, she snaps out of her trance-like state and begins to scream. It is so awfully blood-curdling that I jump, bumping into the wall and sending a picture crashing to the floor. The frame shatters and glass scatters across the floor.

Within seconds, Logan is at my side with an arm wrapped around me, and Vincent places himself in front of me. Both of them are ready to fight off whatever threat has breached the house. Neither of them relaxes when they realize that the threat is Erika.

Joel comes out of his room, rubbing his eyes, and grumbles, "What the hell is going on?"

Then he sees her and backs up a few steps.

Creed has his arms wrapped around her, even as she struggles against him, her arms pinned to her sides. Her screams turn into wails as tears spill down her cheeks.

"I killed them. They're dead," she says through sobs. "I killed them."

I take a step forward, jolting back when a shard of glass pierces my foot.

"They're dead."

She hysterically repeats those two sentences over and over. Logan lifts me into his arms, realizing my foot is cut.

Then everything in the room shifts.

Erika stops crying and struggling. Her bloodshot eyes lock onto me with her nostrils flared and her fangs out.

"Get Isobelle out of here!" Creed shouts.

The last thing I see before I am flying through the trees in Logan's arms is Erika's teeth snapping as she finally breaks free from Creed's grip.

We don't stop moving for a long while, my stomach churning due to the constant motion. We eventually stop outside of the ER doors.

"What are we doing here?" I ask.

"Your foot needs stitches."

"Logan. I don't want to be here. You can just heal me yourself."

He eyes me skeptically. Two nurses exit the automatic doors and catch sight of us standing there. One of them veers in our direction.

"*Please*," I beg.

He huffs and rolls his eyes. Then we're flying off again. I shut my eyes against the wind whipping in my face and send a silent prayer that the nurse assumes she just had a long shift and thinks nothing of Logan and me just disappearing from view.

He takes me out of the city and into the woods. Apparently, he found this place on his hike yesterday. After he heals my foot, he leaves me there for three minutes to go grab food that I'm pretty sure he stole from a food cart in Boston. We sit and talk—and don't talk—until the sun sets. Neither of us have our phones, so we figured sunset would be enough time for Creed and Vincent to get the Erika situation under control.

As Logan runs through the night with me on his back, I can't help but feel guilty for the deaths of whoever she killed. I am partly responsible. After all, she wouldn't be a vampire if I hadn't gone to Germany to find one a month ago.

When we get back to the house, Creed and Joel are in the car, getting ready to pull out of the driveway.

Logan puts me down, and I run barefoot in the gravel to the car.

"Where are you going?" I shout, waving my arms to stop them.

The brake lights make the driveway glow red as the car stops. Creed rolls down the driver's side window and sticks his head out.

"Yes, *princesa*?"

"Where are you going? Where's Erika?" I ask.

"*Carrie* is inside with Buchanan. We're on our way to clean up her mess," Creed says.

"I'm coming," I say.

"No. You're not."

"Creed, this would never have happened if it weren't for me. I'm coming with you."

A muscle in his jaw ticks and he looks straight out the windshield.

"Just let her come, man. She's more stubborn than you are," Joel chimes in from the passenger seat.

"Fine."

I slide into the backseat and ask Logan to grab my sneakers from inside. While we wait for him, we sit in silence; the only sound heard is the hum of the engine. Creed's eyes meet mine in the rear-view mirror for a long moment, breaking away when Logan slides into the seat next to me.

He inserts a disk into the CD player and 60s music starts playing over the speakers. Instead of heading toward the city like I expect, we drive deeper into Belmont. Joel's house lays on the outskirts of town, where he has space for privacy. Homes and shops alike pass by as we drive further. We stop at a house with no lights on. It's a one-story home with a quaint front porch and an oak tree in the front yard.

Creed gets out first, instructing us to stay in the car and wait for his direction. He goes into the house, the front door unlocked, and comes out just as quickly.

"Grab the supplies from the back," he instructs Joel. "I hope you enjoy scrubbing. And put your hair up."

I gulp back the budding nerves in my throat and step out of the car. Luckily, I have a hair tie on my wrist to wrap my hair in a tight bun. Joel heads for the house with two buckets full of cleaning supplies, and Logan and I follow soundlessly. Based on the look on Logan's face, whatever we are about to walk into is going to be messy.

Immediately upon entering the dark home, I'm hit with the strong stench of iron. My entire body freezes and my muscles lock up. The sound of my own screams fills my head. Ren's face flashes across my mind, images of him smiling as he carved into me. The horrible smell of my own blood curdles the contents of my stomach.

"Izzy?" someone calls me, but all I can see is that basement. "Isobelle."

Somebody grabs my wrists, stopping the trembling in my hands. I see Creed in front of me. His hands are wrapped around my wrists.

Logan is at my side, his arm wrapped around my waist the only thing keeping me on my feet.

"What the hell just happened?" Creed asks, concerned wrinkles marking his forehead.

"I—Nothing. I'm fine."

"That wasn't nothing, Iz," Joel says, peeking over Creed's shoulder to see me.

"Really. I'm fine." I shake my head. "Give me a scrub brush."

Joel looks between Creed and Logan, but eventually pulls out a scrub brush for me.

"You can both let me go. I'm fine."

Creed is the first to let go, but his stare lingers for several heartbeats. Logan holds me close to him until I tell him that I'm okay for the fifteenth time.

I won't let what happened to me stop me from helping my friends. We need to do this for Erika.

*I* need to do this.

There are blood splatters across the hardwood floor and cream painted walls. I see the slaughtered couple when I turn the corner into the kitchen. The woman with short brown hair is propped up against the cabinets as if her body slumped down them. There's blood smeared where her body slid. The man is laid across the countertop, his head and legs dangling over the edges.

Both bodies are covered in blood. Their clothes are soaked in it and splatters paint their faces and skin.

"Holy shit," Joel whispers.

"We can't turn any lights on. It'll draw attention. Start cleaning the floor, and I'll get them in the trunk," Creed says.

The way he tells us what we need to do without questioning himself makes me wonder how many times he's had to clean up his own messes like this. I wonder if the Cult Killer makes messes, or if that was something Creed left in his past. I can't imagine what he must have gone through when he was newly turned. Was he alone? Did he have somebody to help him through it?

I want to ask him, but now isn't the time.

He hauls both bodies over his shoulder, piling one on top of the other, and runs them out to the car. Joel and I start scrubbing the floors while Logan wipes down the counter.

We clean for hours. The walls and cabinets are the hardest to get the stains out of. Luckily, Logan found an extra bucket of cream paint under the sink that we use to paint over any residue left behind. By the time we're finished, the sun has begun to rise.

The drive back to Joel's is dead silent. Maybe that's not the best way of phrasing that considering there are two very dead bodies in the trunk.

"I'll be back soon. I need to do something," Creed says as we pull into the driveway.

"What?" I ask.

"Something. Now go shower. You stink."

"Gee, thanks."

I slam the door and watch him drive away again.

"You do stink," Joel adds.

"You think you smell any better?" I rebut.

"We all stink, okay? Let's get cleaned up and agree to never talk about what we just did," Logan says.

I nod, as does Joel, and we all head up the porch steps and into the house.

Erika is nowhere to be seen, but Vincent is in the recliner in the living room reading Pride and Prejudice.

"Erika is asleep," he says.

I smile at him, grateful for his looking after her today, and quietly head upstairs.

This evening, there was another story on the news about the Cult Killer, and I realized exactly what Creed has gone off and done after dropping us off. I want to be mad at him for making their torn apart bodies so public, but that was the best cover we could have used. Their bodies were drained of blood.

That fit the Cult Killer's MO. I just wish I didn't know who the infamous serial killer really was.

I barely ate dinner, my stomach too uneasy to consume an entire baked potato and definitely too queasy to eat a steak.

I wanted to be alone tonight, so Logan slept in his room. That was a mistake I had no idea I was making. I haven't slept by myself since I was taken, and I guess that was for good reason. Every time I shut my eyes, I start to think that he's here, watching me and waiting for the moment to strike.

Ren controlling my sleep is not a privilege I want to give him, yet he has it.

I check my phone to see that it's two in the morning, and I haven't slept a wink. Grumbling to myself, I get out of bed and slide on slippers to go get water downstairs. I'm careful not to make any noise that might wake the others as I make my way out of the room.

When I reach the bottom of the stairs, something catches my eye out the back window. Looking closer, I see Creed standing outside, leaning against the railing and looking out at the lake. Quietly, I go out onto the porch and walk up beside him, mirroring his pose and leaning over the rail.

"Shouldn't you be sleeping?" he asks after several minutes of silence.

"I can't." I shrug.

Still looking out at the water, he asks, "Why not?"

Contemplating whether I want to give him the entire truth or just part of it, I stare out at the moon's reflection on the lake's surface. The night breeze tickles my cheek and sends a chill through my body.

"Logan's in his room tonight. So is Vince." I pause. "In *his* room, I mean." Creed quietly chuckles and looks down at the soil below the porch.

"Since when did you need someone with you to be able to sleep?" he asks.

I take a deep breath, exhaling slowly.

"This is the first night since you found me that I've been alone."

He takes a drag of the cigarette in his hand, the cherry glowing brighter as he inhales.

"I guess I feel safer when one of you is there. My mind is at ease knowing I'm safe."

He stills for a moment, seeming to consider my words, then tilts his head to look at me ever so slightly. He is beautiful in the moonlight, even more so than usual. It isn't fair for all three of them to have the ability to take my breath away by simply existing, yet here we are.

"I thought you quit smoking," I say.

"I did."

"What changed?"

He looks at me fully now, his hazel eyes intense as he looks directly into mine. After a moment, I slowly nod and look down. A soft smile spreads across my face, and out of the blue, I have the idea to take a cigarette from the box laid on the railing. I hold it out, gesturing for him to light it.

"You don't smoke," he states.

"No. I don't."

I bounce the unlit cigarette again, and he smiles with his eyes closed, gently shaking his head.

Then, he takes out his lighter and lights the end of my cigarette.

I've never smoked before. I always told myself that it was the one thing I would never do. My dad always told me not to fall for peer pressure and give into it, and I carried that through my life. If he could only see me now.

I take my first drag and immediately start coughing.

"Jesus," I choke, pounding on my chest with a fist. "How do people do this?"

With watery eyes, I look up at Creed, who shocks me once more. For the first time since I've met him, he is smiling from ear to ear. His teeth are bared and there's real joy in his eyes.

He's smiled before, obviously, but *this*... this is something else. This is real.

I stand there with him for a while, attempting twice more to smoke before giving up on the activity entirely.

By the time I head back into the house and tiptoe into Logan's room, I'm exhausted. I crawl into his bed and immediately, his arms wrap around me. I'm sure I smell like smoke, but he either doesn't care or is too sleepy to notice.

I fall asleep in his arms with the scent of Creed's cigarette smoke stuck in my nose.

Rain patters on the roof when I step out onto the rug in the bathroom. It must have started while I was showering. I love the rain, the gray clouds backlit by the sun, the little drops that land on your arms and head before it starts to pour. My mom loved the rain, too. I remember, one day when I was a kid it was raining, and she took me outside and we danced to our own music in the driveway. Dad came home and saw us drenched in our pajamas and had a fit about how I could get sick and needed to go back inside and change. Albeit, I did get a cold, but that's not the memory that I think of whenever I hear that comforting patter.

The smell of bacon drifts under the bathroom door and beckons me out of the room. Hurriedly, I get dressed and follow the delicious smell downstairs and into the kitchen. Logan is flipping pancakes, and Joel is on his computer, sitting at the counter.

"Mmm," I moan. "It smells amazing, Logan."

He peaks at me over his shoulder and smiles, winking before he turns back to the stove.

"Damn, Betty Crocker, you making us a whole breakfast buffet?" Creed asks as he turns the corner. "*Buenos dias, princesa.*"

He slides onto the stool at the end of the counter, leaving one stool between him and I. After he took care of the bodies yesterday, he distanced himself. He spent most of the day outside smoking or in his room doing whatever he does. At one point, he came down because Erika was downstairs and he wanted to make sure she didn't have a psychotic break.

She's the next to join us, leaning against the end of the island.

"Hey, Izzy," she says, voice soft.

"Good morning," I reply.

She didn't speak to me yesterday when I saw her. I think she was still processing what she'd done. I can't blame her. If I had done what she did to those poor people, I wouldn't be able to process it, either.

It's not her fault, and I know that, but seeing the bloodied state of that couple isn't something that will be leaving my nightmares anytime soon.

"I'm sorry," she whispers, "for—"

"Don't be. You weren't yourself," I say, reaching out to cover her clasped hands with mine.

Logan glances at me and a sad sort of smile crosses his face.

He was in this same position not that long ago.

"Not just that," Erika starts. "I'm sorry for how I treated you. Before I ran away. You were in that barn with me, and what you went through... I can't imagine."

"We don't have to talk about it. I forgive you," I say, squeezing her hands. "We both had a lot to process."

She smiles at me, tears moistening her eyes.

"Thank you."

I nod at her and release her hands.

"Great," Creed says. "You two are back to being girlfriends. You should kiss and make up."

I scoff, rolling my eyes.

"Turn down the perv, Creed," Erika sneers.

He throws his hands up and smirks at us.

"I don't think he's capable of that," Joel remarks, looking up from his computer.

"Don't tell me you wouldn't jizz your pants if you saw these two making out," Creed says. Joel shoots him a look, and he rolls his eyes. "My bad. Forgot you'd rather see Logan and me playing tonsil hockey than the girls."

Joel barks out a laugh, and I can't help but laugh at that imagery. Logan, on the other hand, visibly shivers and shakes off the thought.

He turns around, and I notice pancake batter smudged on his heather gray shirt. He brings over two plates of pancakes with bacon on the side and sets them in front of Erika and me. The pancakes have apple pie filling over the top of them that drips down the sides. He sets another plate in front of Joel, then makes one for himself.

"Where's mine, sweetie?" Creed asks.

Joel nearly snorts out pie filling.

"I'm sorry, I didn't know demons ate real people food," Logan says with a straight face.

I have to smother a smile as Creed looks between Logan and me.

"I'll make you a plate if you say the magic word," Logan says.

Creed's teeth grind and his jaw flexes.

"C'mon," Logan says, holding a hand to cup his ear.

"Jenkins," Creed bites, "*please* get me some fucking pancakes before I rip your spine from your body."

"Better. Could use some work, but that's better."

Logan plates food for Creed and smugly sets it in front of him. He prepares one more for Vincent and covers it, setting it to the side.

Creed nods to the plate and asks, "Where is the old man this morning?"

"Haven't seen him," Logan shrugs.

Creed looks to me next, and I just shrug, shaking my head. He decides to get back to his pancakes and shovels a bite into his mouth.

Logan finishes and starts piling dishes in the sink.

"No, Logan. You are not washing the dishes," I say, getting up and rounding the island with my empty plate in hand. "Let me. You cooked for everyone."

He doesn't move, so I bump him to the side with my hip and he chuckles.

"Fine," he says, "but only because it's so damn hard to say no to you."

Then he leans down and presses a ginger kiss to my lips. With reddened cheeks, I start scrubbing the dishes. Logan heads to the couch to lounge, but Joel promptly reminds him to change his filthy clothes before he even thinks about touching the couch.

Creed comes up behind me, startling me with a terrible impression of Logan in my ear. The cup I'm washing slips from my grip and shatters in the sink.

"Shit," I groan, looking pointedly at Creed.

"Jumpy, are we?" Creed asks, pressing his lips into a line to keep from laughing.

"Asshole."

As I'm picking pieces of glass out of the sink, Erika is sitting eerily still. Looking up at her, I notice that she's as white as a ghost.

I set the glass shards in my hand down on a washcloth and round the counter to get to her. I place my hand over hers and jump a little at the intense trembling. Her skin is slightly clammy, and her eyes are jumping around the room.

"Erika?"

She looks at me with such intense fear in her eyes I might have thought she saw a ghost.

"Erika, what's wrong?" I ask, taking a seat next to her and placing my free hand on her back.

She stutters, trying to say something, but nothing coherent comes out. She gulps hard and shakes her head rapidly. Creed appears on her other side and places his hands on her shoulders.

"Hey," he says, "look at me."

She turns to him and continues breathing choppily, her chest shaky as it rises and falls.

"You're safe. You're not there, you aren't hurting anyone."

I tilt my head, confused for a moment about what he means. Then I realize what's going on. At the house where she killed those people there was a shattered vase on the ground. When I dropped the cup, it must have triggered her.

Creed keeps reassuring her that she is safe, and eventually, he wraps his arms around her to keep her from trembling. She closes her eyes against his chest while he strokes the side of her head.

I have to look away as guilt floods through me. I feel guilty because I'm actually jealous of her. Creed is being more tender with her than he's ever been with me. Here she is, having a panic attack, and I'm *jealous* of her.

I'm a horrible person.

Just then, Vincent walks into the kitchen and stands so closely behind me that I can feel his body heat on my back.

"Go change, we need to start training," he whispers into my ear.

I nod, glancing one last time at Creed holding Erika, and turn toward the stairs.

The image of his hands on her, stroking her hair, and his head resting on her head burns my throat as I find workout clothes to change into. I shouldn't feel this way. Not when I have everything I could ever want with Logan. Even Vincent has warmed up to me recently.

I'm reminded of my conversation with Logan when I was stupid enough to consider the idea of having all three of them.

*What am I talking about?*

Just because he was comforting Erika doesn't mean anything. Even if it does, I don't have any right to be mad. Do I?

Rather than debate the answer to that, I follow Vincent outside and take my frustration out on

him. I think he takes it easy on me today because he lets me land a couple hits. I'll definitely need his blood today because, after only hitting him a few times, my knuckles are screaming at me in pain.

He usually heals me after training, telling me it's better to get used to the pain now than be stunned by it later. He wants me to become accustomed to the pain of hitting someone with bare fists, so that when I do it to an actual opponent, I don't pull my punches to spare myself the pain.

After an hour and a half of working on those skills with him, I run two laps around the lake, followed by stretching so intense that it makes my muscles burn tenfold. Vincent hasn't said anything about my state at all, and I'm grateful, but I can tell he's caught onto my feelings.

"Just ask," I say.

"Ask what?"

"Whatever question has been at the tip of your tongue all morning."

He squats next to where I'm stretching my hamstrings on the grass.

"You're mistaken, love. I have no question."

"You're being polite," I sneer.

"Perhaps."

"That's not fair."

"What?"

"You using that old time-y charm and stupid attractive accent on me. I want to be frustrated with you because you're being too quiet, but I can't, because when you speak it comes out like *that*."

I grab my shoe and arch toward it, pulling myself forward so my entire leg burns with the stretch. Vincent chuckles, and even that sounds gentlemanly.

"I think you needed a distraction. Punching me a couple times seemed like a decent one," he says.

"Thanks."

He gets up and walks back to the house, leaving me to sulk in the grass alone.

I wish I didn't feel the way I do. It's not like I was raised to have feelings for more than one person at a time. Things just... happen.

It's not fair of me. I *love* Logan, and he loves me. Isn't that enough?

As if my thoughts conjured him to me, Logan walks up beside me and takes a seat in the grass. He sits there and looks out at the water without saying a word. My shoulders slump, and I rest my head on my hand to admire him.

"Daydreaming of casting a line?" I ask.

"I wasn't, but now that you mention it," he says, wiggling his brows.

"Next time we're in town or in Boston, we'll get you a fishing pole."

He nods, smiling at me with his lips closed and his crystal eyes sparkling.

"Maybe we can get you one, too. I can teach you to fish."

"Ooo," I coo. "Is that a part of some sexy fantasy of yours? Get me out by the lake, cozy up behind me to show me to cast a line, and end up laying in the mud, on top of me?"

His eyes darken and he clears his throat before he says anything.

"Well shit, Iz. If that wasn't a fantasy of mine before, it sure as hell is now," he says.

His Adam's apple bobs up and down as he swallows.

I giggle and crawl over to him so that I can lean against him while we sit there and listen to the birds in the trees and the leaves rustling in the woods. Everything has turned orange and red now, any signs of summer have left completely. As much as I love the warm shades of autumn, it only excites me for the closeness of winter.

"What's your favorite holiday?" I ask, laying my head on his shoulder.

He hums, thinking about it, then says, "Thanksgiving."

"Why?"

I'm not asking because I think his answer is dumb, but because I genuinely want to know. I know there's a story behind my favorite holiday, so I want to know his.

"My folks always made a big deal of Thanksgiving. It's the one holiday every year where everyone gets together to just be around each other. Jake, my brother, eats an entire sweet potato casserole himself every year. Our Aunt Holly has to make three batches to feed him and the rest of the family."

I picture someone who resembles Logan scarfing down a whole sweet potato casserole by

himself and giggle.

"What about you?"

"I've always loved New Year's Eve," I say. "My mom would let me sleep in until noon and then we'd meet the DiAngelos—Mateo and his family—at the restaurant, even though it was closed, and eat lunch with them. Then she'd take me ice skating until it was time for dinner. She wasn't much of a cook, but on New Year's Eve she would make eggplant parm and homemade tiramisu."

I smile out at the water, remembering the mess she would make in the kitchen. My dad would sit with me on the couch while she cooked and played music to dance to.

"Then we'd all watch the ball drop, and I would cringe away when my parents kissed."

He links our fingers and lays his head on top of mine.

"That sounds amazing," he says.

"We should make Thanksgiving special. Just because you're different doesn't mean it has to be," I say, rubbing my thumb over his hand.

"As long as you're there, it'll be special."

After I took Logan to pick up Mateo's for lunch, Creed and Erika were gone. Erika's car was still in the driveway, so wherever they went, they went together. Joel took his food to the office, so only Logan, Vincent, and I ate together.

I spent the rest of the afternoon sifting through old research I'd done to try to find anything on Vivienne or Ren. For the first time since coming back, I opened all my emails and found that I was fired from the university. They passed my class to another professor until they found a suitable replacement. Of everything that's happened, that hurt the least. I liked my job, but I loved doing my research. I'd have to find another way to pay my bills, which shouldn't be too difficult. Joel offered to help until I found something, which I refused, but he refused to accept my refusal.

Sleep threatens to take me as I sit on Vincent's lap now. We're in the recliner in the living room with the fireplace lit, while he reads the last half of Pride and Prejudice to me. Of course I've read this before, but hearing him read it to me in that voice soothes something in me I didn't know needed soothing. It's like having Mr. Darcy himself read me the story.

Logan's showering, the sound of the water running from upstairs filtering down here. Between that, the crackle of the fire, and Vincent's reading voice, I'm less than ten minutes from falling asleep right here.

The front door opening and closing disturbs my relaxed state, and I look over to see Creed and Erika trying to sneak up the stairs. Erika stops halfway up and tugs Creed's sleeve. I cock my head, careful to stay quiet so they don't notice me watching. My breath catches in my throat when Creed turns around and leans down.

With my stomach in knots, he kisses her.

# CHAPTER 29



"You sure nothing's bothering you, Iz?" Logan asks.

I keep my eyes focused on the movie playing on my TV. After Creed and Erika kissed, I couldn't listen to any more of Pride and Prejudice, so I came upstairs. Logan was waiting on my bed. I crawled in with him and we turned on a random movie.

"Yep."

"Okay," he says. "But I think your cuticles would say otherwise."

I look down to see that I'm picking at my cuticles. I hadn't even realized I was doing that. I drop my hands in my lap and lean back against the pillows more.

After a few beats, I snap.

"Creed made out with Erika, and I don't want to be upset about it, but I am, and I'm so sorry because you're perfect and amazing and I shouldn't be mad over Creed, but I am."

Logan mutes the TV, and I unmute it immediately.

"I don't want him paying attention to this conversation," I say.

"Alright," Logan says. "Creed kissed Erika?"

"Yes. On the stairs."

"And you're mad?"

"Clearly."

He nods and leans back against the headboard.

"You have feelings for him."

"I—" I stop myself before a lie can leave my lips. I told myself I wouldn't lie to him, and I am not about to start now. "Yes."

"If it counts for anything, I thought he had feelings for you, too."

"That makes two of us."

He wraps his arms around my waist and pulls me into him so I'm lying on his chest.

"Creed's... complicated," I say.

He nods and rubs his hand down my arm. Logan kisses the top of my head, then my forehead. I tilt my head up and kiss him on the lips, tasting him as if it will erase my memory for a while.

It's easy to get lost in Logan. He makes me feel special. Loved.

"Want me to distract you?" he says, his voice sultry as his comforting touch turns into something sensual.

"Mmm." I bite my lip, thinking about the possibility of letting myself get lost in him tonight.

"What do you have in mind?"

"A little bit of this," he says, leaning in and kissing my neck. "And this." He sucks on my collarbone and soothes the spot over with his tongue.

"Wait," I say, although my voice gives way to how badly I want this tonight. "I need to show you something first."

"What is it, beautiful?"

I pull the string on the lamp, lighting up the room, and straddle his lap.

"Just let me show you before you say anything."

He nods.

I pull the sweatshirt over my head and bare myself to him. At first, he's confused, then he sees the first scar. The one on my forearm. He immediately starts searching for more, finding the one on my tricep.

"There are two more on my legs."

He pauses, his eyes following the rise and fall of my chest. "I saw the one on your thigh. The other night in the shower."

"You didn't say anything," I say.

"I know. I thought maybe it was still healing from Creed. I didn't think..."

"They're from Ren."

Tears prick my eyes as I force down the memory trying to arise in my head. "Izzy," he says, his voice a whisper, pausing for a moment. "Why didn't you tell me?"

"I wasn't ready to." My voice cracks.

"How did I not notice?" he asks himself.

I hold his head in my hands and look into his eyes as I say, "I didn't want you to."

"*He* left these on you. Forever. I should've—"

"Nothing, Logan. You should've done nothing because you can't do anything. I know you want to, but the reality is, you can't. These are my scars to bear, and I have to live with that."

He shakes his head, conflicting emotions warring behind his eyes.

"I wanted to show you now because I love you. And I trust you. And I want to be open and honest with you. Fully transparent."

He leans forward and presses his head into my chest, holding me and rocking me for several minutes. Then his hands trail up my back and undo the bralette I'm wearing, tossing it onto the floor somewhere.

He takes my nipple into his mouth, and I gasp at the sudden touch. There's a ferocity in him tonight that hasn't shown before. His tongue soothes my tender nipple after he pinches it between his teeth. My back arches into him and my hands find his hair, fingers tangling in the golden locks.

Breaking contact, he lifts me off him and sets me on the bed.

"Get on your knees, baby," he commands. "Get on your knees and say that again."

"Say what?"

"That you love me."

"I love you."

"I love when you say that. Now, on your knees. Put your hands up on the headboard."

With new excitement bubbling within me, I do as he says. He pulls off my bottoms and tosses those on the floor, too. His fingers slide over my wet pussy and he groans in approval. "Always so wet for me, beautiful. Always ready to take me."

"Forever," I say.

He lines himself up behind me, holding my hips in his hands, and thrusts into me harder and deeper than ever. My mouth falls open, and the breath is knocked out of me.

"Relax, baby. Let me fill you. Let me make you complete."

He pulls almost all the way out, then thrusts in again, my ass cheeks slapping against his body with the force of it. I moan loudly and remove one of my hands from the headboard to cover my mouth.

"Say it again," he demands, thrusting into me once more.

"I love you."

*Thrust.*

"I love you so fucking much."

*Thrust.*

He uses his grip on my hips to drive my body forward and back into him, meeting his own movements and making each thrust more forceful than the last. In contrast to his usual tenderness, this roughness lights my body ablaze with something else entirely.

The familiar build up of ecstasy bubbles inside me as he continues at the perfect pace. His moans match my own over the sound of the movie that's still going. One last thrust, and I'm riding my orgasm as it overtakes me. His follows soon after and he slumps down over my back. We both gather ourselves, then fall onto the mattress.

"That was different," I say, panting.

"Good different?"

"Definitely good different."

He spoons me in the middle of the bed, my body matching the curve of his where we lay.

"No matter what, Izzy. I will always love you. That is one thing I'm sure of," he says against my neck.

"I love you, too," I whisper.

Both of us lie there, naked, in each other's arms, as the movie continues. I don't even know what's on anymore, but I watch it, anyway. After a while, I get up to pee and wash off. It's when I am brushing my teeth that I hear something that reignites the anger inside of me in an instant.

Erika moans.

I know it's Erika because there are no other women in the house, and it's too close and loud to be porn. She's not with Joel or Vincent, so either she's flicking her bean much too loudly or she's with Creed.

I wait to hear her again and pin what direction she's in.

She's definitely with Creed.

I storm back into the bedroom and get under the covers without saying anything to Logan. He doesn't say anything, either, and he doesn't try to distract me from what's going on. He just gets up and washes off himself, gets back in bed, and slings his arm over my waist like he always does.

My feet bounce up and down under the covers and my teeth grind together. The noises of them fucking continue into the night, and I fear I'll be getting little sleep yet again.

There is absolutely nothing remarkable about Erika. As much as I want there to be something about her that I find attractive, it's not fucking happening.

Her body is amazing, her voice is even seductive. Unfortunately, neither of those things get my dick hard. The only thing keeping my erection while I rub Erika's tits is the constant image of Izzy that is burned into my mind. Even as I lift myself above the blonde on the bed and sink into her, the thing causing me to moan is imagining that it's Izzy's pussy I'm soaking myself in. She moans, "Ohmygod, Creed."

I imagine it's Izzy's voice.

She tangles her fingers in my hair.

I imagine they're Izzy's hands.

I drive into her, her pussy clenching around me telling me she's close, and still, I imagine it's Izzy squeezing my cock with her pussy as I steer her toward oblivion.

So, when she comes, I spill my load into her wanting pussy, imagining it's Izzy who's now full of my cum and satiated by my cock.

Erika is a loud moaner, so when she orgasms, I'm certain the whole house hears it. She wraps her arms beneath mine and over my shoulder blades, holding me on top of her while she catches her breath, when I want nothing more than to roll over and ignore her for the rest of the night.

Of course she's a fucking cuddler. The desperate ones usually are.

I roll off her and lie on my side, her hold on me releasing so she can curl herself into my chest.

She smells like sultry caramel and salt from her sweat as she lies there, breath deepening by the minute.

I'm desperate for just a whiff of the lavender and vanilla scent that seems to wrap itself around Izzy.

Like a heroin addict trying to satisfy a craving with marijuana, I need a hit of my favorite drug.

As Erika falls asleep against my chest, I'm weighed down with the reality that Izzy is *not* here and that I can't have her. She deserves Logan. She deserves safe, and he's safe. I'm everything but.

Erika doesn't want safe, she wants anything. I fit that box. How Vincent can tolerate not being wanted by Izzy is beyond me, because for me, it tears me apart. Every time her lips touch Logan's, every time he holds her when she breaks down or after she has a nightmare, it tears at the vessels carrying blood to my heart.

She deserves safe.

That also tears pieces of my soul away. She doesn't deserve my flavor of risk. If I let her in, she would be gaining a toxic love. I'm not docile. I won't be the one to sit aside and watch her fall apart while putting out the flames of her trauma. I'd stand in front of her and fuel the flames until every last person responsible for that trauma burned in it.

Not being able to find Ren and pry his teeth out one by one is fucking killing me as it is.

So, no, I'm not safe, and she doesn't deserve me. I deserve to suffer when I fuck Erika because that's what I've made for myself. Instead of being her sanctuary, I'm the gasoline beckoning the flames closer. She doesn't deserve that.

She's had her taste of me. That'll have to be enough. I'll be here to protect her, but I won't be her lover. I can't. Not while she's so fragile and uncertain.

Will my taste of her be enough for me? It has to. But I don't think it will be.

I might spend the rest of my long ass life wanting another taste of her pink lips. Desperate for her touch. I'll be five hundred years old and still craving her sweet pussy. No blood will compare to hers ever again. After knowing what her blood and body taste like, I can never enjoy anyone else the same way.

I fucking hate her because I feel something for her.

When I found out about the mating bond, I wanted to deny it. I couldn't care for a human girl like that. I couldn't let myself endanger her. Yet I've done that already. I do care for her. And I have endangered her.

I hate her because I fucking love her so much it hurts.

*I hate you, Isobelle, because for the first time in sixty years, you've made me love again.*

Logan made breakfast again. Today, he made bacon and eggs. I'm mid-bite when Creed comes strolling down the stairs.

Logan shoots me a cautious look, and I give him a halfhearted smile to reassure him that I'm not going to do anything crazy. We haven't spoken all morning. I woke up and took a twenty-minute long shower, and when I came out of the bathroom, he was gone. I found him down here cracking eggs after I slipped on a pair of leggings and an active-wear jacket.

Creed casually picks up a piece of cooked bacon and bites down on it, the crunch of the bacon between his teeth grating to my ears. He stands at the counter beside me and leans his hip up against it.

"You two had a good night last night," he says, then eats the second half of the bacon.

Logan's back is to me, but I can tell by the way his muscles tense that he's waiting for my reaction.

"Yeah. So, did you, apparently," I deadpan.

That annoyingly attractive crooked smile shows up on his face, grating my nerves further.

"That I did," he says, over-enunciating each syllable. "Who knew Erika was such a good lay?"

Biting the inside of my cheek, I focus on Logan's bare back as he whisks the eggs. He's pouring them into the pan he used to cook the bacon, and my stomach aches at the smell of them alone.

"She has these dimples at the small of her back. They're sexy as hell," he continues, clearly not reading the room. "You don't have those, Izzy. I'd remember if you did."

Clenching my jaw, I try to focus on taking even breaths. Creed watches me and smirks.

"But you do have those constellation freckles. Those are sexy, too."

I slam my fist down on the counter and look up at him.

"Shut. Up. Creed."

"I thought you liked compliments. Every girl likes compliments," he coos.

"Creed," Logan warns.

"Stay out of it, kid. I wouldn't want you to burn our *mate's* eggs."

"Don't you dare call me that. I never want to hear you call me that, got it?" Venom laces my words, and I know I say them with the intention of hurting him, but they don't seem to inflict the wounds I want them to.

"Unfortunately, *princesa*, that is what you are. You're mine. And Logan's. And Vincent's."

"What are you doing?" I turn on him. "Huh? Why are you acting like a dick?"

"I thought I was always a dick."

"Don't. Don't be like this. Be the Creed I know, the one who makes me laugh. The one who gave me the strength to leave my room when I wanted nothing more than to stay there."

He shrugs, leaning down to meet me eye to eye.

"I haven't changed, Izzy. Maybe you've just taken off your rose-colored glasses."

"I know what you're doing."

"Yeah?" He quirks a brow.

"Yeah. You're pushing me away because I was getting too close to those walls you keep around your heart and that scared you," I say, leaning in so our faces are only an inch apart.

He *tsks*.

"I'm not scared of you. You're just making excuses for me that I don't want you to make."

Logan sets a plate of eggs and bacon in front of me, and I pull back from Creed to eat them. He serves himself and stands across from me to eat. The kitchen stays silent while we eat. Then Erika comes down, her hair in a bun, wearing Creed's shirt that goes to her knees.

My blood *boils*. I've never felt this way toward anyone and I wish I had a better reason for it now.

*Creed isn't mine. He doesn't belong to me.*

I try to reassure myself—to calm myself down—and I almost think it's working until she crosses the kitchen and gets on her tiptoes to kiss him right there.

I throw the piece of bacon I was eating on my plate, everyone's attention snapping toward me, and get up.

"I'm going to take my laps around the lake. Tell Vince I'll wait for him outside," I say to Logan.

I get out of the kitchen and onto the porch so fast that no one has time to say anything about my fit or my abrupt exit. Once the crisp air hits me, I bounce on my heels and jog out to the water. Mud kicks up and splashes my legs as I run, but I don't move further from the lake's edge. I like the feeling of running through the mud. The resistance forces me to push harder and harder to keep a fast pace.

My muscles burn so badly, I want to drop and give up by the halfway point on my first lap, but I don't quit. I keep going, willing myself forward until my lungs scream for mercy. Even then, I keep going.

My body tries to slow down as I start the second lap, and I have to push past every mental and physical barrier within me not to. My feet sink and slide in the mud, but I keep my bearings. My body screams at me to stop, but I love the feeling. I embrace the pain because at least this pain is one that I can explain. I know why it hurts so bad.

The pain I feel when I'm around Creed is different. I can't explain it. I have no reason to feel it, yet I do.

They said humans can't feel the mating bond, but maybe they're wrong. Maybe I can and I've just been ignoring the signs. Because that has to be the only logical explanation for the simmering fury I felt when I saw Creed with Erika.

I'm a complete mess when I finish that second lap, bracing myself on my knees as I try to catch my breath. Sweat beads trickle down my face and cling to my eyelashes.

"Don't pass out and make me pull you out of the mud," Creed says.

I look up to find him strolling over to me, arms crossed in front of him.

Looking back down at my muddy shoes, I try to ignore him.

"Come on, you're training with me today."

"What?" I snap, whipping my head to look at him.

"Old man's orders."

I sigh, standing straight and taking a few deep breaths to soothe the ache in my lungs.

"Alright, let's start," I say.

He chuckles darkly and shakes his head. "Oh no, no, no, *princesa*. We're not training here."

"Then where are we going?" I ask.

He turns back toward the house and starts walking.

"A real gym," he says. "Change your shoes. Oh, and your pants, too. They're filthy, and you are *not* tracking mud in my car."

We park along the street outside a boxing gym.

"This is where we're training today?" I ask.

"Yep," he says. "I've been coming here for a while. We'll use my guest pass."

Muttering curses under my breath, I follow him inside. The walls are brick and there are punching bags and fighting mats scattered throughout the gym. In the back are weight racks, and I assume that's where we're going first.

As we walk through rows of equipment, I get the sense that I shouldn't have pushed so hard on my run today. My muscles are already shaky, and now I have to lift weights. Creed, on the other hand, looks like he could handle any of this equipment without breaking a sweat, even on a bad day.

He nods at a couple guys by way of greeting on our way back. Each of them nods to me, but don't let their eyes linger.

"You said you've been coming here for a while?" I ask, as another guy avoids looking at me.

"Since I came to Boston," Creed replies.

We bypass the benches and head for some mats on the floor.

"How many of these guys have you beat the shit out of?" I ask.

He laughs, then looks around the room. "All of the ones I know."

I nod, pursing my lips.

"We're working your core. You pack a mean punch, but without good core strength, you aren't using your full potential," he says.

He grabs a medicine ball and brings it over to me, setting it at my side. He gets down on the mat next to mine and starts instructing me through the motions of Russian twists. He has me start without weights, then he incorporates the medicine ball.

On a break, I ask, "Why do you work out when you don't need to? You've naturally got more strength than anyone here."

"These," he gestures to his biceps, "don't come naturally. Even with the perks that come with what I am, if I'm not in the gym working out my muscles, I'll lose them."

I nod, cataloging that information away with the research I've stowed in my brain.

"And that'd be a shame, wouldn't it? You'd have to depend on Logan for eye candy. Or worse," he pauses for dramatics, "Vincent."

"Okay, eye candy," I say, rolling my eyes, "what exercise is next?"

We go through a few more core workouts and then we stretch before hitting the fighting mats.

He wraps my knuckles and slides on a pair of boxing mitts—the kind that you're supposed to punch.

My abs are aching, but I feel totally refreshed, like my body needed the workout to reset itself.

He holds the mitts out in front of him and tells me to hit them back to back.

I hit one, then the other, repeating the motion several times before he drops the pads. "You need to give me everything you've got, Iz. Not this weak shit."

"Weak?"

"C'mon. Show me what you've got," he says.

I adjust my stance and bounce back and forth before hitting the mitts again. My knuckles burn with the force of my punches, but again, he drops the mitts.

"More," he barks.

I huff out a breath, clenching and unclenching my jaw.

We go again.

*Punch left. Punch right. Punch left. Punch ri—*

He drops the mitts.

"What do you want?" I ask, my voice raised. "I'm hitting as hard as I can right now, Creed."

"I've seen you with Buchanan. You can do better."

The contempt in his voice sets the fury simmering inside me to a raging fire.

He puts up the mitts, and I start punching them again.

*Punch left. Punch right. Left. Right.*

He drops the mitts, but this time, I don't stop. I punch him square in the jaw, and he stumbles to the side. His hand comes up to his face and touches the spot where my fist made contact. Still looking down, his tongue darts out to lick his lip and he draws it in to bite it. His eyes look before his head moves, striking me with immediate regret. I don't let him see that, though. I stand there, looking at him, with my chin held high and my shoulders squared.

His dark chuckle sends a shiver down my spine. Silence falls over the gym and I'm sure there are people watching us. Many of them stopped their workouts the second my knuckles collided with his face.

"Did that make you feel better? Huh, *princesa*? Did that help you get out some of that anger that I've smelled on you all day?"

His tone is biting, and his face is as serious as the dead.

"No."

He steps forward, squaring up as if he wants to spar me. "Come on, then," he says, waving me forward. "Hit me again."

"Creed," I warn.

"Hit me. Again."

Without hesitation, I slam my fist into his nose. The sound of his nose breaking reverberates off the walls as he stumbles back.

"That the best you got?" he eggs me on.

I step forward to hit him again, but an older man steps on to the mat and stops me.

"If you want to let your girl beat the shit out of you, Martinez, take it in the ring." He looks me over. "With gloves and headgear."

"Sorry, Señor Cruz, can't blame me for being proud of her for that punch, though."

The man looks at Creed, observing the blood trickling from his nose. He nods in my direction, an approving look on his face.

"You must've really pissed her off, *pendejo*. Now get equipment on or get out of my gym until you get your head out of your ass," he says.

"Yes, sir." Creed smirks.

He places a hand on the small of my back and ushers me out the gym doors. Once we hit the sidewalk, I step away from his touch.

"I'd set your nose if I were you, before it heals crooked. I'd hate to have to break it again to get it right," I say, and slide into the car.

The car ride back was mostly just us throwing insults back and forth and fighting over the music volume. When I say throwing insults back and forth, I mean Creed saying something he knew would piss me off and me calling him every name in the book.

When we get back to the house, the first thing I notice is the front door wide open. Creed stops the car, and I practically run toward the porch. Creed stops me, pulling me behind him while keeping a hand on me to make sure I stay there. He leads me up the stairs, and we slowly creep through the door. At first glance, there's no blood anywhere.

When we get to the corner to the kitchen, Creed stops, halting me behind him.

"Shit," he mutters.

"What?" I ask, keeping my voice to a whisper.

I walk around him to find Logan, Joel, and Erika unconscious in various places in the room. Logan is on the floor in front of me, his neck bent abnormally out of shape. Erika has her back up against the back of the couch, and Joel is slumped over the dining room table.

I run to Joel first.

"Their necks were snapped, right? They'll wake up?" I ask Creed as I try to assess my best friend.

"Yeah, they'll be fine."

There's a bruise forming on Joel's temple where someone must have hit him hard enough to knock him out. I run my hands over his neck, praying that there aren't any abnormalities, thanking God when I find his spine perfectly normal.

"Who did this?" I ask.

Creed looks around the room, then runs upstairs and returns in seconds.

"Where's Vincent?" he asks.

"He's not here?" Panic floods me. Only one person could have done this. "Vivienne."

*Izzy*

After Logan and Joel woke up, we started looking for Vincent. Joel got onto his computer and started searching for anything he could to find his whereabouts while I came up with the idea to check the house where Erika and I were kept. It's a long shot, but if they took us there, maybe that's where they'll take him.

Dread fills me as the barn comes into view. Memories threaten to consume me, and I shove them down. Vincent is the only thing I can afford to think about right now. Creed stops the car a little ways down the road and we get out to walk in the rain. He tells Logan to wait with me while he sweeps the place.

My phone rings in my pocket and I nearly drop it, I pull it out so fast. "Joel?"

"I've got him. They took him to a building in the financial district," Joel says over the speaker.

"You're sure?" Hope bubbles in my chest.

"Positive. I looked up the ownership of that house, then tracked the same owner to this building. I checked traffic cams and saw them carry Vincent inside, Izzy. I'll text you the address."

He hangs up and sends me the address immediately.

Creed comes out and shakes his head until he sees me.

"Joel found him," I rush out.

"Where?"

"The financial district. We've got an address," Logan says.

"Get in the car," Creed demands. "We're dropping Izzy back at Joel's, then we're getting Vincent."

"What?" I exclaim. "No, I'm coming with you!"

Creed ignores me and starts the car.

The warm touch of Logan's hand on my knee soaks into my entire body. As Creed takes the curvy road back at a dangerous speed, I cling to that heat like an anchor.

"Can we please talk about this?" I shout, ending the uncomfortable silence Creed forced on us.

"There's nothing more to talk about. End of story." Creed's tone is biting.

"There definitely is. You barely even gave me a chance to speak!"

Logan's hand squeezes my knee ever so gently, a sign of reassurance that is undermined by the frustration bubbling beneath my skin.

"She should at least get a chance to say something," Logan says from beside me.

"Shut your fucking mouth, kid, before I throw you out of the car."

"Creed!" I exclaim.

Trees flash by the window, streaks of green against the gray sky. A single raindrop races across the window as the rain starts again.

"Creed," I start, pleading, "please, just let me have a say. This is Vince we're talking about."

"Creed might be right. This is too dangerous for you, Iz."

He must see the utter devastation at his betrayal in my eyes, because he clears his throat and speaks again.

"But she does have a point. She should get to plead her case before we shut her down."

"For fuck's sake," he barks, and Logan goes still. "Fine. Let's hear it, *princesa*. Still doesn't mean I'll change my mind."

I take a deep breath before speaking, but Logan beats me to it, shocking me with what comes out of his mouth.

"You know, your word isn't law, Creed."

The glare Creed levels at him sets every fiber of my being on the defensive. So, I speak up before he can tear Logan apart right here.

"I've done everything you and Vince have asked of me. I spend hours a day training with Vincent and you. I won't be a distraction; I could be an asset. Think about it. They expect me to run in after him, don't they? I can use that against them. I can be a distraction. A-a decoy!" I pause for a breath, refocusing on all their eyes on me, and realize that the car is stopped.

"I'm done sitting on the sidelines. Let me come with you. I can be an asset out there."

Creed's hazel eyes burn holes into my head, and Logan's golden browns soften as mine meet his. Outside, I see Joel step out of the front door. He must not have expected us back here, not without Vince.

"You wouldn't be an asset. You'd be a distraction."

A sharp exhale leaves my mouth as I sink into myself at his words.

"Is that all I am to you? A distraction?"

"Izzy, he didn't mean it like that," Logan tries to comfort me.

Logan's hand squeezes my knee again, and while I love that he's touching me, I'm suddenly repulsed by the gesture.

"No. I get it." I shove his hand away and open my door. "I'm a liability."

Slamming the door shut, I have to force myself not to run as I walk past my best friend and storm into the house. He follows me in, eyes wide.

"What the hell happened?" he asks.

"They won't let me help. So I'm going alone."

"Izzy! Are you insane? You can't walk into a vampire's lair alone and unprotected!" he exclaims.

"Yes. I can. I won't let them go in there and get themselves killed. I can use what Vince taught me to distract the enemy."

I run upstairs and grab the stake I've been making for the last two weeks. I didn't let anyone know I was making it, because I didn't want them to be concerned, but having it under my mattress made me feel safer in my room. I worked on it mostly on the lazy afternoons when we all did our own things. *This* was my thing.

"Isobelle." Joel steps in front of me on my way down the stairs. "Don't do this."

"I have to, Joel."

He flexes his jaw, then steps to the side.

"If you die, I'll kill you," he says after me, his voice cracking on the last word.

I smile back at him before steeling myself and getting in the car.

Following the map on my phone, I drive through the city until the buildings start looking like they cost more and more money. I see Creed's

Impala parked three blocks away from the address Joel sent, likely to hide the fact that he's here. A cherry red car like his isn't exactly common.

I park just across the street, taking a deep breath before getting out of the car. Around the side of the building is a back entrance that is thankfully unlocked. Either they have horrible security, or Creed and Logan beat me to it. Either way, I'm in.

My sneakers are thankfully quiet against the marble floors. I don't encounter anyone as I sneak around the bottom floor, checking every conference room, bathroom, and supply closet until I'm sure Vincent isn't down here. Next is to get to the second floor. I debate taking the elevator, but decide against it and opt for the stairs. There's no way of knowing what's waiting outside the elevator doors until they open.

The second floor has dark wood flooring and gold embellishments elegantly placed throughout the building. Ahead is a hallway, but to my right are grand double doors that catch my attention.

The whole building has an ancient-feeling charm, as if the ancient Greeks and nineteenth century architects collaborated to create it. What strikes me about the intricate double doors is that there's no sunlight filtering through the crack beneath them. Every other door up here, even the ones I can see in the hallway, has sunlight shining under the crack.

I scan my surroundings before heading for the doors, with no idea of what I'll find on the other side. My fingers grasp the handle, my breath shaky as I prepare myself for whatever is waiting for me in there, and I turn the handle.

The doors open before I even pull the handle, sending me stumbling back while I grip the stake in my hand.

"Izzy?" Logan whisper-shouts.

He has an arm holding Vincent up on one side, while Creed supports the other. There's blood all over his clothes from healed cuts and slashes.

"What did they do to him?" I ask.

"They drained him of blood to weaken him," Creed says, looking around the very open space we're in. "What the fuck are you doing here?"

"I came to help, Creed."

"Let's just get out of here. You two can argue later," Logan says, frantically looking around.

"This place is oddly empty," I remark.

As if waiting for his cue, Cameron appears at the top of the stairs, a sickening grin on his pale face.

"Where do you think you're going?"

He cracks his neck and takes a step forward. Logan and Creed drop Vincent and place themselves in front of us, a blockade. I drop to my knees and hold up Vincent's head. He's awake, but barely, grogginess clouding his eyes.

"Cute," Cameron sneers. "You've all come to take back your precious Vincent."

"Let us go," Creed bites. "You don't want to do this."

"It's too late to try to turn me to the light side, sorry."

"That's not what I mean. You don't want to do this because I've been aching for a fight, and trust me, I fight dirty."

Cameron lunges at Creed, the two of them flying back into the wall, cracking it on impact.

Logan stays near us to protect me, but I can see that he wants to help Creed.

I look between Vince and the fight. I know Creed has Cameron handled, but what if more of them come out of hiding? What if this was a trap?

I make a split second decision to press the sharp tip of the stake to my wrist and make a cut. Once blood starts pooling where my skin is open, I press it to Vincent's mouth. He recoils at first, protesting. I whisper to him to drink and press my wrist to his lips more firmly. He takes what he needs from me, not bothering to soothe the pain with his venom this time. At least, not in the sense that I'm used to.

He stops when he has enough strength to stand upright on his own two feet, nodding in thanks before rushing Cameron and pinning him to the wall by the throat.

Creed stalks up to him, blood staining his skin. Whether it's his or Cam's, I don't know. Cam struggles against Vincent's hold, pleading for his life. Then, without any hesitation, Creed rips his heart from his chest. Cameron's body slumps to the floor with a hole torn through it.

I want to celebrate the victory, to spit on him and dance around his corpse. The deep chuckle of someone sinister stops me from doing just that.

I whip around, my head snapping in the direction of the laugh, and watch as a sleek man in a three-piece suit emerges from the shadows of the hallway. His silver hair is slicked back, exposing the vertical scar darting out from his hairline.

"Shame. Vivienne liked that one," he says, a regal sound to his voice that reminds me of Vincent. "Vincent James Buchanan. Brother, I see you've found your way home, after all."

"This is not my home," Vincent says, pulling my arm so that I move behind him.

Logan stands behind me while Creed and Vince stagger themselves in front of me.

"Not this place," he says, looking around the lavish building, "but Vivienne."

"She's not my home, either, Azaizel."

The man—Azaizel—cocks his head, looking past Vincent to lay his unsettling gray eyes on me.

"And *she* is?" He points a long finger at me. "This human with nothing special about her? You amuse me, brother."

"Vivienne is manipulating you. She's manipulating all of you," Vince says, trying to appeal to this unnerving man.

"You're still going on about that, Vincent? You would think three centuries in a tomb would help you move on. Alas, you always were one to hold on to a grudge." Azaizel looks at his hand, observing his too-long nails. "She misses you, you know. She hasn't stopped missing you since the day you locked yourself within the castle. We only uprooted and moved because the sound of your heartbeat in the walls was driving her mad."

He paces to the left, staring through the three of them to get a better look at me.

"And yet, after three hundred years," he starts, dragging out the last three words, "an unspecial human girl was the one to find you. How is that, exactly? How did you," he addresses me directly, "find him?"

He moves eerily slowly around us, circling like a vulture.

"Don't say anything, Isobelle," Vince says.

"No," Azaizel croons. "The girl must speak. It is impolite to allow one to continue a one-sided conversation."

"I don't know," I say.

He barks a laugh, throwing his head back as the gut churning sound leaves his throat.

"You don't know? So, you just stumbled upon the tomb?" He snickers. "And I suppose you don't know how you booked a flight to Germany and rented a car there?"

I keep silent now, tucking myself behind Creed.

"How rude," Azaizel sneers. "Oh well, I'm sure Vivienne will be thrilled to meet you, regardless of your poor manners. Shall we get going, then?"

"We're not going anywhere with you," Creed bites.

"It'll make things much easier if you do," a familiar voice echoes through the room.

I slowly turn around to see the face that has haunted my nightmares for a month standing across from us.

"Hello, vixen," Ren says, a cruel grin on his face.

Each of them grows tenser, their muscles coiled and ready to strike, as they see Ren standing at the top of the stairs.

"You two know each other?" Azaizel gestures between Ren and me. "How splendid!"

He claps and smiles a toothy smile that makes the hairs on the back of my neck stand.

"Well, we've all been suitably introduced. Let us return to Vivienne. She's expectantly waiting for you," Azaizel says.

"Don't make this ugly," Ren adds as he steps closer to where we're huddled.

The light from the overhead chandelier catches the light just right in that moment, a rainbow flashing across Ren's face. I want to run. I want to vomit. I want to curl into a ball and hide.

Most of all, I want to kill him.

"You already did that, remember?" I bite.

His eyes look over my body, and I swear I can feel all four scars burn beneath his gaze. His gaze catches on something and he tilts his head to see around me. Ren *tsks* and shakes his head.

"You killed Cameron," he states. "Pity, I was hoping to do that myself one day. He was an annoying shit, wasn't he?"

The question is directed at me, but I don't grace him with an answer.

"Well, you all have two options," Ren starts. "Option one, you leave sweet Isobelle and Vincent with us and never look back. Option two..."

"We sever your heads from your bodies and use them to play football. Oh, and we take the girl and Vincent, anyway," Azaizel finishes.

"What do you want with her?" Vincent asks.

"*We* don't want anything. Vivienne does. She's... *interested* in the girl."

"I'll go with you. Just leave her be," Vincent offers, stepping forward.

Azaizel clucks his tongue, shaking his head.

"Unfortunately, brother, you and the girl are a package deal in her eyes. It's all or nothing, always has been. I'm sure you remember that," he says.

Vincent and Creed both sink down on their haunches, preparing for a fight. Creed looks back at me, then turns his head back around. He puts up his fingers behind his back so I can see and counts down from three. When he gets to one, he pounces.

"Izzy, run!" Logan shouts.

The three of them engage in battle with Ren and Azaizel. I want to scream for it to stop because I know they're getting hurt, but I can't risk being a liability. Not now.

I sprint for the hallway, since Ren and Creed are currently blocking the stairs, frantically searching for an unlocked door. The last door on the left opens, and I dash into the room.

Immediately, I start piling furniture in front of the door in an attempt to slow someone down should they try to get in. I know it won't stop a vampire, but at the very least, it gives me time to hide.

Once I've blockaded the door as thoroughly as I can, I look around the room. It's an office.

There's a large mahogany desk in front of a window, papers and books scattered across its surface, and matching bookshelves lining the walls. Across from the desk is a large mouth fireplace, the wood in it charcoaled and dusty.

The sounds of the fight filter through the door and walls, shivers shooting down my spine every time I recognize one of their voices as they grunt in pain. There's a loud crashing sound, followed by a gut-wrenching roar.

Logan's hurt.

I shut my eyes, backing up against the bookshelf, trying not to cry as I think about what that could have been or how injured he might be.

I can't think about it because I can't help him. If I think about it too much, I'm going to leave this room. Then what good would I be?

No, I need to stay here and wait for them to win the battle. Then I can help them heal with my blood. *That's* how I can help them.

Something slams against the door. The thick wood groans beneath the impact and the hinges squeak. I tighten my fist around the stake to keep my hand from trembling.

Another slam. The armchair I propped under the handle slides a few inches across the floor. He's getting in, and he's getting in soon. Whether it's Azaizel or Ren outside that door, they're coming for me.

*Slam.*

I find a spot beneath the desk to hide and try to control my breathing.

*Slam.*

The furniture groans as it slides further across the floor.

*Slam.*

The door opens. Heavy footsteps enter the room.

"Isobelle," that eerily regal voice croons. "I can smell you, girl. Come on out."

I gulp back the lump in my throat and come out from my hiding spot. Azaizel is standing in the center of the room, watching my every move. His gaze catches the stake and he snickers. "Put the stick down, girl. You and I both know you can't hurt me with that."

I only grip it tighter.

"Fine," he rolls his eyes, "don't put down the weapon. As you see, I've come unarmed."

"That's not true," I say.

He looks at his hands as if he were holding a weapon he was unaware of.

"You're a vampire. That makes you armed all the time."

"I suppose that's correct."

I dart my eyes toward the door, hoping to see one of my boys coming in for me.

"Your boyfriends are a bit tied up at the moment. Ren is very good at keeping people busy." He takes a seat in the armchair I didn't move to block the door. "Tell me, Isobelle. What makes you so special? Why do you have three vampires out there getting themselves killed trying to protect you?"

I stare at him blankly.

"Ren asked me this same line of questions when he kidnapped me. Why don't you ask him what I answered and stop wasting our time," I say, attempting to hide the shakiness in my voice.

"You are not their equal, yet they treat you as one. You are not unique, yet to them, you are painite."

I pace the room, sticking to the edges as I watch him.

"There is only one possible explanation, but it is impossible."

"What's that?" I prompt, my voice barely more than a whisper.

"You're their mate." He looks up at me, a bewildered look on his face. "But how can you be? You're human. Any such occurrence has not been reported in the entire existence of our kind."

"Maybe you need to find more reliable sources," I say.

"Child, you mock me. Has Vincent not told you our history? Tsk tsk. Well, I suppose we have some time while Ren holds them up out there.

"Vivienne is the first vampire. Well, one of five firsts. She was a part of a group of women who caught the eye of a witch—a very powerful witch at that. This witch promised seven women, Vivienne included, that she could bestow them with talents no man possessed. They completed a ritual, a spell, that turned the women into what history has named *vampires*. Only five women survived the ritual.

"Vivienne has collected us, her loyal soldiers, from every generation that has come after her transition. Vincent and I were among the first to be chosen by her. Though, she was far more smitten with Vincent than any of us others. After all these years, I still believe her to be in love with him. Even after he locked himself away from her and shattered not only her heart, but her mind, her love for him persists."

I shake my head at him.

"She doesn't *love* him. She doesn't love any of you," I say. "She is manipulating you into thinking that you do, but you don't."

"How would you know?" he shouts, rising from the seat. "How would you know the kind of love and adoration we share with her? You are nothing but an unremarkable human girl. I wouldn't be surprised if you didn't know what love felt like at all."

I muster the courage to keep my chin up as he advances on me. I try to come up with a plan to escape him, but each step he takes tears me from my train of thought.

"Do *you* love him, Isobelle?" he asks. "Do you feel for him as Vivienne does? Are you willing to give up everything for him? Your heart? Your soul?"

He is so close now that his breath sweeps my face.

"Your life?"

He tilts his head to the side in a psychotic looking manner, and I take that moment to thrust the stake into his chest. It pierces his skin and I try to shove it further into him. He groans in pain, his jaw slackening and his hands flying to the stake half burrowing in his chest.

I split away from him and make a run for the door.

My whole body slams against the hard wood floor when he grabs my hair and yanks me back, knocking the air from my lungs. I choke as I try to inhale, my lungs refusing to fill with oxygen.

Azaizel wraps his fist around my throat and lifts me to my feet. I can't breathe. He has me in his hold and I can't breathe!

Just *breathe*! I try to will myself to intake air, but barely any gets through my throat.

"Vivienne was really looking forward to meeting you," he says, a nasty snarl marring his face. "It's a shame you've gone and messed that up for her."

*Pain.*

Then the door slams open.

The moment he steps into the threshold, I feel him. Creed.

It's strange knowing that he's there without having to look, but even as I keep my eyes glued to the snarling face in front of me, I know. The sensation on my back where his eyes are burning into my soul would send shivers down my spine if I hadn't already lost feeling there. Instead, every nerve in my body is alight with the pain of what's happened.

The pain of what neither I nor he can stop.

# Chapter 34



**M**y palms sting with the impact as the intricate door is thrown open. On a normal Sunday, I would be fangs deep in some unlucky college girl on the street.

Today is not a normal Sunday.

No. Today, I am horrified as Isobelle stands before me, inches away from Azaizel as he wraps his fingers around her throat. The savage look on his face is enough for me to want to sink my thumbs into his eyes and rip his head off. On a normal Tuesday, I'd rip his fucking lungs from his chest and watch the panic filter through his mind as he dies by my hand.

Today is not a normal fucking Sunday.

He has her in his grasp, rendering her motionless. The glint of something metal in his hand—his hand that's pressed to her chest in a fist—catches my eye. Immediately, I reassess the situation, staring in horror as the gravity of what's happened floods through me.

She's bleeding. The hot scent of her sweet blood saturating the air in the luxurious office.

He has a dagger in his hand. The same hand pressed firmly against her chest. Her chest that is struggling to rise and fall.

He smirks as he looks directly into my stinging eyes and twists the blade. A guttural scream leaves her throat, ending in a choking sob. She's fucking dying, and I'm frozen to the cherry-wood floor.

# CHAPTER 35



Searing, undeniable pain takes hold of my body. My flesh, bone, and muscle being shredded and torn by the dagger buried in my chest. Azaizel pulls it out. The sadistic monster lets me drop to the ground, bleeding and broken and dying.

I feel, rather than see Creed rush him, my vision blacked out at the edges rendering me nearly blind. There's grunting and thrashing sounds as the two of them fight, and I want to shout. I want to scream for Creed to run and get far away from here. From him.

Two warm, rough hands cup my face, and I see the blurry image of a face framed by blond hair come into view. I try to smile, unsure whether I'm successful, because he's here. Logan's here. He's not dead. Part of me thought he had died when I heard him roar.

Then I feel more pain as pressure falls upon my chest. I want to swat it away, to scream at the source to stop, but I can't. I can't move or speak. I can only feel.

Inky blackness fills my vision as my eyes shut against the pressure and the muffled sound of voices rings in my ears. The blurry image of Logan is the last thing I see before my world goes dark.

# CHAPTER 36

## Logan

"**I**zzy, please!" I shout, holding her cheeks in my palms. Her breathing is rattled, and her eyes have rolled into the back of her head. Blood pours from her mouth like saliva.

She's dying.

Vincent is silent as he puts as much pressure as he can on the gushing wound in her chest without breaking every one of her ribs in the process. It doesn't matter. The blood continues spilling from beneath his hands, anyway. It's surrounding her in a crimson puddle, soaking into her clothes and the knees of my jeans.

The sticky liquid spilling from her mouth coats my fingers. I want to force it back into her, to make her heart take it all back and start pumping it throughout her body.

Her heart.

"Her heart," I say. "It stopped."

My voice cracks, and a fist tightens inside my throat.

"What?" Creed shouts.

Azaizel got away. He jumped out the window.

"Listen! It's not beating!" I shout. "Move."

I practically push Vincent off her and start compressions. It's the only thing I know I can do to help her right now.

"Bleed, Logan. Bleed into her wound," Vincent instructs.

Creed falls to his knees at her head.

I bite my palm and squeeze every ounce of blood that I can into her gaping wound. Then I resume compressions. The blood needs to get through her system, right? It can't spread if her heart isn't beating.

"Come on, beautiful," I plead. "*Please*. Come back to me."

Vincent's hand finds my shoulder and stops me.

"You can't bring her back," he whispers.

"W-what? No. She's not—She can't be..."

"She's dead, Logan. Stop it," Creed barks.

"No!" I shout.

Vincent pulls me off her and holds on to me.

Isobelle lays there, motionless, with her eyes staring up at the ceiling, unseeing.

Her chest doesn't rise. It doesn't fall.

Her eyes don't blink.

Her lips don't move.

Her heart doesn't beat.

She's gone.

I lean forward, sobs wracking my body, and press my forehead to hers.

"I love you, Isobelle," I say to her. "I will *always* love you."

She doesn't say it back. Of course she doesn't. She never will again.

# EPILOGUE



Vivienne waits for me in her bed, as she usually does on Sunday nights. Except this time, she looks disappointed.

"What did I send you, Azaizel, and Cameron to do?" she asks, her seductive voice filling her bedroom.

"Retrieve Vincent and the girl," I say.

"Did you do that?" she asks.

"No."

"Not only did you fail to bring me what I asked for, but Azaizel tells me that the girl is dead. You not only failed me, you exceeded my lowest expectations. The girl is dead. I needed her alive."

I kneel at her bedside, bowing my head.

"I'm sorry that I failed you, Vivienne. I won't let it happen again."

She caresses my cheek with her fingers, hooking one of her long manicured nails behind my ear.

"I know you won't, my love," she whispers.

With a swipe of her finger, she cuts the skin behind my ear, opening a scar that's healed already hundreds of times before.

"I do hope I don't need to involve Aurora to motivate you," she threatens with honey in her tone. Sweet, sticky honey that draws you in only for her to clamp her teeth around your throat.

"That won't be necessary," I say.

"Good."

She tips my chin up with her pointer finger and devours my mouth with her own, commanding that I reciprocate the action. I move my lips against hers and battle her tongue the way she likes me to.

She wants someone who will submit to her completely, but also challenge her every once in a while.

If only I hadn't done exactly that all those years ago. Had I driven her away from me, rather than tried to please her, she wouldn't demand to have me in her bed four days out of the week.

She pushes my head back for a moment, her icy blue eyes demanding my attention. "I want you to bring me Vincent James Buchanan. Alive." She pauses for a moment, a cruel frown forming on her face. "And his little *mate*, too."

**To be continued...**

# ACKNOWLEDGMENTS

To my friends who have supported me—Kailey, Kiersten, Sam, Alora, Hailey, and so many more—I am forever grateful. You have all been incredible motivators even when I was in my moments of doubt.

To my mom, thank you for always encouraging me to follow my dreams and being one of my biggest supporters in everything I do in life. I love you.

To my Puerto Rican bestie, Amanda, thank you for being one of my biggest hype girls, and thank you for helping me with questions I had about Spanish, without you Creed would probably be illiterate.

To my street team—Mika, Anna, Lisa, Mina, Raelyn, and Amanda—thank you for blindly believing in me. Your faith in me throughout this process has been unmatched and I am eternally grateful to each and every one of you.

To my alpha reader, Chelsea, thank you for putting up with my irregular writing pace and helping me with your amazing feedback. Your messages as I sent you the "Wattpad" version of When Dawn Rises were part of the reason I kept striving to make this book amazing.

To my beta readers, thank you for all of your amazing feedback that went into making the final edition of this book the best that it can be.

To my ARC readers, thank you for helping me spread the word about this book. Your love and support shown through reviews, posts, and shares means the world to me.

To my editor, thank you for helping me make this book the best version of itself. Without you, I'd be missing commas everywhere.

To my family, thank you for putting up with my constant nagging about the process of writing and publishing this book. And I apologize for all the future nagging about my other books.

Finally, thank you to the bookish community for allowing me to turn this dream into reality. Without the love and encouragement that you have shown me, I doubt When Dawn Rises would have ever seen the light of day. When I joined the bookish community in 2020, I never expected to be taken on this wonderful journey.

Thank you for everything, and I cannot wait to see what the future holds.

# ABOUT THE AUTHOR

Jalen Noel is a new author specializing in all things romance. She is an Arizona native who wrote a snowy winter novella and is currently working on her debut paranormal romance series. The Crimson Sun series will kick off with book one, When Dawn Rises, in January of 2025. Jalen loves spending time outdoors when the weather is nice, watching movies with a hot tea, and binge-reading like her life depends on it. She dreams of being a full-time author one day and encourages everyone to follow their desires, no matter what others say.

My website: https://www.authorjalennoel.com/